NAOMI LOUD

FIRST EDITION

Cover Design: Mallory Parsons (TikTok: @mal_reads)

Editing: Louise Johnson, Literary Maiden Editing

Proofreading: Salma Rafaf and Christana Tremblay

www.naomiloud.com

## CONTENT WARNING

This is a dark romance and may contain triggering situations such as voyeurism (non-con), exhibitionism, sexual coercion, findom, cults, childhood SA (implied), predatory behavior by a parental figure/religious leader, torture, gore, murder, humiliation (non-sexual), themes of shame and guilt, religious trauma, kidnapping, praise, degradation, nightmares, suicidal thoughts (quick mention), alcohol and drug use (weed) and explicit sexual situations for 18+.

*For those who never wanted salvation and who found comfort in their own darkness instead.*

# 1

**Fifteen years old**

*My hand grips the handle of the knife, the blade meeting soft skin as I plunge it into their body with the full force of my hurt and rage. Face contorting in pain, betrayal etched deep in their searing gaze. Their body slumps slowly down, nearly lifeless, to the ground with a deafening grunt.*

I jolt out of my daydream, slamming back into reality. I'm locked inside this barren room with nothing to do but let my mind wander. I have had this particular vision often but never told anyone. Not even my sister Lucy. No. This, I keep secret. Visions like these could only mean I've been kissed by the devil himself.

Sitting listless on the bed, tucked into the furthest corner from the locked door, I shake the lingering images from my head and refocus on the wall in front of me. The metal springs from the thin mattress beneath me dig into my thighs but still, I sit and stare. I have not moved in what feels like hours. I wouldn't know, there are no windows here. The beige paint of the room is so old it is turning yellow. Cracked at the corners where the bedroom walls meet.

Bedroom.

If you can call these four walls that.

I listen to a fly struggling against the overhead light. The quiet echoes even when there's nary a sound being made. It bounces off the walls and hurls itself back onto me like small pebbles pelting my skin.

I could always read from the pages of the book left on the small bedside table beside me to pass the time. But it doesn't matter.

I can recite the words effortlessly from memory. It has been a required reading ever since my mother taught me how to read. It recounts the genesis of our entire existence here on earth. Penned by my father, Jasper Lincoln, leader of Sacro Nuntio. He is the reincarnation of the archangel Raphael, blessed with a healing touch so profound, he manifests miracles at will with just a touch.

His words are Holy. As so are his testaments.

A framed picture of him hangs slightly crooked above the bed. I have that picture memorized as well. His aging, wrinkled white face follows me no matter where I am, thinning gray hair combed to one side, beady brown eyes always watching. In every room I enter, he is there, watching over me. Over us. Always wearing a narrow but serene smile, portraying his devout role as the harbinger of all things good and saintly.

Wringing my hands together and licking my parched lips, I wait. My left thigh twinges, making me wince and resettle on the mattress. I lift up my blue cotton dress gingerly, uncovering the metal-chained cilice wrapped tightly around my thigh. The metal garter pinches and cuts no matter how I sit, the metal spikes digging into my already tender skin. I itch to take it off, if only for a few minutes.

But I need my bleed to have stopped for my atonement to end.

It's my first.

Just shy of sixteen, I have become a woman.

I wasn't ready. I had shamefully tried to keep it a secret but my mother found me trying to scrub the evidence off my nightgown and shepherded me into this room as soon as I was discovered. I have known about these rooms since I was a young child. Our mothers and older sisters have disappeared for a week every month for as long as I can remember. Sequestered and hidden until they are cleansed, the elders deeming them worthy of reentry to society.

The chained garter was an uncomfortable surprise, however, one that made my blood seethe with feelings I couldn't even properly describe.

Just this blunt and hazy knowing that this is somehow wrong.

Finally, I hear the door unlock and my heart jumps into my throat. The hinges creak, and my father appears, his long bony hands unfurling and the same serene smile that adorns the frame above me appears on his face.

"My child, come," he utters softly.

I stand up quickly, favoring my right leg and finally exit the stale air of the bedroom, my hand tucked into my father's and the cilice still indented into my skin.

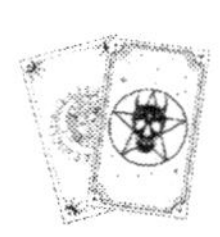

I AM to be wed today.

It has been a few lunar cycles since my first bleed, and I have only just turned sixteen. Somehow, I feel different. The rhythm of life has changed now that I have been welcomed into adulthood. Gaining more duties around the commune, added responsibilities, and I have even been privy to conversations I was excluded from beforehand. Most importantly, I was formally introduced to my future husband, Patrick. We have been in courtship for a little over two months now. The introduction was unnecessary since I grew up with him. A brother of sorts. Not in blood but in faith—carefully chosen by our prophet. My father.

My mother clasps the final button of my wedding dress, and takes a step back, beaming. It's a simple dress in construction, swishing against the carpet as I look at myself in the full-length mirror in my mother's bedroom, the long sleeves covering my arms to the wrist. The only intricate detail is the long row of satin buttons lining the back of the dress, up my spine and reaching all the way to my neck. My black curls are braided into a crown around my head, wild-flowers from the garden weaved into the plaits, and dark brown eyes shining with eagerness for this day to unfold. I am even allowed a touch of makeup, typically forbidden, due to the importance of the day. I cannot help but preen silently and inconspicuously at the sight of my reflection. I look pretty and my heart flutters with the thought, my cheeks flushed with excitement.

My mother squeezes my shoulder tenderly and I find her gaze in the mirror, smiling softly back at her. *Patrick is a good man*, I think. Of good faith and from a good family. He is twenty-four and builds houses with his father for the community. I do not question that I will eventually fall in love with him.

All in good time, as my mother likes to say.

There is a rustle at the door and my eyes snap to one of my sisters entering the bedroom. She smiles slyly and drifts in, light on her feet.

"Lucy!" I can't help my excitement and my mother tuts softly to lower my voice. I twirl around, the dress billowing with the movement and I quietly giggle as my youngest sister embraces me with a gentle laugh of her own.

"You look beautiful," she says, squeezing me tightly in her arms. "I have come to fetch you, father wants a word in his study."

"A word?" I repeat as I pull away. "But it is almost time..."

She shrugs her shoulders. "He says it is urgent. He needs to see you before the wedding."

My stomach falls suddenly, I'm not sure why, but my throat goes dry as I look towards my mother. "But—"

"Go," she responds flatly, her eyes harder than ever before. Then, she clears her throat and smiles. "You do not want to make him wait now would you?" Waving her hands towards me, she effectively shoos me out of the room.

Thankfully, everyone has already gathered in the gardens readying themselves for the ceremony, lowering the chances of someone seeing me in my wedding dress. I still hug the walls in precaution, shuffling quickly to my father's quarters located in the north wing of the main house. I climb the few sets of stairs quickly while still trying not to perspire. Finally, I reach the third floor and knock on the door of his closed study. I hear his booming voice telling me to enter.

"My child. Please," he says as I walk in, brandishing his hand which still holds the pen he was writing with. "Close the door behind you."

I do as I am told, my throat even tighter than before, an eerie—yet unfounded—feeling beginning to crawl up my spine like a slithering snake.

"Sit, sit," he coaxes.

Nervously, I settle into one of the chairs facing him.

He steeples his hands together on his desk and rests his chin atop his fingers, a knowing smile appearing on his weather-worn face.

"It is your wedding day," he states.

The urge to say something insolent is hot on my tongue while I sit before him in my white dress. "Yes," I simply answer, "it is." My fingers dig into the aging chair cushion under me as I wait for him to continue. Eventually, I realize he is waiting for me to speak again. I clear my throat, digging my nails further into the foam cushion. "I am quite pleased with your choice of husband, Father. Thank you."

"Good. Good," he mutters, standing up. He crosses the room in a few short strides and locks the door behind me.

My heartbeat skyrockets, body motionless. The air fills with an ominous chill that I cannot understand but can only *feel.*

"Now. We need to discuss the matter of your maidenhead." He sits back down, facing me with that same serene smile he always carries and I suddenly feel sick.

"My..." I cannot even utter the word out loud without my cheeks burning.

"As you should know, your virginal state is a gift meant only for God. It is not for your husband to take," he says, studying me with an expression I have only seen him use when watching one of his wives. I swallow hard, not able to understand why I'm suddenly so uncomfortable. He stays silent while continuing to observe me until finally, he speaks again, his voice lower, almost secretive but curt. "And so as a shepherd of God, I make it my sacred duty to become the vessel for this offering. Now. Before your union with Patrick."

The dress I'm wearing suddenly feels two sizes too small, choking me at the neck.

"I do not understand," I utter, my voice slightly trembling.

My limbs are frozen as I watch my father stand up and slowly close the space between us, his fingers trailing against the small sliver of skin still visible near my nape. The goosebumps that rise from his touch are not... *righteous.*

I still do not understand what his words really mean, but if I believe the fear rising up my throat, and this deep subconscious wail telling me to run—then something here is deeply wrong.

"Come." My father's voice is lower than before, his hand reaching for mine.

The part of me that is shocked and utterly disturbed by what is slowly unfolding is locked somewhere inside of me, letting him pull me up from the chair and towards the couch facing us. My body trembles, my skin crawling with foreboding but I follow and sit down while he crouches in front of me.

I stare at my knees and listen to his breath hitch while he pushes my dress up and up and up.

My vision begins to blur at the edge, my chest feeling like it is about to collapse.

And yet, I cannot help but think bitterly about my mother, wondering if the small speck of darkness I saw in her eyes before I came here was her knowing what was to come. Knowing she was allowing this, and still leading me to my slaughter.

I cannot hear a thing by the time he uncovers my thighs, the left one now permanently marked by months of cyclical repentance. He swipes his gnarled index over the scarring and finally stands up.

I am a statue, stone carved from shame.

How can this be? How can this be right?

But then my hearing returns. Sharp and crisp.

The pull of his pants zipper echoes like a detonation inside of me and I finally snap.

I will lose myself within the feeling threatening to kill me if I do not act now.

"No." My voice is barely a whisper as I hastily tug my dress back down my legs.

I cannot look at him. I can't.

His hand strikes my cheek, whipping my head to the side. I'm shocked into silence, my palm on my burning flesh while I look up at him with wide eyes.

Anger flares his nostrils like a bull. "You will obey me, child," he hisses through clenched teeth, looming over me, his pants half undone. He tries to shove me into lying on my back, but I resist. I don't think he was expecting me to fight, and I use it to my advantage. Struggling to my feet, I gather all my strength and push him off me.

"No!" I scream with all the breath still left in my lungs. No longer thinking rationally, I grab the small stone sculpture beside me and strike him in the head as hard as I can.

He stumbles backwards, eyes etched in shock and in the span of one long blink, I watch him trip over his own feet, arms flailing, his temple slamming against the corner of the desk. He crumples to the floor like a sack of bones, face first into the rug.

I force air into my tight lungs, my trembling hand slowly covering my mouth as I gape in the horror of what I have done.

"Father?" I croak.

I fall to my knees beside him and tug on his shoulder but he remains unmoving.

"Father?" I repeat again, tears now streaming down my cheeks.

I try moving his face to the side but realize in horror that a pool of blood has begun to form under him. His dark orbs remain unblinking.

I let go of him, sucking in my breath, a low pained gasp traveling up my throat.

*No, no, no, no, no, no, no.*

I scramble to my feet, moving away from my father's body, desperate to distance myself from what I have done.

I've killed my father.

I've slain our prophet.

The realization and its implications carve themselves into my skin—no deeper still—into my now-damned soul.

I stand in the middle of the study, paralyzed while my body trembles uncontrollably.

I hear laughter drift up from the open window. My gaze

jerks towards it and then back to my father. The dichotomy of both things is barely making any sense and I suddenly know that there's only one way out of this. Only one way out of this unforgivable sin I've committed.

Adrenaline and unadulterated fear strum through my veins while I reach for the door, unlock it and *run*.

# 2

**Twenty-two years old**

The vinyl creaks underneath my weight as I slide into the diner booth, my younger cousin Bastian sliding in after me, and my best friend Byzantine settling across from us. The restaurant is a damn near ghost town at this time of night, my eyes quickly sweeping the place trying to find where the hell Martha can be hiding.

I finally spot her and wave her over.

"Evening sugar," she says, beaming at all three of us as she walks over to our table. "Haven't seen the likes of you in these parts in a while. Hungry? Of course you are, Lord look at youse. Skin and bones every single one of yas!"

Martha is quite possibly as old as the diner, her graying hair dyed an unnatural shade of red, black eyeliner always smudged, but she also makes the best boysenberry pie in SoCal.

"It's been a busy year," I say with a side grin, giving her a quick wink.

"I'll say," Martha replies, hiding a small sniffle and giving my shoulder a soft pat.

A busy year is the understatement of the century, having to take over as the leader of the Sin Eaters after my father died in a shootout last year. At twenty-two, I'm now responsible for the most powerful crime organization in the city of Noxport, California. But my age doesn't keep my men from falling in line. It's a family legacy I wasn't quite ready for but I've managed. Especially with Byzantine and Bastian at the helm with me. One as my second-in-command, and the other as the best hacker you'll find on the West Coast, maybe even the country.

"Some coffees and a piece of that world famous pie, would you Martha?" I say, flashing her my equally world famous smile.

"Of course dear, of course." She sticks her pen into her tight bun before turning around and shuffling back to the counter, yelling something unintelligible to her husband who's loitering in the back.

"I wanted some pie too… " Bastian mutters beside me.

"Well next time try speaking out loud, it might help," I

respond in exasperation, picking up a sugar packet and flinging it at his face, but Byzantine is quicker, somehow intercepting the flying thing mid-air from across the booth.

"Knock it off," Byzantine grunts.

I let out a loud laugh. "He'll be fine. The kid barely speaks, it's unnerving." I pretend to shiver, my shoulders shuddering in exaggeration. "I can't believe we're fucking related."

Bastian says nothing, choosing to simply glare at me.

"Not everyone can be as loud and annoying as you, Connor. I'd fucking shoot myself if that was the case," Byzantine says dryly while standing up, probably heading to the counter to order some more pie. My hand lands on my gun, the urge to whip it out just to fuck with him undeniable. My holster snaps open at the same time as the bell over the door chimes and a rush of white staggers inside.

There's a girl under all that white—fifteen, maybe sixteen—her eyes wild as they flit across the restaurant. Her gaze lands at our table for half a second, before quickly fixing on the floor, her chin tucked to her chest, features barely visible as she walks to a table and sits down facing away from us.

"Is she wearing… a wedding dress?" Bastian whispers.

"Now he speaks," I utter, his elbow finding my ribs in a short jab.

I don't have time to question it myself before I hear Martha's loud squawk, rushing over to the girl. It's quiet enough in the diner that we overhear what Martha says from all the way over there.

"Sugar are you alright? What happened?" she says, her tone high-pitched with worry. "Are you hurt?" Concern twists her features.

The girl responds in a low whisper I can't hear while Martha flutters about her like a startled bird. After a short exchange, she swivels around, pours a glass of water behind the counter and brings it promptly over, quickly setting it in front of the young girl.

Byzantine is back at our booth with our coffees when I catch Martha's attention and give her a quick jerk of my head, calling her over.

Flustered, she practically runs to our table.

"What's going on?" I ask.

"Oh dear," Martha whispers, busy wringing her shaky hands, eyes wide with worry. "Oh dear, oh dear, oh dear," she continues to repeat while glancing back to the table where the girl is still sitting eerily motionless, back ramrod straight. "I think she's a runaway… from that weird culty commune a few miles from here. I don't know how she even got here. Did you see her *dress*?" She hisses the last word and I nod.

I'm not sure what makes me so goddamn charitable all of sudden but I pull a wad of cash from my coat pocket and hand it over to Martha while telling her, "Find her a place to stay and keep her off the streets."

Her eyes go watery as she nods profusely and I'm suddenly suffocating under the emotion swirling around in her gaze. I need to get out of here. This whole situation is grating at a feeling I can't even describe. I stand up. "Let's go," I bark at the guys, giving the girl one last quick glance before heading for the door.

"But what about the pie?" I hear behind me.

"Jesus fucking Christ," I bite out. "Fuck the fucking pie Bastian," I yell, not even bothering to check if they're following me. I know they are. I get the hell out of the diner as quickly as I can, gulping down the evening air as I head for the car.

When I finally tear out of the parking lot, Byzantine riding shotgun beside me, the last thing I see in the rearview mirror is the lone shadowy figure of the runaway sitting alone at the diner table, Martha on her way back to her.

# 3

I watch the dildo slide into Prisha's pussy, the harness digging into my hips with every thrust—but I don't care. I'll tolerate the slight irritation if it means I can slide my fingers over her dewy brown skin, tug on her open bottom lip and hear her small gasps as I circle her clit with my other hand.

I'm enamored. I'm obsessed.

She's fucking divine.

But I also know as soon as she comes, I'll orbit out of

this near perfect veneration of her body and itch for her to get the hell out of my apartment. So I lose myself in the moment, my skin bursting into goosebumps when I finally hear her moan out my name like a siren's song.

I love being a top, it's like performing on my very own private stage, I get high off the breathless compliments I receive alone. I couldn't care less about their gender as long as they worship me.

Prisha's body starts to shake under my own and I quickly pull out, chasing her orgasm with my tongue flat on her clit, needing to taste her one last time. One last hit.

But I can already feel myself crashing. She needs to leave.

Besides, I have shit to do today. A business to run.

She lets out a small satisfied hum. "You're amazing," she sighs and I can tell she could go for another round but I've lost interest. I smile against her skin, kissing her thigh softly trying not to be a *total* bitch, while my hand is patting around the bed for her shorts. When I finally find what I'm looking for I drag them next to her and stand up from the bed, stark naked aside from the strap-on.

"You were great," I tell her with a wink while I unclasp the harness, climbing out of it and throwing it back on the rumpled duvet to deal with later.

First things first: kick Prisha out as gently as possible so she doesn't end up hating me.

"I'm sorry to rush this," I say with a small pout. "But I have a meeting in about an hour and I need to shower first and…" I trail off hoping she gets the message. There's a flicker of hurt in her eyes before she blinks it away, forcing a smile on her still-flushed face.

"Of course," she says shyly, quickly gathering her

clothes and hopping into her shorts, her top now halfway on. "I'll get out of your hair."

While she gets dressed, I reach for the back of my bedroom door and slide my short pink satin robe over my shoulders, not even bothering to cinch it closed. Finally, I walk her to the front door, a wide open smile slapped on my face but inside I'm resisting the urge to shove her out of here.

"I'll call you," I chirp as she gives me a sheepish wave from the outside hallway. Closing the door, I quickly bolt it behind me. I let out a deep sigh, flipping my long black hair off one shoulder and head to the shower.

I wasn't lying about that meeting.

"I'M HERE!" I yell out to Sunny from the hall, trying to overcompensate for my tardiness. I bite back a smile as I suck in a much needed breath, my heels echoing across the hall. Turning a sharp corner, I practically skid into our joint office. I know such a dramatic entrance isn't needed but that's just who I am around my best friend, especially when I know damn well that I'll find her glaring at me from her messy desk. And oh, how surprising, there she is throwing daggers at me as I make my way to my own desk facing hers.

"Morning babes," I sing-song, pretending I don't notice her sour mood. She's lucky I didn't call her my gloomy baby. A nickname I appointed her due to her constant morose attitude—to put it lightly—for the first few years of our friendship. She hates it.

"You're late," she says with annoyance.

"Am I?" Mocking innocence and raising an inquisitive eyebrow.

Before sitting down, I readjust my leopard print pencil skirt and power up my desktop, my long acrylic nails tapping on the keyboard as I enter my password. The nails on my index and middle finger are noticeably shorter on my right hand, which leaves the straights very perplexed.

"Lenix," she deadpans, her eyes dangerously close to an eye roll.

"Sunny?" I wrestle my wide grin into a small smirk and finally look directly at her. She doesn't say anything more, just stares at me with big hazel eyes and finally, I crack.

"Ok fine, I'm *sor-ry*." I over pronounce the two last syllables just to annoy her further and give her a small exasperated eye roll of my own. "I got caught up with something," I say slyly, looking her up and down, knowing full well she's picking up on my insinuation. After all, we've been best friends for years now.

"Let me guess," she answers dryly.

"No need." I flash her a smile, wiggling my shoulders. "I can give you all the juicy details instead."

Sunny finally breaks her scowl and laughs. "I'll pass thanks. But I'm serious Len, you need to stop pulling this shit. I can't always pick up the slack, you know."

I can't help but to feel guilty but I *also* can't help but to whine a little. "But you're so good at this. You can't deny that my strengths are not here in the office, but out there," I say, pointing in a random general direction. "I'm the party and you're the planning. Tell me I'm wrong."

We met nearly five years ago, both working at a bar near Old Town called Sammies. I was the resident party girl, and I quickly took Sunny under my wing. We hooked up a few times at the very beginning but our relationship quickly turned into a steadfast friendship and she's been my person ever since. She's the strongest person I've ever met, and I'm so proud of how far she's come.

Sunny groans loudly, dropping her face into her open palms, her messy auburn bun flopping atop her head with the sudden movement.

She knows I'm right.

We started our own event planning business last year and naturally fell into the roles that made the most sense for our dynamic. I'm the face of the business while she takes care of things behind the scenes. My special talent is schmoozing potential clients into giving us their money. It's basically a business casual version of flirting, which happens to be my favorite pastime.

Besides, she's being taught by the best. Her boyfriend Byzantine has at least a decade of experience cooking the books for the Sin Eaters and owns more than half of the bars and clubs across town. Which is a lot considering how big the city is. The beaches might be beautiful but Noxport has a dark underbelly like any major metropolis. His specific skills sort of translate—I suppose? Not that I've really asked.

Our business has been steadily growing ever since so we must be doing something right.

"Anyway, what's this meeting about? New client?" I ask.

Sunny pops her head up and settles back in front of her computer looking guilty. "Of sorts."

"Of so—"

Before I can even finish my question, I'm cut off.

"Ladies," a deep smug voice drawls from the door.

My heart drops to the very depths of hell knowing exactly who that voice belongs to. Bespoke three-piece suit over broad shoulders, eyes as black as his slicked back hair, sun-kissed white skin, square jaw and a perfectly trimmed mustache over full lips. When my eyes finally land on the devil himself, I'm not surprised to find him leaning lazily against the doorframe looking like a bored king gracing his royal presence to the masses.

# 4

## Connor

"Oh for fuck's sake," Lenix exclaims and I flash her a side grin, pushing myself off the doorframe and strolling into their small office, peering around half-interestedly.

"So this is where the magic happens," I say, sliding my hands into my perfectly tailored navy slacks. "Cute."

"Sunny!" Lenix practically screeches, looking like she's

about to launch herself over the desk and wrestle her best friend into finally looking at her. "What is *he* doing here?"

I chuckle, dropping my ass down on the green velvet couch close to the door. "What darling? You can't even say my name now?" I give her a mock pout I've seen her do a thousand times before. "You wound me," I say, placing a hand over my heart to further taunt her.

"I swear to fucking God Connor—"

"Okay, everyone shut up," Sunny interrupts our bickering—right when it was getting interesting—and stands up facing both of us, hands on her hips. She looks like she's getting ready to scold a bunch of unruly children.

"Lenix," she says firmly, her index pointing straight at her. "Did you not just tell me I was the planning part of this whole thing? Well, this is me planning."

Lenix's mouth slams shut as she listens to her best friend nullify her petulance towards me and I laugh under my breath. At the sound, Sunny's shoulders shoot up to her ears, spinning on her heels to face me fully. "And *you*." That same pointed finger is now being shoved against my shoulder. "You're the boss of the biggest crime organization on the West Coast for Christ's sake, maybe start acting like it."

I drop the smile, seeing Lenix trying to conceal a smug look on her face and I roll my eyes. "I liked you better when you were terrified of me."

She lets out a small huff and falls back into her desk chair. "Can you two be civil for one fucking second while we discuss this? *Please*."

"What do you even need planning for anyway?" Lenix asks with slight disgust.

"My birthday is coming up." Her eyebrows shoot up, but I don't let her comment before continuing, "I need a reason to have some of the most important players in the city in one room. Perfect excuse really," I say while casually stretching my arms across the back of the couch.

"Which is?" she asks.

"Wouldn't you love to know, darling," I drawl, pinning her with my stare and feeling her body tense from across the room.

I could do this all day.

"So," Sunny jumps in, sounding all business-like, which makes me smirk remembering the party girl I first met three and half years ago. "Not only will this be the biggest event we've ever planned but this will also be the most influential party of the year. This could be huge for us, Len."

She stares at her for a beat and finally exhales long and deep. "Fine."

"Fine?" Sunny repeats.

"Fine," she answers glumly, crossing her arms over her chest. "How long do we have?"

Sunny perks up. "April, so a little over two months."

"It'll cost you a pretty penny," Lenix tells me with a superior look, a challenging glint in her eyes.

"Shocking," I deadpan while standing up and smoothing my hands over my suit jacket with a bored expression. "Anyway, this has been quite the delight." I take one last glance at Lenix, winking at her. I swear her ears burn red before I head for the door. "I'll have Byzantine forward you the details," I tell Sunny from over my shoulder, not even bothering to wait for a confirmation, and walk out of the office.

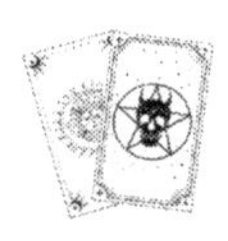

"What's up with the porn 'stache anyway?" I hear Byzantine say from above me.

I'm out of my three-piece suit and into red swim trunks lazing beside the pool while I take advantage of the small lull between meetings. My days mostly consist of networking with local officials, busy working on building up the legal business side of the Sin Eaters. This typically means supplying weed to dispensaries, tax breaks for our bars and businesses, and most importantly getting my puppets instated right where I want them.

He hands me a tumbler full of mezcal with a smirk and I snap it out of his grasp with a huff.

"Are you going to ask me that every time you see me?" I bite out.

"I'm never satisfied with the answer," he says, sitting beside me dressed in all black, boots included.

I glare at him but say nothing more. Draining the glass of its contents, I talk myself out of smashing it against his skull, changing the subject before I actually do.

"Saw little miss sunshine today," I say while leaning back into the sun, referring to his girlfriend's namesake.

"Yeah, she told me," he answers distractedly, looking into the distance, swiping a tattooed hand over his shaved head. A tell that his mind is somewhere else.

"Little miss *not so* sunshine was also there," I add with slight amusement.

Byzantine chuckles, stretching his body on the deck chair, closing his eyes, a lopsided grin appearing on his lips. "I know." He reaches for his whiskey and takes a sip before continuing, "You were at each other's throat again?"

"Hardly… I just find it amusing to rile her up, it's just so — easy," I say absently as I look for the joint I rolled earlier. Finding it near the ashtray, I pop it between my lips and light it up, taking in a lungful, my muscles relaxing almost immediately.

"You two got along so well at the beginning," he muses.

"And?"

"And remember what you told Bastian when he asked if you two were fucking?" My adrenaline spikes but I say nothing, simply taking another hit of the joint. When I don't answer, Byzantine answers for me. "You denied it. Said she'd hate you by now if you were.'"

My nostrils flare, questioning if I should just kill him so he can shut the fuck up already. Effective. A bit inconvenient.

"Get to the point," I say through clenched teeth.

"Well, looks like she finally hates your guts," he says with a laugh, his eyes still closed against the sun. "Not hard to put two and two together, brother."

"Trust me, that's not why," I reply slyly.

Well, it might have a little to do with it but it's far from the reason why she can no longer stand the sight of me. I can't help my shit-eating grin, a sick thrill traveling through me, knowing full well why she hates me, and *fuck* does it turn me the fuck on.

Is it a little sadistic? Maybe. Fuck knows I'm not a great judge of character for those things. Has it kept me entertained for over two years now? Absolutely.

"Anyway," Byzantine mutters, standing up. "Not my business, nor do I really care."

"So why the fuck did you bring it up?"

"Because I know Sunny is dying to know and well…"

"And she's got you thoroughly whipped?"

"Happily so," he says while walking away. "I'll see you later, Ron Jeremy."

The glass I fling in his general direction shatters against the wall near the sliding doors. Byzantine doesn't even flinch, barking out a laugh, and disappearing into the house.

# 5

Closing my apartment door behind me, I kick off my heels with a satisfied sigh, sliding my feet into pink furry slides and shuffling into the kitchen. Ewan, my orange tabby cat, trails behind me, chirping to be fed.

I moved into this place about a year ago. At twenty-nine, it's my first time living on my own without any roommates, and I didn't realize how much I would enjoy it. Most importantly, how much I'd love decorating it to my own taste. Everywhere I look, it screams Lenix—like my pink couch, which is my prized possession. Some might call it tacky or gauche, but I would just call them boring.

Byzantine got me a sweet deal in the downtown condo building he used to live in before he met Sunny. Now they live in Garden Heights, an affluent neighborhood, close to Connor's mansion. I have a sneaking suspicion he pulled more than a few strings to get me this place but I must admit, I didn't ask a lot of questions. And I'm certainly not complaining if it landed me with this view.

I pour myself a glass of rosé and feed Ewan before he disowns me altogether. I slide the patio door open and step onto the balcony. My condo faces the ocean, as well as the sunset, the sun now dipping low on the horizon. Sitting down, I let out a long satisfied sigh, my eyes captured by the water reflecting the glowing rays.

Then my phone buzzes on the glass table, startling me.

My blood boils when I realize who it is. I snatch it up and hiss, "What."

"My, my," Connor tuts, his tone dripping in amusement. "Is this how you treat all your clients?"

The sun has suddenly turned into a giant ball of fire heading directly towards me, my anger burning my cheek, while my fingers hold on to the phone much too tightly.

"Only the psychopathic ones," I answer with a sneer he can't see but hopes he hears.

Connor laughs, it's low and heated and makes my heart slam into my throat. "What are you wearing, darling?"

"Don't call me that," I bite out.

"Oh, little Lenny doesn't like that, does she? Or would you rather I call you what you really are?" he says mockingly. Not to mention how he knows I hate being called Lenny.

Still, the heat that spikes through my lower stomach is positively mortifying.

"You're such an asshole," is all I find to say. I'm so disappointed with my comeback that I consider chucking my phone over the balcony, totally horrified that my body still reacts to him. Especially since I'm certain he somehow *knows* it does which makes it at least ten times worse. I exhale loudly through my nose. "What do you even want, Connor? I'm busy."

"Well, I figured since we'll be working closely together for the next couple of months, we should at least be on speaking terms."

I scoff. "Why would we be working closely together? Don't you have better things to do than micro-manage your own event?"

He laughs. And I wince.

"I think you underestimate how much I love control, darling. I'll see you tomorrow morning."

My scathing comment is burning on the tip of my tongue but it fizzles out like a flame underwater when I hear the tonal hum of my phone. I reconsider flinging my phone into the ocean, my body practically vibrating from our interaction.

One day, I'll get him back for what he did.

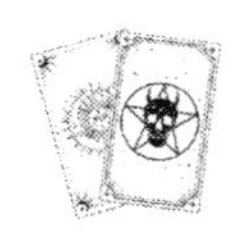

*Forgive me.*

*Father. Please, father. Please.*

*Forgive me.*

I let out a startled scream, my bedroom pitch black, fighting off the duvet cover as if I'm under attack. My left thigh is burning, but I'm still too groggy to decipher if the pain is real or just a messed up figment of my imagination. Reaching for the bedside table, I turn on the light, my personal demons scurrying back away into the darkness like cockroaches. My breath is ragged while I fling the covers off my legs and look down. There are large welts on my left thigh, almost exactly where the cilice used to be. I've managed to pinch myself so hard in my sleep that bruises are blooming across it.

"Fuck," I mutter out loud.

I slide my shaky thumb over it, my heart pumping far too fast but I can't seem to calm myself down. My fingers trail across the faint scars still adorning my skin. They're barely visible, but I know they're there and that's enough.

They speak of another life entirely. A time before Lenix was even born. And suddenly the shame of everything that has happened or *might* happen flays me alive and I can't stand the sight of any of it.

I will do anything to suppress the feeling.

Can you even call it that?

Feeling.

Such an innocuous word for something that makes me feel like I don't deserve anything good. Such a simple word for something that makes me feel like I've been branded as the town pariah—even when no one knows anything about my dirty little secrets.

But my secrets are not so little.

And one day I'll burn in hell for them.

# 6

## Lenix

*It is cold today. The wind cuts through my thin cotton dress while the metal mouthpiece lodged atop my tongue tastes like rust and sin.*

*What I have locked around my face and head resembles a horse's bridle, and I am ashamed to admit that this is not the first time I have been forced into it. I have a hard time keeping quiet. I'm too loud, my laughter too shrill. It might have been distressing at first, but now I just bide my time and try not to let the drool slip down my chin. Shifting on the wooden bench, I try to keep my eyes on the ground, forced to sit in the town square for everyone to see.*

*I was caught gossiping by one of the elders. Brother Evans.*

*I hate him.*

*There I said it. I know I should not think ill of the elders but I cannot help it.*

*I hate him, I hate him, I hate him.*

*My lips quirk an inch around the device keeping me from speaking, proud of my internal defiance when I should be lost in thought, deep in repentance, asking for forgiveness.*

*The bridle is for my own good. That is what the elders told me when they locked me in it. A reminder to submit. To listen and emulate the demure nature of my sisters. But all the while it feels like something is missing. It continues to rattle inside me, especially when I am left mute like this. It shakes and groans but it has no name, just a feeling. This unknown essence of just knowing that something is wrong with this place.*

*But I would never dare to accuse.*

*Never dare to question.*

*From sunup to sundown, I am forced to sit here, and I count the hours by the slow drag of it against the blue sky.*

*The commune's chosen sinner. If only for the day.*

*I'm sure in less than a week, I will find one of our mothers or maybe a fellow sister sitting where I am now. It is not uncommon. We are sinners, every single one of us. It does not efface the shame I feel when I have been found at fault. Only my father, our savior, can save us from ourselves.*

*Sometimes, I wish there was another way.*

*Another path to redemption.*

Trying to apply mascara, my hand shakes while my mind lingers inside memories I wish I could forget. My eyes are welling up with tears but I absolutely refuse to ruin my makeup, so I widen them and flap my free hand trying to dry up the water threatening to fall. It doesn't stop my lower lip from trembling and my body's reaction to the heightened emotions. It's seriously cramping my style. I need to get it together.

Twisting the mascara closed, I take a step back from the bathroom mirror, my bare feet sinking into the white shaggy carpet. Ewan quietly purrs against me, curling himself at my feet, pawing my calf, vying for my attention.

Remembering that the brain can't differentiate between fake or real smiles, I grasp at straws and force myself to smile. Trying desperately to offshoot the sinking feeling currently residing in my chest.

It's not working.

I'm usually so good at repressing this shit. My skin crawls at the thought of even having to come close to the memory I'm trying to ignore. But I need to if I want the foul thing to sink back into the darkest depths of the unclassified part of my brain. I do it anyway—with the help of an imaginary ten foot pole, unwilling to get any closer than necessary.

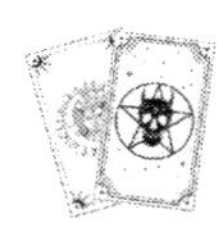

My car idles while I stew in mind-numbing morning downtown traffic. Sunny is going to ring my neck again. I was already running late but may have taken another extra ten minutes at the drive-through ordering a large latte. Hopefully buying her coffee will help assuage my lateness. Or is she still in her tea phase? Either way, I'll apologize profusely to the only person I would ever apologize to because I can't handle her being upset with me.

Eager to get there I drum my fingers to the beat of the

pop song blaring out of the car speakers. I'm either antsy or just straight up anxious, I'm not really sure. I bite my lip, humming a bit too loudly, distracted and impatient.

Glimpsing out of the open car window, my eyes lock with a person standing on the sidewalk only a few feet away from me. My body reacts, doing a few things at once. First, my body locks up with a surge of adrenaline so intense that it convinces me I might be having a heart attack while simultaneously trying to scooch down in my car seat. Second, my arm shoots forward, the car horn blaring.

"*Fuck*," I choke out, trying to signal to the other drivers around me that this small freak out was a total accident and not me trying to be an asshole. My forehead is prickling with sweat, my body shaking much too aggressively as I turn my attention back to who I think I just saw. But they're gone.

Did I just imagine that?

Was that what it was? A figment of my imagination? I'm having trouble even swallowing as the cars in front of me begin to move and I drive away from the near-fatal embolism I just experienced.

There's no way I just saw who I think I just saw. My mind is trying to find every excuse to convince me it wasn't them.

And if it was them, they wouldn't have recognized me.

How could they?

I look nothing like the child who ran away.

Nothing like the sinner who killed her father.

# 7

## Connor

I watch Lenix park across the street from her office building, mindlessly running my index finger and thumb down my mustache while I lean beside the front door. It's a habit I can't break since I let it grow out. I'm sure it makes me look like some kind of Machiavellian villain but who gives a fuck really.

Her long bronzed legs are the first thing out of her

black Saab. She's tall—taller than most in heels. It only accentuates the air of royalty she carries with her anywhere she goes, and people can't help but stop and stare. Her straight black hair is pulled back into a high ponytail, accentuating her face and neck, lips painted a deep red, her dark brown eyes looking almost feline by the bold lining framing them. Today, she's wearing gold—and I'm like every other fool who can't stop staring. Her dress pulls high up her thighs when she climbs out and my jaw tightens. I try to look away but my gaze zeroes in like a goddamn sniper ready for the kill instead.

She crosses the street and I can tell she's biting her bottom lip even from here. Something is making her nervous, a wild look in her eye, and it's certainly not me since she hasn't spotted me yet. I've had years to perfect the casual, slightly arrogant pose I adopt now, leaning near the entrance, my hands tucked into my pants pockets.

When she does finally notice me, her steps stutter for a millisecond before she sends me a death stare but continues on her path inside the building. I follow right behind, the click of her heels, the only sound echoing inside the silent lobby while we head to the elevators. She continues to ignore me while we wait, her eyes fixed on the descending floor numbers as if she can will it to go any faster. The doors ding, sliding open and we walk in.

Somehow, this loaded silence percolating between us is as entertaining as when she's slinging insults my way so I happily let her stew knowing she'll eventually crack.

By the second floor, she does.

"When did you become such a suit guy?"

I smirk in surprise—of all the things I thought she would say.

"Bothered?"

She scoffs under her breath, pressing her painted lips together, her eyes still locked on the blinking numbers above us. "Why would I be *bothered*?"

I shrug a shoulder, my mouth watering at the thought of taunting her. "You're the one who brought it up… " I take a step closer, expecting her to move away but she doesn't. She just continues to stare straight ahead. "Does the sight of me in a suit excite you?" I say in a low conspiratorial tone. "Tell me, do I still make you wet, darling?"

My fingers graze her forearm and she flinches, the doors dinging open at the same time. Flustered, she turns and glares at me. With her heels, we're at eye level—and something about it excites me. My lips curl into a provoking smirk, waiting for her to speak.

If a look could kill, I'd be in hell. But I'd do it again and again just to see her like this.

Pure fire. And I'm the gasoline.

"You're so full of yourself," she grits out as I let her push me into the elevator wall. My grin widens when she wraps her hand around my throat. "That was years ago Connor, get over it already." Her grip tightens before giving me a quick shove, releasing me. Turning away, she walks out the doors. From over her shoulder she says, "Or better yet, sign the damn papers."

That same sick thrill blazes through me as I follow her out.

"What papers?" I ask innocently, matching her quick strides through the hallway.

"Ugh!" Stopping dead in her tracks, she swivels around, looking ready to attack me, and I give her a bright smile. Her eyes narrow. Her chest rises. But then she closes her eyes and takes a large breath in. "You know what? Fuck this and fuck *you*. This little game you love to play anytime you see me, even after *months* of blissful absence where I managed to avoid you, which, for some reason, feels impossible lately," she says in exasperation, rolling her eyes dramatically, then looks back at me with a sudden cold stare. "It's boring me. *You're* boring."

She quirks a brow arrogantly while saying it, then turns back around and heads inside her office. I chuckle mirthlessly, following her.

"I'm anything but boring, Lenny."

"Who's boring?" Sunny asks, distracted by whatever's on her computer screen.

I flop on the couch, my expression still amused while Lenix shoots me a searing glare before she sits down at her desk.

"Connor," Lenix answers.

"Connor's boring?" Sunny repeats.

"Yes," she responds primly.

Sunny finally looks up, seeming to realize how absurd this whole exchange is. "What are you two even on about now?"

I open my mouth to answer but she cuts me off. "I changed my mind, I don't care. What are you doing here Connor? I thought we were meeting later with Byzantine."

I shrug, fixing a disinterested look on my face. "I was in the neighborhood. Thought I'd show Lenix the yacht club."

"Why me?" she whines.

"Because you're on my payroll now," I reply, not bothering to look up, adjusting my cufflinks instead.

In reality, I have a million more important things to do right now than being here. But here I am nonetheless, unable to resist the chance of goading Lenix in person. I've never really dwelled on *why* I get such a kick out of it, or the likely chance that I'll fuck my fist tonight remembering our little exchange. It's just a fact. Like that irresistible urge to strangle a kitten when it gets too adorable to look at.

Both girls fall silent while they stare at each other, looking like they're having a telepathic argument and by the sudden look of despair on Lenix's face, Sunny's winning. Finally, after a rather long stretch of silence, she stands up.

"Fine. Let's go."

ONE THING my father taught me before he died and bequeathed all of this shit to me was: if you want to rub elbows with the city elite get yourself a membership to the Noxport Yacht Club. I've been an active member for over a decade. The people who frequent it are chock-full of platitudes, centuries of stuffy traditions, and so heavy with prejudices that I'm shocked the club hasn't sunk into the surf from the sheer weight of it.

However, there's nothing the wealthy love more than a charismatic asshole. But I'm also a snake in the grass. I'll make deals with the husbands over a thousand dollar bottle of brandy before fucking their wives and making their daughters cry. And I hate brandy.

The nervous staff shepherds us into the prestigious gilded ballroom with the large windows facing the water. Lenix takes notes, asking a few key questions and I try to join in. Slowly, she turns my way, and glares at me, effectively conveying with her dark brown eyes that I'm not welcome. She gives me a quick jerk of the head, and I slide my tongue over my teeth, considering immediate retaliation for her dismissing me—in front of the staff no less.

Looks like she needs a reminder of who she's dealing with. I match her gaze, and her expression cracks for half a second before turning hard again. Satisfied for now, I flash her a smile and stroll back into the lobby. Settling in one of the chairs, I decide to catch up on some emails.

After a while, she reemerges, exchanging information with the club's event manager and we head out. The establishment sits at the very tip of the pier, distancing itself from the more crowded and public part of the boardwalk. Lenix is still actively pretending I don't exist, but I lead her down the wood-slatted walkway anyway and she surprisingly follows.

"Ignoring me isn't going to deter me you know," I finally say.

"Maybe I'll kill you in your sleep," she mumbles with her arms crossed. "See if that deters you some."

"Sounds hot," I drawl, pushing my hair back into place. "But you'd have to be in my bed for that."

She groans loudly. Tensing up, she hurries her step, back stiff, tight fists tucked to her sides. I'm speeding up behind her, chuckling to myself when I see her freeze in front of me. It's visceral and so sudden that it leaves me frozen along with her. It lasts only a second until she looks around with a frantic jerk of her head and finally dives behind the door flaps of one of the large tarped tents lining the boardwalk. I look around, my vision narrowing into quickly assessing any threats but I don't see any.

What just happened?

I follow Lenix inside wondering what the hell just got into her.

I find her trembling, her eyes as wild as when I saw her earlier this morning.

"Care to explain what just came over you?"

"Nothing," she answers quickly, biting her lips, her knuckles white. She looks around trying to seem genuinely interested in her surroundings.

What is this place anyway?

The atmosphere feels heavy, even the sounds feel somehow muted in here. Deep blues and dark burgundies decorate the tent, the strong smell of incense burning my nose. I don't recognize half the shit I'm looking at behind the glass cases near the cash register. Until my eyes land on a poster pinned to the wall.

Before I can roll my eyes into the back of my skull, an older woman walks out from the back. Her shoulder-length hair is stark white against her pale white skin, a pair of reading glasses dangling from her neck, and my attention zeroes in on the tattooed markings she has on her hands, looking almost ceremonial.

"Here for a palm reading?" she asks.

I'm about to tell her to fuck right off when I hear Lenix next to me say, "Yes, he is."

My lip curls in disdain. Over my dead body.

Lenix and I lock eyes and she smirks. She seems to have gotten over her little freak out long enough to stare at me with dazzling over-confidence, her expression daring me to say yes.

What she doesn't know is that having to exist deep inside the underbelly of Noxport for well over a decade has turned me into a bit of a mind reader myself. And what I see behind the hard steel of this little tough guy act she's putting on is a small desperate plea to just play along. To give her this inconsequential win.

I must be high off that incense because I suddenly feel the need to entertain this fucking bullshit.

Without saying a word, I promise her retaliation for this little stunt she's pulling and her almost inaudible gulp satisfies me enough for me to sit down at the small table where the palm reader is already settled, patiently waiting for me. Luckily there's no crystal ball in sight.

Lenix follows suit, sitting beside me looking pleased with herself but I can't help but notice her quick glances over her shoulder toward the exit. Clearly, something is worrying her but I play dumb for now and pretend I don't notice.

"Left hand, palm up please," the lady says.

Begrudgingly, I unfurl my fingers and place my hand where she asked. She takes her glasses hanging off her neck and places them gently on the tip of her nose. Taking my hand in hers, I fight back the instinctual flinch attached to the vulnerability of the moment.

We fall silent as she bends over my palm, the pad of her finger tracing the lines carved in my skin like she can actually *see* something. What a waste of my fucking time.

And I have only myself to blame.

"You have her life line etched in the palm of your hand," she finally says, her voice barely a whisper.

Great, she's speaking in fucking riddles.

"He has what?" Lenix asks for me, sounding as incredulous as I feel, sitting on this too small plastic chair inside a charlatan's tent.

*Jesus fucking Christ.*

"*Her* life line," she repeats as if somehow that's what was needed to make this all make sense.

"Whose?" I grunt in annoyance, less because I'm

curious and more because I want this whole interaction to be over as soon as possible.

Her shoulders are still hunched over while staring at us both from behind her glasses, eyes flitting back and forth between us two. She finally raises her index finger stacked full of silver rings and points it directly at Lenix.

"*Hers.*"

# 8

The room is dead silent.

Both Connor and I haven't said a word, as if we've both completely short-circuited. The moment only lasts a few seconds but it feels like forever.

*What the hell did she just say?*

Connor clears his throat beside me which jolts me into finally responding to this absurd claim. I give her a tight smile. "First of all, that's impossible. Second of all, I'm not sure I know what that *actually* means."

I shoot a hard look toward Connor and he just stares back with a blank look on his face.

*Great.*

I wish he would at least say something.

"You've been bound before." She pauses, eyes dancing back and forth. "And have experienced many lives together," she states vaguely.

That makes Connor finally react, yanking his hand away from her and standing up.

"Lady, you've got the wrong couple. All that past life shit has nothing to do with us." He then startles like he just realized what he said, and blurts, "We're not a couple. I just meant that's not us. You've got the wrong *people.*" He swipes his hand through his black hair and then rubs his neck, a small tell that he's more flustered than he's letting on. And I fight the urge to scoff at the sight.

The palm reader stays silent, a small smirk on her lips, studying us.

Maybe getting Connor to have his palm read was a dumb idea after all.

Meanwhile, I'm still sitting on the chair facing her, sweating like I'm at the doctor's office about to be told I have a week to live.

"Tell me," she says to Connor, carefully taking her glasses off and letting them hang off her neck. "Do you have a birthmark over your heart?"

His eyebrows pull down, his forehead wrinkling in aggravation.

"What the hell does that have to do with anything?"

"Answer my question."

From the corner of my eye, I see his hand slip into his suit jacket. Alarmed, I spring to my feet but I'm too late. Connor is already pointing a gun at the poor woman's face.

"You better watch who you're fucking talking to."

"Connor what the hell!" I grab his raised arm and pull it down. "Have you lost your fucking mind?"

I turn to her, ready to get on my hands and knees to apologize for his appalling behavior but I'm left speechless when I find her sitting still, her eyes fixed on Connor. Her expression is flat and unimpressed as if having a gun pointing at her head isn't much of an event in her day to day life.

"Well?" she says, carefully clasping her hands together and placing them atop the table. "Do you?"

The fiend beside me shoves his gun back into his holster, straightens his suit jacket, and swipes his hand over his mustache.

He pins her with a stare, giving her a sinister smile, then walks out.

I'm left stunned—a multitude of things pulling at my attention. Eventually, I turn back to face the palm reader and hand her a twenty from my purse.

"Sorry about that," I mumble. Suddenly feeling awkward.

"Don't you worry, child. You did nothing wrong," she says warmly, hands loosely clasped together, eyes wrinkling with a kind but knowing smile.

A chill racks my body at her words, trying to tamp down the irrational fears overcoming my senses. My gaze lingers on her, not knowing what to say.

"Come back if you ever need questions answered. Him too." Pointing at where Connor was just standing.

My throat is dry, the words stuck in my throat while I give her a shaky smile and walk back onto the busy boardwalk. The sun feels suddenly too bright, like I've just resurfaced from a long journey to the underworld.

I look around, expecting to find Connor but he's nowhere in sight.

Well. At least I was able to get rid of him.

Even if that whole experience left me creeped out and itchy.

Then, like slamming into a brick wall, I remember the reason I beelined into the tent in the first place. My breath catches in my throat as I look around nervously, but don't see any familiar faces looking back. Friendly… or otherwise.

I quickly make my way back to the office on foot, trying to shake away the bizarre morning I just had but the heightened paranoia seems to follow me all the way back.

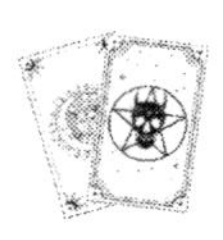

I SIT ALONE in our regular booth at Sammies, glaring at the TV hanging over the bar, a Paloma sweating on the table in front of me. Both Sunny and I quit working here a year and a half ago but we still love to come back once in a while. The Sin Eaters still own the place, but Byzantine is a lot less hands-on now that he isn't stalking Sunny on a nightly basis. The boys' booth became our booth too.

I still can't make sense of anything that happened today. I've replayed everything multiple times in my head over the past hour. I clink my nails on my drink while I think but the more I think the more I have questions.

What the hell did she mean by us being *bound*? Connor and I? Laughable. And never going to happen, except for—actually never mind. I've never been the one to believe in this type of thing. But that was until Byzantine barrelled his way into Sunny's life, and somehow convinced her he remembered all their past lives together.

After that? It's a little hard to ignore the possibilities that some things are just unexplainable. Us humans don't know much about anything.

And this bizarre occurrence was only *one* of the troubling things that happened today.

I'm being followed.

I can't even bear saying his name. But if I close my eyes, I can still see his face watching me with intent. So it's best to just keep them open.

It wasn't him. It can't be him.

It's getting harder to gaslight myself when I'm almost positive I saw him twice today. My hand trembles as I reach for my drink and down the rest. It does nothing to soothe my nerves.

I should just go home.

I slide out of the booth, bussing my own table—because old habits die hard— before grabbing my purse, giving a small wave to the staff and walking outside into the dark.

# 9

Running my tongue over my teeth, nostrils flaring, I climb the imperial staircase two by two. At the top of the stairs, the hallway splits into two separate directions and I turn right, storming into my study. It's where we conduct most of our Sin Eaters meetings. Byzantine is already here, Bastian too, along with other men from our crew.

"Everyone out except you two," I bark, heading toward my desk next to the large window.

"We weren't finished," someone says behind me.

I turn fast on my heels, eager to see which idiot thought it was a good idea to undermine me. Diego stands near the fireplace to my left and by the expression under his full black beard, I can tell he's regretting every decision he's ever made. He's a big guy, bigger than I am, but that doesn't prevent me from lurching towards him and grabbing him by the ear, dragging him out into the hallway. If I'm going to make him bleed, better not do it on several thousands worth of designer carpet.

I slam my fist hard into his gut and he immediately wheezes and doubles over onto his knees. Before he even touches the ground, I bend my leg and knee him in the nose. I can feel *and* hear the bone crack before his eyes roll back and he lands hard on his ass. Bastard better not have damaged my hardwood floors.

Stepping into the study, I glare at anyone who isn't my best friend or cousin.

"I said get the fuck out." Striding through the room, I rake my hair back in place "And get that piece of shit out of my sight."

A chorus of *yes sir* can be heard before the door closes and Byzantine and Bastian simply stare at me questioningly. Ignoring them, I take my suit jacket off and carefully fold it over the chair before finally sitting behind my custom-made mahogany desk. I grab my phone and check my emails.

The two of them haven't stopped staring since I reentered.

"What," I say flatly, my eyes still looking down.

"Bad day?" Byzantine asks, clearly entertained by my sudden outburst.

"He had it coming," I growl.

"Sure." He sinks into the chair in front of me and Bastian follows suit.

My muscles grow tight, slamming my phone down as I finally glare at them both. Byzantine is sporting an amused look on his face, his lopsided grin in prominent display while Bastian just seems uninterested as usual. He reaches for his laptop, most likely trying to evade any more of this interaction.

I can tell my second-in-command is mulling his words over and I bet Sunny has already told him that I met with Lenix this morning. My body is vibrating with the promise of knocking this fucker out if he even utters a word about it. I smirk, goading him to do just that.

He holds my stare for another few seconds, but finally just sighs, clearly conceding. Leaning forward, he hands me an unsealed manila envelope.

"What's this?" I ask.

"The names you asked for," Bastian answers for him, eyes still locked on his screen, bleached, almost white, blond hair falling over his forehead.

Ripping the thing out of Byzantine's hands, I fish out the papers tucked inside and give it a quick glance. Some names I recognize and some I don't.

"Good," I mutter.

I drop the papers and envelope on the desk, stand up and head for the wet bar. I pour myself two fingers worth of mezcal and slam it back. I pour another, dropping some ice cubes into the tumbler this time before heading back to my desk.

"Not in a sharing mood?" Byzantine quips.

"Jesus fucking Christ, does everyone have a death wish

today?" I grit out exasperated. I sit back down and grab hold of the papers again. "Pour your own damn drink."

He chuckles while standing up, making himself a whiskey and then one for Bastian who takes his with a quick nod.

"Who's everyone?" My best friend asks, continuing his grating questioning.

I close my eyes, and inhale through my nose, smoothing over my mustache, my jaw clenching so hard that I can feel it all the way up to my fucking skull.

"I swear to god, if you don't get out of my ass, and stop asking me stupid fucking questions, I'm going to reach over this goddamn desk and cut out your tongue."

Byzantine doesn't react, not even a flinch. Just sits there, sipping on his whiskey, assessing, eyebrow slightly raised, green eyes glinting with mirth.

Bastian eventually cuts the tension by closing his laptop. "Later." He shoves his computer in his bag and promptly walks out the door. All the while, Byzantine continues to stare and I continue to fantasize about ringing his fucking neck.

Finally, he places his now empty glass beside him and stands. "Let me know if you need any more intel on some of those names. I'll have Bastian find out more."

I give him a nod and he leaves.

The room falls silent but I'm still breathing hard. I haven't been able to calm down since I pulled my gun out on that palm reader. It's not like I feel any remorse. She had it coming with all that fucking drivel she was on about. But it's left me rattled. And that's a hard feat to achieve.

Distracted, I don't notice my hand moving up to my chest like it has a life of its own. My finger rubs my chest directly over my heart as if soothing a small, near imperceptible, twinge. As soon as I realize what I'm doing, I yank my hand away.

*What the fuck am I doing?*

That psychic's question, or whatever the fuck she was, echoes in my head.

"*Do you have a birthmark over your heart?*"

I spring out of my seat and head for my bedroom at the end of the curved hallway. Passing closed doors and largely unoccupied rooms, I begin unbuttoning my dress shirt, revealing my chest underneath, my body so heavily tattooed now that you can barely see the skin anymore.

Crossing the threshold, I trek across the room, walking right up to the floor length mirror in the corner near the walk-in closet. I stare at my reflection, my muscles taut. I'm feeling fucking ridiculous but all of a sudden I'm on my hand and knees pulling a plastic box from under the bed.

Inside, I find a photo album from when I was young—when my mother was still around. It's one of the few things she left behind when she walked out on me and my father twenty-three years ago. I flip through the laminated pages, the smell of a home lost wafting through my nose with each page turn, finally landing on a few pictures of us at the beach. There's one of me, waving at the camera in nothing but a bathing suit and a green bucket hat. Must have been six or seven. I take the picture out of the plastic and look at it closely. It's grainy but unmistakable, my birthmark like a small splatter of paint directly over my heart.

# 10

## Lenix

Hunched over my oval kitchen table with one leg raised up on the chair, I peruse the binders stuffed with an assortment of color SKUs and fabric swatches thrown haphazardly around me. I'm working from home today, trying to land on a coherent theme for Connor's event. My glass of rosé is perched precariously on one of the many piles on the table while I riffle through the thick binder next to me.

It's been a few days since that bizarre morning with

Connor. He's been radio silent since then and I only have the palm reader to thank. My response was to push the errant thoughts of what transpired that day far down somewhere where I don't have to stumble on it anytime soon. It's second nature, like a muscle I've trained to do my bidding.

The thought of him being spooked is almost laughable though. He's always been hot-headed but to go so far as to pull a gun on an innocent bystander? What a ridiculous show of power.

I've conveniently omitted telling Sunny about it. I don't like keeping secrets from her. But it hasn't prevented me from doing just that for most of our friendship. The guilt of keeping so much from her nearly knocks my breath out of my lungs when I linger on the thought for too long. But these secrets are different. I'm the only one who needs to bear the memories of what I've done.

Then there's the secret I share with Connor. The one I've been keeping for over two years now. But the reason I've kept that one hidden from Sunny has a lot more to do with pride—and absolute mortification. The thought of hearing her tell me *I told you so* would be enough for me to wither up and die. I wish what I'm keeping from her could be as simple as us hooking up once or twice. That was never the problem. Frustratingly, it was the best part of that damn affair. But I'd stab Connor in the heart before I would ever come close to admitting that to him.

Pompous asshole.

My phone rings from under a pile of strewn papers and I curse under my breath while looking for it, hoping I'll find it before the call ends. My hand finally lands on it and I fish it out, feeling slightly victorious. I notice it's a blocked caller ID, but don't think much of it since I have a panoply of businesses, venues and suppliers calling me at every hour of the day.

"Hello?"

"Penelope…"

My free hand shoots out as if trying to defend against an unidentified threat, knocking my wine right off the table. The glass shatters on the floor, mirroring the shattered pieces of my mind as the name that's been long dead echoes in my ear.

"Who is this?" I say, trying to keep my voice as steady as possible. But a slumbering part of me knows. I could trace his face in the dark with just the sound of his voice.

I should hang up. *Just fucking hang up.*

But I'm utterly frozen, victim to the seconds creeping by, waiting for him to speak again.

"Has it been so long that you do not recognize the sound of your own brother's voice?" Frederick says tauntingly.

I'm suddenly so nauseous that I fight the pool of saliva accumulating in my mouth threatening to turn into bile. I swallow hard, desperately trying to collect myself but my whole body is shaking. My reaction is visceral. Every single memory I've been trying to keep captive under duress is let loose. I don't know if I'll survive this resurgence when I've gone so long without looking at any of it.

The commune.

My sisters and brothers. My mother.

The cilice cutting into my skin.

My too-young body in a wedding dress.

The blood seeping into the cracks of the floorboards. My father's dark eyes suddenly lifeless.

My escape.

The gravel digging into the soles of my feet while I ran and ran and ran. The harsh wind with no end in sight.

Then finally a light in the distance. A diner.

And an angel named Martha.

I blink long and hard. Once. Twice. And finally, find my voice again. "How did you find me?" I croak, the memories clambering to resurface while I struggle to take a breath.

I hear him laughing dryly through the receiver before he says, "We were always going to find you, Penelope. It was an eventuality."

I swallow hard, opening my mouth, closing it, then finally. "How do you even have a phone to call me with?"

My mind is so scattered that it's focusing on the wrong things instead of the most glaringly important ones. Like the one where my brother is threatening to bring me back into the flock.

"When Father died, I was brought forth as the new messenger of Sacro Nuntio. There is an allowance for a few frivolities when having to deal with the ungodly… such as yourself, sister." His tone drips with disgust and superiority.

My blood heats, boiling me alive from the inside out.

"So you're having Patrick follow me? You can't even do it yourself?" I say incensed. Patrick, my ex-fiancé, doing my brother's dirty bidding. I silently chew my lip raw waiting for his response.

I still don't understand how he's been able to pin me down. I legally changed my name. And the only online presence I have is of the business and typically, I try to keep my face out of the pictures. The demure sixteen year old he knew is not who I am now.

"Come home, Penelope. You can do it willingly or by force. Either way, your life in Noxport ends. I am giving you until the end of the week. By his touch, we live."

He hangs up and I'm left clutching my phone so hard against my face that I'm sure I've left a dent on the side of my cheek.

By his touch, we live? By his *fucking* touch?

Hearing that Sacro Nuntio saying leaves me disgusted and lightheaded. Not only that but hearing his inflection and choice of words reminds me of how much effort it took for me to change the way I spoke when I first ended up in Noxport. Valley speak was the fastest thing to pick up and was my shield for years until I morphed into the person—or is it a persona?—I am today. I'd walk around downtown and just listen. As silly as it was, to me it sounded like freedom. It tasted like defiance on my tongue and it wasn't long until I began to crave it. I was already cursed. Ungodly. What was one more sin if it felt this good?

My brother is out of his holier-than-thou fucking mind if he thinks I'll willingly leave the life I've created for myself and come *home* without a fight.

I just need a plan.

# 11

## Connor

Leaning against my SUV, shades on and hands tucked deep in my dark blue jeans pockets, I watch Lenix jog towards her building. I'm in plain view of her front door but she hasn't seen me yet.

Light brown skin glistening in the afternoon sun, her long black hair pulled away from her neck, swishing this way and that while she runs.

I let my mind wander for just a second, a

millisecond even, revealing a flash of a memory from two years ago. Of Lenix flushed underneath me. My fingers digging into her hips as the fingers of my other hand slid into her open mouth, her hot tongue curling for a taste, a staccato of breathy moans I could feel on my own skin.

*Jesus.*

I sucker punch the vision as far away as possible while the present Lenix nearly jumps out of her skin at the sight of me. I push myself off the car door, a smirk on my lips.

"Boo."

I'm expecting a barrage of expletives to leave her mouth but instead, she just sticks her hands on her hips, her chest heaving beautifully while she catches her breath.

"I'm busy." And turns towards her building.

I follow her. As one does.

But before reaching the door, she stops and swivels around. "What are you doing?" she says, crossing her arms, clearly annoyed.

"We need to talk."

She side-eyes my cocky grin. "About?"

"The event." I run my index and thumb over my mustache, lowering my voice. "What else darling?"

I notice her eyes quickly dart around, scanning her surroundings before landing back on me. She schools her features quickly and gives me a small smirk of her own.

"Oh? Not about your little freak out from the last time I saw you?"

I internally wince. I should have known she'd bring it up. I somehow wished she'd suffer from a sudden bout of amnesia.

"You've never seen me 'freak out', as you put it." I drag my gaze up and down, my eyes narrowing and decide to put a little more venom to my tone. "You wouldn't speak to me so brazenly if you had."

She scoffs. "Is that supposed to scare me? Or better yet *impress* me?"

"Why would I care about impressing you, Lenny?" I say while looking away disinterested.

My little jab doesn't land as expected.

She just smiles. "And yet, here we are."

I glance back, quirking a brow. "Meaning?"

Stepping closer to me—and then even closer still, she leans in.

"You're obsessed with me," she says as her nail trails down my shirt. It hovers close to where my jeans and shirt meet, her finger dipping between the two, finding the skin underneath. The hair on my arms raises but I don't move a muscle. With her lips now close to my ear, she whispers, "Do you miss me? Is that it?"

That's enough to jolt me back into the land of the living, and I swat her hand away taking a large step back. "Miss you? All we did was fuck a few times. Don't be delusional."

Her expression goes from hooded eyes to cold hard stare in a split second. "My point exactly." Jamming her index finger into my chest. "So why don't you sign the damn papers, and stop being such a psycho."

"*Christ*, that again?"

"That again?" she repeats incredulously. "Do you realize how unhinged you sound?" Before I can formulate a quick comeback, she turns around and punches in the code for the front door and opens it. "If you even *think* of following me up, I will pepper spray you right in the eyes, I swear to fucking God."

I laugh but stay put. As much as it pains me to do so, I

let her have the win and watch the door close behind her. I imagine fucking that little attitude right out of her, while I readjust my hardening cock currently pushing against my jeans.

But I also rather enjoy her like this. Why would I ever sign the papers when it lends to the best kind of foreplay?

But obsessed?

Please.

Making my way back to my car, I climb into the driver's seat and fish out a joint from the small metal box in the middle compartment and light it. My head hits the headrest behind me before taking my first drag, eyes closed. I take a few seconds to allow the high to roll in like a fog through my limbs and eventually let my eyelids flutter back open.

My gaze lands on the car parked only a few feet away. I can barely discern the person driving it, only what looks to be a man. For reasons I can't really explain, I'm suddenly on high alert.

For the next few minutes, I stay low, smoking my joint while I observe the car and the guy sitting inside: talking on the phone, keeping his car idle, but most importantly his attention seems fixed on Lenix's building.

There's something about this whole situation that makes me fucking *itch* for a confrontation. Not one to suppress those urges, I pop the car door open and jump out. In a few quick strides, I'm beside the driver's window. The idiot doesn't notice me until I bang my fist on the car door and he jumps. At first, he just stares at me like a gaping fish out of water, so I motion for him to roll down his window.

As slowly as humanly fucking possible, he does.

When there's finally nothing between us, I ask with irritation, "You waiting for someone?"

"Wh—why?"

"Well, you seem pretty fucking interested in that building over there." I point over his car, joint still between two fingers. "So what's your reason?"

"No reason," he answers quickly, looking like a rodent caught in a trap, twitchy and full of shit.

Calmly, I flick the joint into the streets and reach for the gun tucked in the back of my jeans and press it to his temple. "So then I would encourage you to get the fuck out of my sight before I shoot you in the fucking head."

He splutters, his eyes growing wide while his hand reaches blindly beside him, shifting the car into drive. I take a step back, flashing him a toothy smile like I'm just being neighborly. His car jerks forward, and then finally drives away while I give him a small wave, gun still in hand.

*Fucker.*

Finally, I walk back to my SUV and drive away from Lenix's building myself.

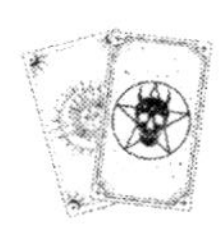

PULLING open the door of The Chelsea, I walk in. The bar is one of many the Sin Eaters own in the city, located in an up and coming neighborhood near the city center. It's an unassuming kind of place, with barely a sign outside the door, but inside the atmosphere is warm and unpretentious.

My gaze sweeps the room trying to locate the president of the Black Plague MC, eventually finding him in a back corner booth. Hands in my pockets and a grin on my face, I unhurriedly stroll over. It's mid-afternoon, the place isn't busy, still the few patrons in here can't help but to swivel their heads as I walk by.

"Took you long enough," McGregor says gruffly and

slightly irked, bringing his hands to the pilsner sweating in front of him. His club runs out of Pueblo Quieto, a landlocked town two hours outside of Noxport.

"I had more important business to attend to," I reply with a cocky smirk while I slide into the worn black leather booth directly in front of him. He grunts his displeasure but says nothing as I flag the waitress for a drink.

The Sin Eaters and the Black Plague have been doing business for more than two decades, there's never been any bad blood between us and have always stayed allies. Still, Noxport is a port city and I hold monopoly with what comes in and out, illicit or otherwise.

The waitress brings me a mezcal on ice with a slice of orange without me having to ask and I give her a wink as well as a hundred dollar tip for a job well done.

Taking a sip, I study him from across the table, the liquor smokey and smooth down my throat. "Tell me why I'm here."

McGregor takes a swig of his pint, sweeping his long rusty brown hair out of his face before speaking. "We want to expand our drug trade, widen our territory and start importing from Russia," he answers, his Scottish accent peeking through even after decades of living overseas. He settles back into the booth, straightening his cut before crossing his tattooed arms over his broad chest. "We need access to your ports to do so."

"Is that so?" I cock one eyebrow, my interest peaked. I keep my expression impassive with a hint of arrogance but inside, I'm rifling through all the possibilities and advantages this could hold for the Sin Eaters. Most importantly, free shipping for any drugs coming out of Russia. I've had a contact for years now but was unable to do anything with it since I didn't have the trade routes. Until now. All I need for them to do is put our drugs alongside their shipment, and once in Noxport, my men simply remove it from the crates and the Black Plague is none the wiser.

Ignoring my sarcasm McGregor continues, "Ten percent for every shipment coming through Noxport."

My glare grows serious, my typical amusement effectively erased while it's my turn to lean into the booth, left hand splayed over the top. "I don't even get out of bed for ten percent. Think again."

His nostrils flare, but says nothing, eyes turning hard while he seems to mull over what I just said. "Fifteen," he finally says.

Settling back, I stare him down from over my drink, thinking over his offer. I place the glass back down and swipe my hand over my mustache before answering. "Twenty, and we get first pick on any product you bring in."

McGregor curses under his breath, looking anywhere but me until his gaze finally circles back to mine, his palm reaching between us both. "Deal, *blaigeard*."

I chuckle mirthlessly and shake his hand, then jerk him towards me and over the table, nearly spilling his beer. "And next time you call me a bastard in Gaelic, I'll slice your balls clean off, you understand me?"

By his expression, I can tell he doesn't know if I'm kidding or not, and that's exactly how I like to keep it. His gaze studies me for a beat until he pulls away. "Got it," he says.

"Good," I reply, signaling to the waitress for another round. "Now let's drink."

# 12

Laying on my back in bed, I stare at the ceiling. The insomnia is like an unwanted visitor sitting heavy on my chest. I haven't moved in what seems like hours. Not since I woke, startled from a dream—or more like a memory from another life.

A time when I wasn't so bold. Or rarely had an original thought of my own.

I didn't know any better, I know that.

I should have compassion for that younger version of

myself. The one who was brainwashed from the time she took her first breath.

Instead, I hate her. I can't stand her. I would kill her if I could.

But Frederick's phone call rattled the ghosts dozing in my head. They're now haunting the long halls of my mind, poking at things that shouldn't be touched.

Now I'm wide awake, replaying the dream in my head. I was with my sister Lucy, playing in the wild flowers up the slanted hill from our house. Lucy wasn't, *isn't* my only sister but we were the closest. She's five years younger, and we also share the same mother.

I lost everything that day—thirteen years ago. I never even had time to grieve the people I left behind. It was just too much to bear, a pain that was so acute it felt cold. And so that's what I did, I froze. I haven't let my emotions thaw since. And if I have any control over it, they will remain frozen as long as I have breath in me.

But this dream is a loose cannon, threatening to unearth feelings I can not and will not deal with. As I continue to stare at the ceiling, I can feel a lone tear escape my left eye. It travels down my temple and into my hair. I pretend I can't sense it rolling down my skin. If I lay perfectly still, maybe the feeling will eventually leave. Like evading a wild animal, I play dead hoping this expanding sadness inside me will disappear and go attack another poor unsuspecting soul.

Not me. Please just… not me.

The duvet tucked tight over my chest begins to feel like a trap, and I'm suffocating under the weight of it. I jerk upwards and fling the damn thing off me.

I can feel the restlessness settle deep into my bones. It's early, maybe four or five in the morning but I can't just sit here and dwell. I need to do something before I snap, so I jump out of bed and head for the closet. I slip into some leggings and a sports bra, then tug my running shoes on and bolt out the door.

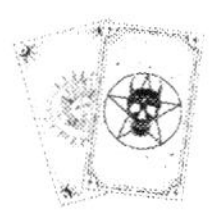

I PARK my car at the foot of the wooded hiking trail. I've driven in near trance-like determination up here as if this was the remedy to all my problems. Not sure what over-came me to think that I'm the kind of active person who hikes but there was no convincing me otherwise.

There's not a soul around and a small voice inside tells me this is how eighty percent of all crime shows begin but I decide to ignore it. Stepping out in the still crisp night air, I inhale deeply and head for the trail, weaving between the trees.

My muscles were already tired before I even began, and five minutes into the hike, they're now throbbing but I'm too stubborn to quit now. Eventually, the heavy breathing and the constant push of my body up the path pulls me into a state of serene quietness. Like I've somehow slipped underwater, even the rustle of the cool breeze through the leaves above me has become muted. I focus on the need to climb and climb and climb. And eventually, after the longest thirty minutes of my life, the terrain evens out and I realize I've reached the top of the hill. A small twinge of victory pulls at my heart as if this hike meant something else entirely but I don't linger on the feeling and flop onto the dry dirt at my feet.

The pebbles bite into my back while I lay there, arms spread up near my head but I pay them no mind. From my peripheral, I watch my chest rise and fall, as I slowly catch my breath. The twinkling stars above are slowly disappearing, slipping back into the depths as the night sky turns into early morning. I listen to the sound of my own breathing while my heart eventually returns to a normal speed and finally I stand back up.

I realize I can see the expanse of the city outline from this high up. And somehow, the change of perspective from this vantage point makes me think I can do anything.

It's a false belief. But I embrace it.

For a small fleeting moment while I watch the sunrise over Noxport, the rays bouncing off the glass of the taller buildings, nothing really feels that dire. There's hope in every sunrise, and I'm privy to this one. I let it tingle through my tired limbs, my eyes falling closed for just a moment as I let this strange feeling sink in. A feeling I don't quite recognize.

But it doesn't last long.

This feeling can only exist here. And I can't stay here forever.

The small tranquil smile I didn't even realize was on my face in the first place disappears. I take one last long look at the city, and the ocean even further out melting into the horizon, and turn away.

My calves scream all the way down, but I barely take notice, lost in thought. The same thoughts I managed to hide from on the way up. The trail ends and my thoughts darken, walking gingerly to my car. Inside, I sit in silence, biting my lip and chastising myself for feeling so weak. My insides are threatening to crawl out of me. I can't remember the last time I've felt this rattled. I hate it.

But I refuse to cry.

I jam the keys into the ignition, my hands shaking. I

choose the loudest EDM song I can find and tune out. By the time I park in my building's underground car park, I've managed to regain some kind of composure and wrestle my persona back into place. Lenix does not do morose. Lenix is fun, flirty and casual. I flip down the car mirror, patting the few stray tears that are on my cheek, fix a smile on my face and climb out of my car.

# 13

## Lenix

I'm on my way home, stuck in the late Friday afternoon traffic. It's nearing the end of the week and my brother's threat is grating at me with every passing second. I know it's not an empty threat. Not when I still remember a few instances when women would disappear and then reappear a few weeks later—or even months. No one would dare say anything out loud but we knew. Upon their return, everyone would act like nothing was out of the ordinary. A sister had simply lost her way and been found again. I couldn't see it then, but now looking back my stomach sinks recalling the look of defeat in their eyes when they were eventually brought back into the flock.

There's absolutely no way I'm going back.

I know what waits for me if I do. I've been gone too long. There wouldn't be repentance for my sins, only damnation. I would be used as an example for all. I would have to pay for what I did to my father.

A pedophile. But a holy one.

It's the only thing that matters to the elders—and now Frederick.

There's no love lost between my brother and I. I don't secretly wish to save him like I do my sister. Or any of my siblings even. Being thrust into the real world, allowed me the vocabulary to understand the dynamics within the commune. A goddamn cult is what it is. The reins of patriarchy are so insidious that I know I've lost my brother from the corruption of it all. He's brainwashed—just how I used to be. But it's harder to save someone in his position, to make him see the light when he so willfully benefits from the system held in place. He's not a victim.

And nor will I be. Ever again

I glance distractedly to the car idling beside me. That's when I see him.

Patrick. My ex-fiancé. The one I was meant to marry that day.

He hasn't even looked my way but my adrenaline spikes nonetheless. *Fuck.* I need to make a decision fast. And when the traffic finally starts to move, I try to lose him. But after a few random turns into streets that are leading away from my condo, his car is still trailing behind me. My chest tightens as I mentally think through the options I have.

They're limited but one continues to pop up, demanding my attention and finally I crack.

I connect the Bluetooth and make the call.

It rings and rings until *finally* Connor picks up.

"Is this a butt dial?" he says, voice bright, instead of hello.

I roll my eyes out of frustration. *I wish.*

"Are you home?" I say impatiently, skipping the dumb pleasantries and getting straight to the point, my grip tightening around the steering wheel.

"No. Why?" he says, finally being serious.

"Where are you?" I ask while checking my rearview mirror.

"I'm having a drink at The Chelsea."

"Are you alone?"

"Yeah, Bastian just left. What's going on?" I can almost hear concern tinting his tone.

"I don't have time to explain right now, but meet me outside in fifteen."

I hang up before he has time to decline and speed towards the bar, his car still following me from a block away, my heart in my throat.

When I finally park in front of The Chelsea, Patrick has lost all his stealth—he knows he's got me cornered. He parks right beside me. I do a quick sweep of the parking lot but Connor is nowhere to be found bringing my adrenaline to an all time high

*Great.*

When my ex-fiancé climbs out of his car, I quickly lock my doors, sitting practically paralyzed in my seat, my fingers white-knuckling the steering wheel.

"Where the hell is he," I say under my breath as I watch Patrick approach my window and crouch low to look into it, a placating smile on his lips that gives me the fucking creeps and reminds me of my father's.

All of it was fake, I've come to realize, even their smiles.

The asshole tries to tell me to open my car door but I give him the finger instead, keeping my gaze facing forward. He slams his palm into the side window and I flinch.

His voice is muffled but I can still hear the warning in his tone. "Open the door, Penelope."

I close my eyes for a beat, taking a deep breath, trying to stay calm. I'm about to call Connor again when I see the front door of the bar swing open and he strolls outside, glancing around. At the same moment, Patrick tries to open my locked door, his body jerking in frustration while he forcibly pulls on the handle.

What he doesn't see is Connor taking notice. I watch through the window as his body straightens, dark brows narrowing, his expression quickly morphing from casually entertained to deadly, and my heart can't help but to soar at the sight.

Feeling slightly more confident about the situation now that the resident psycho is close by, I unlock my car and push my door open, slamming it hard into Patrick. He stumbles back but eventually regains his balance while I step out.

I give Connor an apologetic look but his gaze is locked on the man trying to drag me back to the cult. A flicker of recognition travels across his face before he steels his expression. None of us say a word while we watch Connor casually pull out a metal cigarette case and take out a joint, flicking his zippo open and taking a long drag before looking back at the man in question.

With the joint still tucked between his index and middle

finger he points to Patrick and says, "You." While taking a slow step forward. "Didn't I have a gun to your head last time I saw you?" he says, tone dripping with tedium.

Surprise roots me to the spot, my head snapping to my ex-fiancé. He looks slightly befuddled, opening his mouth and then closing it. However, that small moment of confusion on his part propels me into action. Back straight, head high, I walk towards Connor and slide my arm around his. His body jerks, his gaze suddenly on the place our arms are linked but I pay no mind, readying to drop the bomb that might solve all of my problems or make everything ten times worse.

"You can tell Frederick, I'm not going anywhere," I say with a smug smile, I try to pull Connor even closer, but he's not budging. "And if any of you ever try to get close to me again, you'll have to go through my *husband* first."

# 14

## Connor

The word *husband* hangs heavy between us while I try to wrap my head around what the fuck is happening. Lenix's arm is still tucked tightly into mine, her face calm but I can feel how tense her body is leaning against me. I'm about to open my mouth to deny any such thing, but she stealthily kicks my shin and I realize with sudden clarity that I've led myself right into this trap.

Not to mention that this is the same guy I saw in front of her building the other day and it doesn't take a fucking dummy to realize he's been stalking her. Not one to shy away from scaring the living shit out of people, I pull out my gun on him yet again and push Lenix behind me.

I can hear her hurried whisper near my ear before I can decide if this guy is even worthy of the bullet inside the chamber of my gun.

"Don't," is all she says.

There's a split second where the urge is bright and heady, but there's enough of a plea in her tone that I reluctantly shove my Glock back into my holster and stalk straight to him instead. He flinches, a small whimper escaping his lips. His reaction gives me the smallest of pleasure. Or at least scratched the itch some.

Finally, I fist his shirt into my hand and drag him up close to me, his shaky breath fanning across my face.

"I don't know what the fuck is going on here. And trust me, I'll soon find out. But if I ever see you near… " I pause for half a second, my expression still blank, swallowing hard, unwilling to call her by the word currently feeling like sandpaper on my tongue. "*Her* again. I'll skin you alive." I release him from my grip—not before giving him a hard shove first and he staggers back. I spit on his shoes, stare him straight in the eyes and smile.

Shockingly, the idiot finds the nerve to point a shaky finger at Lenix and says, "You are dancing with the devil, Penelope." Before scrambling to his car.

*Penelope?*

I don't have enough time to wonder who the fuck that is before I take quick note of his license plate to relay to Bastian later. Finally, I turn slowly towards Lenix while I hear the tires screech behind me, the car pulling out of the parking lot in haste.

Her eyes are wide, rattled and flustered. But there's also the ghost of a smile on her face. And just like a chameleon changing its colors, I watch as Lenix gracefully shakes the fear off and crosses her arms in defiance, her grin now wide and arrogant.

"What?" she says with a small innocent tilt to her tone.

My fingers flex, fighting the urge to wrap them around her throat and squeeze. Or maybe slam her into the wall and fuck her. Whichever quells the fire the fastest. Instead, I fix a blasé expression on my face, swipe my hand over my mustache and keep my voice steady. "Care to explain?"

She pushes her tongue into her cheek and raises her eyebrows as if thinking. "Which part?"

My restraint snaps and I stalk forward, her eyes going wide when my fingers find her throat. Her body stumbles backwards but I squeeze her neck just hard enough to keep her steady.

"Maybe the part about me being your husband?" I bite out.

She schools her expression as soon as her initial shock is under control, a condescending glint to her eye.

"Well," she says, raising her hands up to my shoulders and giving my suit a quick sweep as if fixing my outfit. "Considering you *are* my husband…" She then hums as if recalling something. "You remember, don't you?" My blood burns but her eyes burn even hotter before she continues, "Since you think it's *so* funny not to sign the papers, I figured I might as well get something out of the single worst trip to Vegas I've ever had."

I could kill her. I *should* kill her.

I let her go, no longer wanting to touch or even be close to her.

But the most aggravating part of all this is that she's not lying.

"For fuck sakes Lenix, don't be so overdramatic."

"Overdramatic?" she says, her eyes wide in disbelief. "Connor, this isn't a joke."

"Darling," I reply while walking towards my car parked away from hers. "You must be as delusional as me if you think I'll go along with this for even a second longer."

"Wait." The sound of that one word holds more weight than anything she's said since she showed up here. I stop, my back still turned but look over my shoulder and find her demeanor completely changed.

Nervous. Shoulders slightly hunched. Hands wringing together.

She takes a large inhale and closes her eyes before her stare lands back on mine.

"I need your help," she says in a near-whisper.

*Fuck.*

That shouldn't make me feel anything—including empathy. But here we are. Plus Byzantine would have my head if I left Lenix high and dry, considering that she's Sunny's best friend.

I tell myself this is the only reason and turn on my heels, walking back to her. "Are you going to tell me what the fuck is happening then? And why that asshole called you Penelope?" I hold in the urge to crinkle my face, the name not tasting right for Lenix's explosive flavor.

She bites her lips, her shoulders dropping. "I'll tell you everything, I swear. Just—just not here okay?"

I let the silence fall between us, letting it stretch for far too long, savoring the way she squirms before finally dragging a palm over my face, then stuffing my hands into my pockets.

Exhausted from this turn of events, I let out a long exhale. "Fine, let's go."

# 15

I sit rigidly on one of Connor's large gray couches in his sprawling living room. Everything about his place screams modern architecture, including the floor to ceiling windows facing the ocean. My feet are tucked underneath me, tugging on my skirt that's ridden up my thigh. By the look of this place, he doesn't entertain all too many people in this one room. It looks pristine, ripped right out of a home lifestyle magazine.

I stare at a lone beauty mark on my knee, trying to

avoid Connor's glare as he sits in front of me in a chair that doesn't even look like it's meant for sitting. It looks hard, uncomfortable and most importantly—expensive.

Finally, he clears his throat and I slowly focus my attention on his. "Speak," he says.

My eyes narrow, a few choice words at the ready but swallow them back down. My fingers find my hair, and I twirl them around a strand trying to fight the nerves crawling all over me. What comes out of my mouth however, are half-truths.

"My ex-fiance has been stalking me."

His eyebrows shoot up in surprise.

"What?" I ask.

"You've been single the entire time I've known you."

"Yeah, well we all have our origin stories don't we? Our relationship didn't end well. He became obsessed. He—he threatened me and… I've been running away from him ever since." Oh how the lies taste sweet on my tongue. Connor doesn't need to know who's actually after me. Just that I need protection.

Connor fixes his gaze on me—studying, examining—and for a second I think he won't believe me. Instead he says, "Why did he call you Penelope?"

"Lenix is my middle name." Another lie.

"So I'll just kill him," he says flippantly.

"No. Jesus," I huff out in exasperation. "That's not the solution to every fucking problem."

"Isn't it?" he replies with a shrug, leaning back in the chair and rubbing his mustache contemplatively.

"I just need… protection." I fight an internal cringe. I hate giving Connor this much power but I have no other real choice.

Connor quirks a smile as if I just gave him a compliment. I roll my eyes.

"What's in it for me?" he finally says.

My nails bite into my thigh as I try not to hurl an insult straight at him. "I don't know Connor, maybe just be decent for once?"

His grin grows even wider as he stares me down, leaning forward, his arms on his knees, hands loose in front of him. "I'm anything but decent, darling."

Against my will, I feel my cheeks flush. I'm appalled by my own body's reaction to him. A villain with a royal air that has always made my throat go dry.

"Can you be serious for once in your miserable life?"

"I am being serious."

I jump to my feet.

"You know what? Never mind." I'm way too stubborn to continue to beg *Connor* of all people. I would rather place myself in direct danger than continue trying to convince him of something he clearly doesn't want to do. But before I can storm out of the room, his hand wraps itself around my wrist and I freeze.

"Sit back down, Lenix. We're not finished." His voice is hard and flat, what I imagine he sounds like as the leader of the Sin Eaters.

I try to yank my arm out of his grip but he's stronger. He tilts his head to the side and looks me up from the corner of his eyes.

"Sit. Down," he says with the same tone, a small chill traveling down my spine at the sound.

I stifle a hard swallow, my knees buckling slightly under me, but I manage to stay perfectly still, my eyes never breaking eye contact.

"There's more to this story, I can tell but..." he adds

musingly, his hand sliding up my arm, leaving goosebumps in his wake. "I'll help you."

I exhale, relief traveling quickly through my limbs, until the devil himself opens his mouth once more.

"I have some conditions."

I pull my arm away and look down at him from where I'm standing, indignation burning hot inside my chest. "Wasn't you forcing us to stay married after all this time, condition enough?"

"Hardly," he says as he motions me to sit back down with a quick flick of the wrist. I eye a vase on a side table near his chair and daydream about smashing it over his head before finally sitting my ass back down on the couch with a huff. As if plucking the thought right out of my head, Connor's glare lingers while he slowly pushes the vase further away.

He leans back into the chair, looking me up and down as if appraising me. I bite into my lip, the pain centering me while I wait for him to finally voice his conditions. I can't help but to speak first. "What is it Connor? Out with it."

He smirks.

"If you want this to work in your favor. You need everyone to believe we're actually happily married." Connor's lip curls into a sneer as if him even saying those two words together is making him physically ill and my stomach sinks. I hear his words before they're even uttered out of his mouth. "That includes Sunny."

"She doesn't need to know for this to work," I say quickly in protest.

"Oh yes she does. If your ex-fiancé is like any other loser out there moaning over the loss of ownership." He gives me a hard stare, daring me to react. In my head I do, the vase's already in pieces around him. In reality I sit still, my hands balling into fists to fight the urge to rip his eyeballs out of his skull. "Your best friend of all people needs to believe the lie."

I take a long inhale, while I let what he just said sink in.

"She won't buy it," I mutter.

"Make her. And oh," he says abruptly, raising a finger as if he just thought of something. But I know better to believe it—everything is calculated when it comes to Connor Maxwell. "You're moving in."

"What?" I practically screech.

Connor runs his tongue along his front teeth while he watches me react, seemingly enjoying every second of this.

"Regretting roping me into this yet?"

"Fuck you."

"Careful darling… if you want my help? You'll behave like a good—"

"Don't you dare say what I think you're about to say."

He chuckles low with fire in his eyes. "Stop making this harder than it has to be. And besides I don't know why you're the one bitching and moaning about this. *You* came to *me* with your little problem."

I wouldn't call being forced back into a life of servitude and God knows what else a little problem but I bite my tongue and swallow the hard pill Connor is currently shoving down my throat.

"Fine," I say, stubbornly crossing my arm over my chest. "Anything else *your majesty*?"

"You accompany me to any social function I need to attend. As long as this little arrangement lasts."

"Why?"

"Some of the men I deal with are old school, being married gives me something for them to relate to. If I'm married, I become more trustworthy in their eyes. There's a few closed circles I'm still not invited into for exactly that reason. Also," he trails off, waving a lazy hand around. "I might have fucked a few of their wives."

Connor's devious grin is enough to give me a heart attack. I've never seen someone so full of themselves. This time I don't react, instead I stand up.

"As long as you don't continue to fuck their wives, you have yourself a deal Mr. Maxwell." The words slip out unencumbered and I regret them immediately. I manage to keep my expression neutral, ready to get the hell out of here and enjoy my last night of freedom before I'm ensnared into what might be the stupidest decision of my life.

I brandish my hand towards him and he stands up, taking my hand in his to shake. But then he pulls me towards him and I stumble into his chest, his familiar scent of cedarwood and orange blossom warping my senses. His other hand lands on the small of my back, keeping me in place. His lips find the shell of my ear while my heart beats wildly in my chest.

"This is going to be fun," he growls.

# 16

Leaning on the rails of my balcony, a joint hanging loosely between my fingers, I watch the smoke curl up and up against the city's night sky and sigh.

I wish I was smoke.

In the same way that I wish I wasn't bound to any one thing. Incorporeal. Free to just… be.

Freedom is a fickle word, when it feels like I've been imprisoned my entire life. If not chained by my father's influence, it was from the fear of being found, the fear of being caught, for people to know I'm a fake. That Lenix isn't even real. Who am I behind the charade of hoping I'll never be found… when I've been lost since the very beginning.

And now this.

Was this really my only choice?

To make a deal with the devil?

It definitely felt like it at the time. I'm unsure why turning to Connor for protection was my initial reaction in the first place. I avoid examining it any further. I dodge the questions floating around in my head as if I'd be in danger if I looked directly at them—a black hole threatening me into extinction. Pulled in to never be seen again.

A classic deal with the devil. I might not have signed my name in blood, but it's just the same.

Connor isn't someone who makes casual deals.

I've been warned my entire childhood of this and yet, I signed my soul to him, in a desperate attempt not to go back where I'm falsely promised salvation.

And maybe it's because I'm pleasantly stoned from the joint I'm still smoking, but my mind begins to wander, and then wanders a little *too* far.

*You two have been bound before…*

I startle, my back straightening as if I've been caught daydreaming in class. Where the hell did that come from?

To even give what the palm reader said any kind of weight is laughable. I force myself to relax once more, taking another long drag of the joint while I hurl the thought into a corner of my mind to never think about again.

Especially, when there's more important things to consider like the very real chance Sunny is about to disown me… or kill me. Or both. The guilt I feel about this whole situation and the web of lies I've run head first into is making me sick. How the hell am I going to pull off making her believe that Connor and I are in love, let alone married? It sounds utterly impossible and my brain is overheating just trying to come up with a lie that doesn't sound like I've been possessed by a Stepford wife or something.

I audibly groan and turn to the table, stubbing the joint into the ashtray with a bit too much force, the metal table creaking underneath the weight of my small jerky stabs. I quickly give my whole body a stretch, trying to rid myself of the tightness I feel everywhere—it doesn't work and I grumble back inside. At least it's Friday night, I can avoid Sunny for a few days and try to come up with a realistic lie over the weekend.

I walk over to the kitchen, the tiles cool under my feet. I have a half-drunk bottle of rosé in the fridge but that won't do. Not for the mood I'm in. I slide the bottom freezer door open and fish out the bottle of tequila. I set it on top of the counter and turn around to find a glass, although I strongly consider drinking directly from the bottle. Already knowing I won't be finding any lime or lemon anywhere in my kitchen, I pour myself a drink minus any of the frills. Straight up will do. It goes down smooth—maybe a little too smooth.

I deliberate putting the bottle back but decide against it and drag it with me along with the glass into my bedroom.

I need to pack.

My mood sours even more.

Well. If this bullshit is unavoidable might as well turn it into a dance party. I grab my phone and find the perfect curated playlist for the mood I want. For this stupid and absolutely insane moment in time—and I have no one else to blame but me. Ewan jumps on top of the bed, stretching his entire body, claws included, with a wide yawn and then gives a small meow looking for an ear scratch. I do so distractedly while pressing play and throwing my phone back on the bed next to him.

I've always been great at finding small pockets of joy in even the darkest of times. It's my speciality. Because life is ridiculous. And not ridiculous in a light and whimsical way but in more of a 'is this a sick cosmic joke?' kind of way.

If I don't laugh, I'll cry and that's just not an option for me.

The first few notes of one my favorite songs come on and I pour another drink while I start dancing around my bedroom. Ewan watches me from the bed, one of his hind legs stretched straight above his head like he interrupted his cleaning just to watch me prance about the room. After he's had enough of my antics he resumes his bath and I disappear into the walk-in closet to unearth my suitcase.

After finding it collecting dust in the back, I drag it out and plop it on the floor. It's gaping wide open, ready to be filled with whatever the fuck I find worth bringing with me to Connor's. Eventually I fall into a rhythm, the music, paired with the tequila warming my stomach, keeps my broody thoughts at bay for now. I spend the rest of the evening drinking and packing while taking breaks singing in front of the mirror in just my underwear and a loose shirt.

A few hours later and half the bottle gone, I fall asleep on the heap of clothes that I groggily promise myself not to forget to pack tomorrow morning.

Tomorrow… when I'll willingly upheave my entire life and move into Connor's god awful mansion.

# 17

## Connor

Fresh out of the shower and stark naked, I stroll into the bedroom while toweling my hair dry. Noticing my phone light up on the bedside table, Lenix's name flashing across the screen, I smirk and pick up.

Not letting me put a word in, she says, "I'm here," her voice curt and a little hoarse.

"Ok… and?" I deadpan.

She stays silent for a beat before adding, "Well aren't you going to come out and help me with my things?"

"No," I reply with all the seriousness I can muster.

"You're such a prick," she hisses before hanging up on me.

I laugh to myself, pulling on some sweat cut offs and head for the stairs, half considering just staying completely naked just to see her reaction. I'm not a complete heathen, I'll come out and help. It's just so easy to fuck with her and trigger a reaction.

But by the time I arrive down the stairs, walk across the house, and into the foyer, she's already trying to jostle the front door open. As if I would just keep my house unlocked and unprotected for anyone to walk in as they see fit. After quickly disarming the alarm, I open the door to find a somewhat bleary eyed and disheveled version of Lenix that I only recall seeing once before—in a suite in Vegas two years ago.

Her baggy white t-shirt is slipping off one shoulder, paired with light pink sweats and black furry slides that look more like slippers than anything else. My perusal eventually lands on a crate on the ground at her feet.

"What's *that*?" I say in disdain.

"Ewan," she clips before shoving a duffel bag into my arms. I don't budge, continuing to block the entrance while I glare at her.

She huffs loudly and rolls her eyes. "My cat," she says like I'm some kind of fucking idiot.

My scoff pairs well with her dramatics. "You're not bringing a cat into my house."

"Watch me." The crate now securely in her hand, she shoulder-checks me as she passes, walking all the way into the middle of the foyer before turning back around. "The deal was that I moved in. You never said anything about me not bringing Ewan with me."

"Well if I would have known you own a feral animal, I would have stipulated it last night," I say between clenched teeth.

She shrugs her shoulders. "Not my problem." Bending down, she opens the caged door. "And my baby's *not* feral." The orange monstrosity in question pokes its head out, placing a tentative paw on the marble floor and I immediately hate everything about it. It gives me a crooked look that seems to say the sentiment is mutual and eventually peers up at Lenix, who picks it up off the floor.

"He'll stay in my room, he won't be a problem okay?" she says with a sigh.

The cat purrs loudly, trying to paw its way up her shoulder while she scratches its head. She looks so innocent then, standing there, stripped bare, eyeing me wearily like I'm about to rob her of something she actually loves.

My chest twinges and I rub it absently while I shrug the duffel bag she handed me over my shoulder. "Where's the rest of your shit?" I ask instead.

"I'll get it later," she mutters while looking around. "So where's my room?"

"Room?" I bite down the smile wrestling to get out and keep my face serious.

Lenix's breath catches in her throat.

"You must be joking." Her voice rising with every vowel out of her mouth.

"What did you expect?" I say, my lip curling into a mischievous grin. "We're married aren't we?"

Her face turns red and I half expected her to fling her pet in my face in retaliation. As much as this amuses me, I release her from her misery and laugh, cutting the tension between us.

"Don't you worry your pretty little head, Lenny. Upstairs, on your left—end of the hall."

She blinks for a second too long as if rebooting and finally winds back to life.

"I hope it's as far away as possible from yours, you insufferable twat," she grumbles under her breath, spinning on her heels and heading for the stairs.

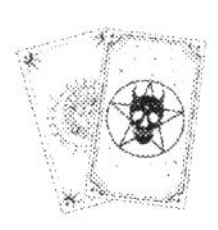

I HEAR the pads of her bare feet across the cement before seeing the rest of her. I take a peek from behind my dark shades while I sit, unmoving, on the deck chair near the pool. My throat goes dry when she finally falls into my line of sight. She looks like an actress on holiday straight out of the 1960's.

Long black hair over one shoulder, a sheer white robe that covers absolutely nothing billowing behind her as she walks. Her one piece bathing suit—somehow sexier than a bikini—is a light shade of pink that pops against her golden brown skin, and the large-framed sunglasses that hide most of her face are perched delicately on her upturned nose.

My eyelid twitches and I look away.

She delicately slides herself down onto the deck chair beside me but says nothing, pulling her phone out of thin air and begins to scroll, ignoring me.

I'm grinding my molars, trying not to lose the little game I've decided we're playing on who's going to speak first. While I do so, I quirk my head to the side and sweep my gaze across her body. Her skin looks like it's literally sparkling and I'm conflicted with the dual urge to lean over and taste her or ignore her as much as she is me.

"What?" she snips, her eyes never looking up from the screen. Trying to be subtle, her hand still finds her robe and lays it across her left thigh as if trying to cover the small row of scars that I've noticed before but never pointed out.

"Did you lather yourself in a vat of glitter or something, you're fucking blinding the entire neighbourhood."

"Wow," she drawls, still not looking up. "Who's dramatic now? It's just some shimmering tanning oil. Look away if you're so bothered."

I stand up. The need to lounge near the pool is suddenly trumped by the need to get as far away as possible from Lenix.

*Great, this is already boding well.*

I look down at her from my height, and she finally, oh so slowly, matches my gaze.

"I need you ready by eight tonight," I tell her.

"Ready?"

I smirk. "Time to play, *wife*."

Although her sunglasses hide most of her face, I still notice her pursed lips. Pleased, I turn away, quickly leaving before she can come up with an excuse.

# 18

## Lenix

Knowing that our little agreement came with mandatory *pretend* wife duties, like rubbing elbows with the elite of Noxport, I'd come prepared. Standing in front of the closet in the bedroom that will now be mine for the foreseeable future, I peruse the dresses I brought with me. I'm trying to figure out which one would be appropriate for tonight's event but given Connor gave me absolutely zero detail, I'm having a hard time choosing.

Grabbing my phone to ask him, I send out a quick text.

I regret my decision as soon as I hear footfalls on the hardwood floor heading towards my room and then a quick knock on the closed door. Hurriedly looking down to make sure I'm decent, I tighten my short silk robe around my waist, and march over. Opening the door just a creak, I poke my head out.

"I didn't ask you to come all the way over here."

He grins and places his wide palm on the door, pushing it open. "I was in the neighborhood."

I relent with a sigh, letting him in and step back, my feet sinking into the plush cream carpet. He strolls in, looking unnervingly dashing with his black hair slicked back, and dressed in a perfectly pressed dark gray pinstripe suit. His navy blue collar is still unbuttoned, allowing his tattoos to peek through. He tugs on his sleeve as if fixing them, the gold watch on his left wrist glinting against the light. After an unnecessary examination of the room, acting as if this isn't his own house, his black eyes finally land on mine.

"Show me."

I vaguely point to the closet, curious to see what he would pick out himself.

Traipsing over, he takes a look. Reaching out, his fingers softly graze the different fabrics and a shiver inexplicably travels down my body at the sight. I shift on my feet trying to shake the feeling, the silence between us widening while I wait for him to say something.

"This one," he finally says, glancing over. My words get stuck in my throat when I notice the softness in his gaze. As if noticing my reaction, Connor blinks and the hardness usually outlining his eyes slides back in place. He quirks his typical arrogant smile and heads for the door. "Be ready in an hour, darling."

"Quit giving me orders like I'm one of your lackeys," I

mutter before he disappears into the hallway. But my retort falls flat when he doesn't answer and leaves me standing there, in a room in his own house, about to put on a dress that he picked out for me.

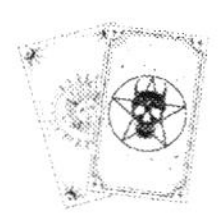

Connor waits by the front door, head down, distracted by his phone. The sound of my heels on the marble floor alerts him of my presence, and he slowly raises his gaze. There's a flash of surprise, eyebrows slightly raised but it disappears quickly. I'm no dummy, I know I look hot.

The vintage floor-length silk dress he picked out for me is perfectly tailored, hugging my curves, the thin straps showing off my shoulders. It's mostly backless with the soft red fabric dipping low down my lower back, a long slit traveling up my left leg, ending a few inches above my knee. That, paired with drop pearl earrings and black stilettos—I'm dressed to kill.

"What?" I ask innocently, sliding my phone into my black clutch.

"Have I ever seen you in this dress before?" he says, his eyes looking slightly unfocused as if trying to recall something.

"No—why?"

"No reason." He gives his head a small shake and smiles, bright and wide, the spark in his eyes igniting while he gives me another one of his slow once-overs. It's then I realize the color of his pocket square.

Red. Just like my dress.

My heart squeezes and it's my turn to be taken aback. Thankfully, by that time he's looking away, opening the front door. I school my features before he glances back and offers his hand. "Let's go, darling."

I place my hand in his, which immediately feels way too weird and quickly take it back. His eyes travel to me and then away. Did he just look disappointed? I say nothing while he leads us to the car parked right in front of the door. It's not his regular SUV however, it's a vintage Aston Martin. I raise an eyebrow when he looks back at me, having opened my car door which is surprising in itself.

"Nice car," I state, stepping into the passenger seat.

He shrugs, flashing me a devilish smile before closing the door, then strolling over to the driver's side.

I watch him in silence as he starts the car, shifting the stick into drive and pulling onto the long driveway. His wide hand confidently curls around the stick shift, veins bulging anytime he shifts gears. Watching Connor drive manual does things to me that I would rather die than to admit out loud. Still, I let my thoughts wander, imagining that same hand around my neck, his hard body pinning me to the wall—I clear my throat. Swallowing hard, I yank myself out of the vile thoughts I was swimming in and ask, "So what's the story?"

"About?" he says, his eyes still on the road.

"Us," I answer with a slight sarcastic bite. Connor chuckles, and I clench my jaw. "Can you stop thinking everything is just so hilarious." Which only makes him laugh even harder.

I'm this close to punching him hard in the arm when he shoots me a quick amused look before shifting gears, looking back to the road. "We already have a story."

The slight curve of his lips infuriates me further but I try to keep my cool before answering. "Not sure this type of crowd will find a Vegas wedding all that tasteful."

"Oh darling, is our honeymoon already over?" he says in a mocking tone, feigning being upset.

"I swear to God, Connor," I reply in exasperation.

He laughs. "Fine, fine. These people have no idea we've known each other for years. So let's just say we met over the Christmas holidays. And that it was some love at first sight, whirlwind bullshit and we eloped a few weeks ago. Happy —" he turns to me with a smirk—"wife?"

"No, not really." I blow out a frustrated breath. "Fine, tonight we eloped, but we'll need to come up with a better story to sell it to the people that *actually* know us." Then something hits me. "Shit, we don't even have any rings."

Connor seems unfazed. "We eloped remember? Shopping for the perfect ring as we speak."

I glare at him fixedly, and then sigh. "Fine."

"Ready, Lenny?" he says in a teasing tone as he parks.

His right hand slides up my uncovered leg, and I immediately swat him away but not before goosebumps break out all down my skin. I can tell he notices but says nothing. Besides, it's a normal reaction to being touched. Nothing else.

"Stay," he says, jumping out before I can reply.

A few moments later, he's opening my car door and my eyes are practically rolling into the back of my head. He holds out his hand and I take it, even if it's with slight petulance.

"This gentleman act doesn't suit you," I tell him while he gently pulls me out of my seat.

"Don't worry darling," he says while dropping my hand and fixing his tie. "I can be your favorite asshole behind closed doors." He winks and leads us inside.

# 19

## Connor

I can barely remember what charity this event is for, but the cause is irrelevant, it's the people that matter. If Lenix thinks she can manipulate me into pretending we're happily married then I'll use it to my advantage, and squeeze every opportunity I can get out of this fucking shitshow.

I leave my keys with the valet and lead Lenix up the stairs, her hand daintily placed in mine. Halfway up, she tries to rip it out of my grip like she did earlier but I squeeze her fingers tightly while keeping my eyes straight ahead. She eventually gives up.

The venue is decorated like every other boring upper crust event in this city. White flowers, gold accents and enough champagne provided in crystal flutes to serve tonight's guests until they're pleasantly catatonic.

I eye the waitstaff as soon as we walk into the ballroom trying to get my hands on said champagne so I can lull some of my near-manic energy into a quiet roar. I can't tell if the feeling is stemming from the uptight crowd I'm having to shmooze tonight or the girl whose hand is still in mine.

Not to mention the dress she's wearing.

*Fucking Christ.*

And by the look of the people around us, I'm not the only one noticing the vision she is in that silk dress.

We're not three steps inside before someone is already heading our way. I groan inwardly seeing that it's Roddrick. He owns a chain of hotels near the water—and is absolutely useless to me. Definitely not the reason I came here tonight, but a big enough player that I can't kill him for the way he's eye-fucking Lenix without repercussions. Luckily, I've caught a server's attention quickly and two champagne flutes make their way to us first.

I lean into Lenix, and whisper, "Play nice." And circle my arm around her waist, my fingers splayed loosely against her hip, her signature vanilla and jasmine scent slowly enveloping me. She tenses up but says nothing, taking a sip with a tight smile.

"Connor!" Roddrick's garish voice booms loudly around us, his hand already brandished towards me and I reluctantly let go of Lenix to shake the man's hand. "My, my," he says while clapping my shoulder with a little too much force. "I haven't seen the likes of you around here in a while."

The need to stuff my entire fist into his mouth is burning hot in my veins but I keep my face stoic, adding a small grin to the mix to hide my displeasure, while I take a large step back from his grating presence.

"Been busy. You know how it is," I answer, my arm finding its way back around Lenix's waist.

Roddrick's beady eyes track my movements, his gaze slowly taking in her body before landing on her face. His tongue darts out to lick his thin upper lip like the fucking lizard he is before speaking again. "And who might this be?"

Before Lenix has time to even open her mouth, I jump in.

"My wife," I say matter of factly, my mask serious yet warm.

"Oh." His eyes grow wide in surprise as he takes in the information, and the same sick thrill I can never seem to name slams through me.

"Lenix," she says, her voice smooth as honey. "It's a pleasure Mr…?"

"My, my. Where are my manners," he says, shaking away his shock and barking a laugh. "Call me Roddrick, dear." He takes her offered hand into his, leans in and gives it a quick kiss, my fingers curling tighter into her hips at the sight. His eyes slide to mine and then back to her before saying, "Connor married… what fascinating news. Given his reputation, I always thought he would stay the most eligible bachelor in Noxport."

Finally letting go, he straightens, watching Lenix closely as if hoping for some kind of reaction from her.

She looks at me with soft eyes and smiles. If I knew any better, I'd think it was real. And then, shocking me, she leans over and kisses my cheek. I swallow my surprise and smile back at her.

"His *reputation* is what first attracted me to him, isn't that right Connie baby?" Her voice is sickeningly sweet. Taking a slow sip of her champagne, she looks around the room, a bored look on her face, effectively dismissing Roddrick.

He clears his throat. "Well, congratulations are in order. It was lovely to meet you, dear. And Connor, always a pleasure." Without waiting for much of an answer, he walks away to find his next victim.

Well, damn.

Lenix might be more useful than I originally thought.

She turns to me, stepping out of my embrace, my arm falling to my side. She smiles, a mischievous twinkle in her eyes. "You might know these people personally, but it's my *job* to know who's who in this town. Roddrick might have not known who I was but I know more about him then you probably do, including his very low status within this world. If you're going to make the most of our agreement. At least *use* me well."

Discarding my glass on a nearby table, I ignore the images her last sentence is evoking, smoothing my palm over my mustache. I look her up and down before grinning back at her. "How would I use you, exactly?"

I know Lenix picked up on my little innuendo but chooses to ignore it. "Since I roped myself into this mess, I might as well try to make it fun," she says, her lips curling playfully.

Before I can even respond, she turns her back to me, her ass so perfectly displayed in that *fucking* dress, that I have no other choice but to follow her to our table.

I thought Lenix would fight me the entire time, a prisoner of her own fate. But seeing her now, shoulders straight, a sultry sway to her hips, I realize I've misjudged her. Right before my eyes, she slips into a second skin, becoming a honey tongued vixen in the blink of an eye. It's almost as if playing a different person is second nature to her.

I'm suddenly very curious indeed to see where this will lead us.

# 20

I let the drone of the voices wash over me while I focus on cutting a small piece of salmon from my plate and raising it to my mouth.

Connor sits to my right, his hand loosely curled over his glass of mezcal in front of him, a finger distractedly playing with the lip while he listens to Mayor Hawkins command our table with a funny story across from us.

How we ended up at the mayor's table is beyond me. Observing Connor tonight has made me realize how much he *is* the devil in disguise. He could almost seem innocently normal if it wasn't for his dark aura pulsing with every breath he takes. It's hard to avert my gaze for long.

And a quick study of everyone at our table confirms I'm not the only one whose eyes can't help but to gravitate to him. Even the mayor's eyes seem trained on Connor while he continues to regale us with his grand tale. A small twist of envy grips my stomach, until my eyes land back on Connor, and realize his gaze is on me. My stomach then twists for another reason entirely.

The slight curl of his lip seems to fuel Hawkin's story, who swerves into a tangent and I internally groan. I've barely registered a word in over five minutes but my face is fixed into a pleasant smile while I chew my food politely. When my eyes aren't pulled back to the man beside me, they're subtly observing the other ten people at the table.

Just like Roddrick earlier, I know them but they don't know me. As much as I love attention, there's a time and place for it. Right now, I'd rather keep my cards close to my chest, melting into the background as Connor's unassuming wife. Although I know I'm the reason I'm in this mess to begin with, the thought of people picturing me as just that, tastes bitter in my mouth. I feel like I'm losing all sense of agency just sitting here.

There is a silver lining, however. Since no one is expecting anything from me, controlling their perception of who I am becomes a lot easier. Just one more persona to mold into creation and add to my arsenal. It's second nature at this point.

"Henry," Connor says, addressing the mayor like they've been old chums for years. "That was one hell of a story. You sound like you were quite the ruffian in your heyday."

God. I fight the urge to roll my eyes. Did he just use the word *ruffian*?

Hawkins lets out a boisterous laugh. "Just the young being young! I'm just happy the internet didn't exist back then." He winks my way as he speaks and I hold in a full body cringe.

Something about him feels slimy but I can't place what. Well, other than he's a politician who clearly knows who Connor is and *what* he does. I'm sure he's as squeaky clean as every other politician in this city. Which is not at all.

I stopped believing that men in power were anything but evil the moment I heard the door lock in my father's office all those years ago.

And Connor is no exception.

But at least, if not busy impressing the elite of Noxport, he wears his sins like badges. They define him. He is unapologetically himself. And maybe that's what attracted me to him originally. That and a faulty sense of self-preservation. I danced too close to his fire and got burned.

And now here we are.

"So…" he says, the mayor's eyes focusing back on Connor. "Tell me how you two met."

As if on cue, his hand slides over my thigh and my spine straightens. My *husband* answers for us, his voice steady and silky, "Us two?" His fingers slowly caresses the fabric covering my leg. I struggle not to push him away. He knows I can't make sudden movements so I let him have his moment as I sit demurely still. His head turns to me and he pauses studying me as if drinking in the face of the woman he loves. He reaches over with his free hand, his finger tracing my jaw and I fight the instinctive flinch.

"It was love at first sight." His voice smooth and downright enamored.

I'm suddenly dying of thirst. But I keep my expression calm, serene. *Smitten.*

I nod, and smile bashfully, the words catching in my throat. I reach for my champagne and take a sip, looking back to Connor and his dark, smoldering eyes.

"Never met a woman quite like Lenix." He continues to gaze at me with such tenderness, it glues me to the spot. "Sometimes I need to pinch myself to believe that all of it is real. That *she*'s real," he says in awe.

The table fawns over his admission, obviously not picking up on the double meaning. I shift in my seat, nerves traveling up my body and cross my left leg onto my right. I immediately realize my mistake when his hand finds my naked leg, the slit in the dress uncovering my entire thigh to his covert ministrations.

*Fuck.*

My fingers curl around my fork, the sudden urge to stab his hand with it as strong as the little voice in my head nudging me to just let him continue. At least, it would make this drab dinner a little fun—or slightly thrilling. He continues to butter up the mayor and the conversation finally shifts to the people sitting to his right. Something about the upcoming mayoral elections.

I haven't paid much attention since his fingers began traveling up my thigh, my skin ablaze under his touch. This is so fucking stupid. Absolutely idiotic. I haven't let him touch me like this since we woke up in Vegas, married and hungover.

So why now?

Luckily, the table is draped in white linen, his hand and subsequently my lower body hidden underneath it. My brain goes blank as I uncross my legs, his fingers immediately finding the small opening to the center of my thighs.

Connor's body is so relaxed, one tattooed hand still lazily playing with his glass, answering questions when prompted while the other is smoothly sliding up and up and up. I almost convince myself that I'm imagining all of it. My heart pumps faster as I reach for my flute again, if only to have something to hold. His knuckles graze my inner thigh and to my utter disgust I widen my legs just an inch.

I think I might have lost my mind.

Because this is Connor we're talking about. My rational brain is mortified, but my body responds to his touch like a kindling flame.

Especially when I know there isn't any lace separating his skin from mine. After a slow, torturous trail upwards, his thumb finds me wet under his touch.

His head turns the smallest amount towards me, his eyes slamming into mine from under his long lashes, one dark eyebrow raised. There's a hint of surprise in his hooded gaze. I'm flustered by my body's response, but somehow find a way to channel all of it into a smug look, unwilling to show him the crack under my armor.

His lips curl as he takes a slow sip of his drink. His thumb delicately strokes my pussy, dragging upwards to my clit. And oh, does it throb in desire.

But I don't let myself enjoy it. I don't let myself anticipate what he might do next. My body might be betraying me, but I refuse to submit to his touch. I may be playing the part of his loving wife but I still have agency and I will not surrender to his seductive allure.

My sanity barrels back into me and I fling his hand away, the attention turning to me as I do. I hide the sudden movement under the guise of standing up, clearing my throat and smoothing my dress before speaking. "Apologies, I just need to freshen up."

I give the table a tight smile and look down to Connor. The same hand that was moments ago somewhere it *should not* have been, curls around my own, while he presses a kiss to my knuckles. He then traces the thumb over his lips, his gaze searing into me and I lick my own lips in response. "Hurry back, *wife*," he whispers.

# 21

## Connor

Lenix hasn't said a word since she climbed into the car and slammed the door with way too much force for a vintage Aston Martin. I cringed at the sound but didn't comment. Too busy replaying that perfect tension filled moment where Lenix let me touch her unabashedly.

A similar tension winds between us now and I revel in it, my heart hammering to the beat of her quick breaths beside me. Her arms are tucked tightly over her chest, shoulders up to her neck as she stares out the front window, but I don't think she's staring at much at all.

The gates leading up to the driveway open in a silent welcome, and I make my way up to the house. I can almost *feel* Lenix about to go off and my lips twist in anticipation.

I finally park near the front door, the engine purring itself to sleep, the inside of the car falling as silent as a graveyard.

Until her voice pierces it.

"What the fuck was that?" Her voice is a lot steadier than I would have expected. I assumed she'd lead with her dramatics—which are a lot more fun to handle than this.

"I could ask you the same thing, darling," I reply in jest, and with a smile.

"Don't you fucking *darling* me," she hisses.

There she is.

And fuck does her feistiness make me want to do every little dirty and depraved thing I can think of to her.

Fuck her into submission, for starters.

I smirk. Pulling the car keys out of the ignition, I give her a side-eyed look that seems to rev her up even more.

"If you want to pretend you weren't wet with just my fingers near your cunt." I pause, my thumb and index finger finding my mustache. "Be my fucking guest Lenny. I don't care if you lie. It won't change the fact that you willingly opened your legs for me while we were surrounded by a table of Noxport politicians."

Her mouth opens and closes, obviously trying to come up with a rebuttal but landing on nothing. She huffs loudly instead, followed by a small groan. Pushing the car door open, she gracefully, if not a little hastily, climbs out.

I'm out of the car before she rounds the hood, heading for the front door.

"You're the absolute worst," she says from over her shoulder, tone laced with venom.

"Darling—I'm the devil you know," I respond while casually strolling right behind her.

"Yeah, and look where that has gotten me." She turns on her heels and glares at me, crossing her arms in defiance. "In fucking hell."

"At least hell has a pool," I quip as she tries to open the door.

Finding the door locked, she throws her arms in the air as if this is the last straw.

"I need a key to this place. I'm not your prisoner."

"But you would be so pretty wrapped in chains," I say darkly, a cocky grin curling my lips while I climb up onto the doorstep.

She's practically vibrating when I near her, and unlock the door. Storming in without another word, she takes her heels off before starting for the stairs. While I disarm the alarm, I track her movements. The casual action of her taking off her stilettos in front me makes my dick twitch for reasons quite unknown and most likely unimportant.

She's halfway into the foyer when she stops as if just remembering something and turns back to face me.

"And what's with the whole *wife* thing?" she says with a bite, hands landing on her hips.

"As in the whole reason we're stuck in this mess?" My eyebrows lazily rise to match my arrogant look.

"Don't play dumb with me Connor, I swear you had a fucking boner everytime you said that word tonight. And before you try to deny it, I don't think the idea of me being your wife is what turns you on," she says, walking towards me and jamming her index finger in my chest. "I think what turns you on is the ownership attached to the word itself. Don't forget that I know you, *husband*." Her nail digging into my skin. "You get off on power. It's the one sure thing that makes you feel worthy. But don't forget, power is a fickle thing."

*Well shit.*

She's not completely wrong but what's the fun in admitting it?

I take a step back, stuffing my hands in my pocket and head for the kitchen.

"Whatever helps you sleep at night, darling."

I can feel her practically implode behind me, most likely trying to find a way to get the last word in but failing. Instead, I hear the soft pads of her bare feet head for the stairs and I pretend the sound doesn't tickle at my senses. A sound way too domestic to enjoy, especially when it's coming from her.

After pouring myself a nightcap, I head upstairs. At the top, Lenix's cat comes zipping out of the shadows and I lurch out of the way, almost spilling my drink.

"Little shit, what happened to keeping it locked up?" I mutter out loud, ignoring the fact that I was startled in my own house by that feral creature. It disappears down the dark hallway and into Lenix's bedroom.

Her door is ajar.

I know what I'd find behind it if I pushed it open. It's proving quite easy to summon images of her naked body when I've seen it before. When I've touched it—*fucked* it before.

It's hard to forget.

When her soft moans were the most alluring sounds I've ever heard.

I still fuck my fist to the echoes of it.

She's been harder to get out of my head than expected.

Especially when her ignoring me makes me want to push her buttons even more. And me holding those papers over her head for the last two years has been entertaining—to say the least.

My hand twitches on the bannister and I realize I've stopped in my tracks, staring at her door like a creep.

Not that I mind the thought…

Begrudgingly, I shake myself out of it, denying myself the urge to open her door and truly bask in how much of a creep I can be.

*Christ.*

All I need is one last tryst with her. To get it out of my system, so I can start focusing on something else. It's not like I've been sitting around for two years just thinking about her. I have an empire to run for fuck sakes. But having her in my house is making this dormant urge burn me alive.

I'm usually not the one to deny myself of anything. If tonight is proof of anything, it's that Lenix can be swayed. Her body still craves the pleasure it knows I can give her.

All she needs is the right temptation.

# 22

## Lenix

I'm drifting back and forth somewhere between here and wherever we go when we dream. My eyes are closed, and I let out a small hum of contentment. But then my mind walks clear into the land of the living and my body jolts awake, eyelids springing open. Although a part of me knows where I am, it takes a few moments for everything to lock into place. Nestled in soft dark green bedding, my eyes bounce around the room putting all the missing pieces back into place.

Dark red velvet curtains frame the wide windows to the right of the four poster king size bed. A dark brown antique desk tucked between the two. Even from here, the drapes look expensive, and feel like they should belong in an extravagant turn of the century mansion—not in the modern era. But oddly, they don't feel out of place, simply adding an eccentric flare to the room.

I groan into one of the many pillows strewn around my head. This bed might be the most comfortable thing I've ever slept in. And that only adds to my frustration. I think I would rather sleep on a sad single mattress in a broom closet than this. It would pair well with my current penance.

What did I do in a past life to deserve this?

I guess that isn't really an offhand remark and more a real question when your best friend has firsthand experience with the whole… reincarnation thing.

Does it mean we all have connections like Sunny's? Maybe not as intense, but a connection all the same? I wonder where I've been, or *who* I was to have ended up here, in one of Connor's guest bedrooms of all places, masquerading as his wife in order to evade my fervent brother and the cult I was born into.

When I lay it all out, it sounds absurd. It makes me feel far removed from myself, disconnected, like it's impossible for all of this to be real.

Is this really my life?

*Ugh.*

Flinging the covers off of my body, I lay there having a small existential crisis. When my brain finally decides to unfurl itself from the fetal position, I throw my legs over the side of the bed and sit up. My satin tank top is askew from sleep and I fix it distractedly while my toes curl into the soft carpet underneath me. Ewan immediately finds his way between my legs, butting his furry head against my calf.

My gaze lands on the bedside table, another piece of furniture in this place that looks more expensive than anything I could ever afford.

Filthy rich bastard.

But then my eyes catch on my phone sitting face down on it and my heart squeezes. Nothing good can come from that screen. It's only been two days since my altercation with Patrick. It's just a matter of time before I hear from my brother again.

Anxiety tightens my throat, and I swallow hard. I don't even know if me being married is going to dissuade Frederick.

I can already hear his voice echo in my head, his cadence so similar to my father's. *Don't you think you have sullied yourself enough Penelope? Binding your soul to such an ungodly man?*

If only he knew. Or maybe word has already traveled back to him. Connor is not only ungodly, he is the very incarnation of all my sins. The punishment I deserve.

But my brother's voice isn't the only one I hope not to hear through the phone. Just the thought of having to lie to Sunny when I'm already keeping so much hidden from her is enough to make me hate myself.

How the hell did I end up here?

Suddenly, I'm out of bed and halfway across the room before I can even form another sad and morose thought. Future me can deal with all this shit, while present me can pretend nothing is wrong.

Taking a quick peek into the hall, I half expect Connor to spring out of the shadows like something straight out of my nightmares. Satisfied that I'm all alone this early in the morning, I wander down the hallway.

This isn't my first time in his house. But this is my first time exploring the second floor. I do know his bedroom is somewhere towards the other end and my curiosity takes a hold of me, my feet light on the hardwood floor as I try not to make a sound.

Noticing a door ajar at the very end, I take small, soft steps closer and closer until I reach the end of the hallway. Would he really leave his door open like that? It feels like a taunt. And I almost turn around to spite him and prove him wrong. *Almost.*

I can see his bed from the doorway. The room is obscured in darkness, his thick curtains, similar to my own but navy blue, are drawn shut. The space looks double in size compared to the guest room, even his bed looking bigger than mine. I can barely make out a body at first but then my eyes finally adjust and I see him slowly materialize in front of me. The black sheets are pulled down to his stomach, one arm sprawled above him. There's not an inch of his body free of tattoos. His chest rises softly, up and then down. I can barely assess what I'm seeing. How almost innocent he looks, sleeping like this.

Unguarded.

I don't think Connor understands how similar in our lies we are. He might think he's good at hiding it. But a fake can always spot another fake and his entire personality is as perfectly constructed as mine. An act he effortlessly hides behind.

Even the few times we hooked up, we never fell asleep beside one another. He or I were gone as soon as it was over. So I've never *seen* him asleep. Never watched him like this.

And it's almost more frightening than any other side of him I've seen before this.

Because this is real. This is Connor when no one else is looking.

Then, like watching a double exposure photograph come to life before my eyes, my vision blurs. Suddenly light-headed, my heart skips several beats and I take a step back from the door but I can't unsee what I think I just saw. A flash of a dead body, a knife through their heart. Blood. So much blood. It appeared overtop Connor still sleeping in bed as if this other image existed right there too and somehow shared the same time and space but existed in two different realities. A flicker like tuning the radio to the right station and then it's gone.

Hastily, I rub my eyes. My rational brain clearly thinks I just lost the plot and what I witnessed was just a remnant of the dreams I woke up from.

But no.

This feels different. And so real that I would rather never think about it ever again.

Before Connor catches me watching him sleep, I tiptoe back into my room. I stand in the middle of it, unsure of what to make of what just happened.

*What the hell did I just see?*

Thinking a shower can set me right, I move listlessly to the ensuite. Eventually, under the billowing steam of the water pressure, I convince myself that it was indeed just a figment of my imagination, and let the water glide down my skin hoping it washes away everything else sticking to me.

But I can't deny that it's getting harder to evade what I've been running away from for years. I've been stuffing everything behind the closed doors of my mind. Now it's bursting full and I fear I can't even come close to them without everything escaping like bats out of hell.

What will become of me when my past threatens to unmask who I really am?

And who is that but a liar? A monster.

A wretched soul bound for eternal misery.

# 23

## Connor

I'm in my study, pacing near the fireplace, glaring at the portrait of my father hanging over the mantle. Bastian and I both look like him: dark hair and features, roman noses, which isn't surprising since our fathers were fraternal twins. They are long gone now.

Not sure why I keep that damn thing hanging in my office still. This house used to be his. I inherited the place when he died, gunned down by the Gravediggers, our rival gang. I wasn't at the docks when the shooting took place and I will live with that regret until I most likely find the same fate as my father before me.

I don't picture myself old. Not because I have a death-wish but more like I can't comprehend what the fuck I'd be doing at that age. I would rather put a bullet through my own head than grow bored and then just wait for death to come. I wait for no one. Not even death.

I took over the Sin Eaters when I was only twenty-one years old. I had no fucking clue what I was doing but pretended I did. Eventually, with the help of Byzantine and Bastian, I became who I am today. Ruthless and cunning, leading one of the most feared crime organizations on the West Coast. It wasn't easy, I've had plenty of close encounters with death. Bullets emblazoned with its namesake, but somehow I always manage to evade it, sending my enemies to perish in my stead.

Hearing steps nearing the study door, I look over. Bastian strolls in, his white-blond hair looking freshly bleached, dark eyebrows pinched together as he looks down at his laptop, holding it while he walks.

"I have some more intel on Governor Morrissey," he mutters while plopping into the one-seater near me, his eyes still roving across the computer screen.

The Governor is Mayor Hawkins' uncle. Nepotism at its finest. And also the reason why I've spent the last year cozying up to him. Hawkins is malleable and turns a blind eye to most of the illegal activities I partake in, but he's also not a complete idiot.

As one would hope.

He has his eye on a chair in the Supreme Court and only a select few know how truly corrupt he is. And I have a feeling his dear ol' uncle doesn't know the extent of the bribes he receives on any given day.

Is that to say that Morrissey is a saint? Hardly. But it's proving more difficult to pinpoint what angle to approach him with when his nephew isn't allowing me into some select spaces.

I've been working on the long game. And Lenix might be the very key to unlock some previously locked doors. Hawkins knew my father, and knows who I am underneath the polish. But my public persona precedes me. And most of these men are stuck in decades long past, where a married man is inherently more trustworthy than if he's single.

Sitting on the leather couch near Bastian, I watch him continue to type on his keyboard and wait for him to speak but it looks like he reached his talking quota for the day.

"And?" I bite out, kicking his shin with my winged-tipped shoe. "Are you going to tell me or just fucking sit there staring at your screen?"

Looking up, his eyes almost black and nearly lifeless, he stares at me for a long miserable beat. Probably the most reaction I'll get from him. Fucking weirdo.

"He has a mistress here in Noxport. Pays for her condo downtown," he finally says.

Well, well, well, *this* I can use.

"Let me guess. Barely legal?" I say half amused, half disgusted.

"Yep."

How painfully unoriginal. It's always the most God-fearing ones out of the group too. Blackmailing the governor with this almost feels too easy. But I'm not above this kind of chess move. If he's dumb enough to do it, I'm smart enough to use it against him. I just need to play my hand at the perfect time and place. So I'll sit on this valuable tidbit of information until the timing is just right, then I'll strike.

In the meantime I'll use my other valuable chess piece —the queen.

Lenix is a shiny new toy I can finally play with. She'd castrate me if she ever heard me say that out loud. Doesn't stop me from dragging my tongue over my teeth, my smile growing wider at the thought.

Bastian promptly stands up. "I'll have the intel ready for you by this afternoon," he says nearly incomprehensibly. He's already closing his laptop when I realize I should inform him of my new… complications.

"Wait. I need to tell you something," I sigh. Jesus fucking Christ. Why am I getting flustered?

Bastian doesn't sit back down but studies me like a code he's trying to decipher. "Does it have to do with Lenix staying in the bedroom down the hall?" he says flatly.

"You noticed?" My voice rising with surprise.

He rolls his eyes. "Or the fact that you've been married for the past two years?"

I choke on my tongue and stand up feeling suddenly awkward sitting there like a jackass while Bastian reads my horoscope or whatever the fuck you call this.

"You knew?" Is all I manage to say while raising an eyebrow.

He just shrugs his shoulders, the same unimpressed look he always carries around glued on his face. "You pay me to know this kind of shit."

"Why didn't you say anything?"

"Wasn't my place to say something was it?"

It's my turn to stare at him, admittedly a little dumbfounded.

"We're not together," I mutter, the words stumbling out awkwardly

"I don't care," he drawls, aloof as always.

Although bizarrely relieved that he knew all along, his robotic responses are beginning to grate at my nerves. Before my fist finds his temple, I head over to my desk looking for the cigarette case and the joints waiting for me inside.

"You're lucky you're my cousin or you'd be six feet under right about now with that fucking attitude," I mumble around the joint between my lips. I light it, taking a long drag then finally, look at him.

He gives me the tiniest grin, a barely there glint in his eyes. "Try me."

I can't help but chuckle. Bastian might be the brains but he's far from innocent. Unlike Byzantine and me, the kid doesn't have a single tattoo, save for *memento mori*—remember you must die—tattooed across his chest. His blond hair and nose ring are the only other modifications he has on his body. But he doesn't need a single thing to make him look deadly. His presence alone is enough. That and the fact that he barely says a fucking word. People find him unsettling. And if we weren't blood, I'd feel the same way too.

"Fine. But I need you to find someone for me," I reply.

"Who?"

"Lenix's ex-fiancé." I keep my face blank, unwilling to show how much saying that sentence affects me.

Bastian eyebrow rises, staring in question, but I don't offer anything more.

He nods and walks out of the office.

# 24

## Lenix

It's Tuesday night and I haven't been in the office since Friday afternoon. I'm avoiding the inevitable. I know that. I'm pretty sure Ewan, who's quietly purring beside me, even knows it. I've been pushing off having to look Sunny in the eyes. My body shudders at the thought.

So I've been skipping the office for the past two days, telling her I'm too busy with vendors for Connor's event to stop by. I can tell she knows something is up. But could she ever guess that the *what* is me being married to the devil himself?

The very one she warned me about three and a half years ago. I mean, technically she doesn't have a leg to stand on. Byzantine isn't exactly the fucking Pope either. But somehow he's always seemed a lot more stable compared to his best friend. Connor feels like a grenade, or simply put, a ticking time bomb.

I'm home. No—not home, but wherever I can call this place. It's dark out and I'm feeling on edge. I haven't really seen Connor since Saturday night. Technically, Sunday morning if you count me watching him sleep.

Great. That didn't sound creepy at all.

I fish out half a joint from a small circular plastic tube that I keep in my purse for just that, dragging my body downstairs and out the large sliding patio door. The silence is comforting as I walk as quietly as possible, not bothering to turn on any lights outside. The dim glow of the underground pool is enough for me to find my way to a deck chair near the back of the property. I sit with a small pleased hum, dropping my phone beside me and bringing the joint to my lips.

I fill my lungs with smoke, the high like a comforting blanket over my senses while I watch the stars shimmer above me. I sit there for a while just zoning out until I've relaxed enough to notice that the itch that started Saturday night, and that I haven't yet scratched, hasn't subsided.

It might even be getting worse.

I cross my legs thinking it will help ease the ache between my thighs, but it only heightens it.

I've been achingly horny since the charity event, and my irritation rises at the thought of who landed me in this current parched state.

It would be so easy to find someone else.

And fuck Connor clean out of my system.

Instead, I reach for my phone. Turning down the volume and luminosity, I find the video I'm looking for in a hidden folder.

My eyes lock on the screen, my body heating almost immediately—I was halfway there already. I lay back onto the seat, sitting in a loose criss-cross position, and let my legs fall wide. My fingers travel down my sundress and slide under my thong, finding my clit. I suck in a breath, already so sensitive to the touch.

My buzz is strong enough now that I forget my surroundings, my attention zeroed in on the video playing on my phone and on my fingers dragging slow, hard circles against my clit.

*I'm so close…*

A teasing tone breaks through my fantasy. "I wish I was recording this."

"Fuck!" I yelp, so startled that I fling my phone clear across the yard. I scramble to sit in a less compromising position and look up, knowing full well whose eyes I'll find focused on me.

Connor's expression is shadowed by the darkness surrounding us, only illuminated by the bluish light of the pool floating across his face as he continues to stare me down. Still, I could make out his smug look in the darkest of nights.

"Naughty little wife," he tsks.

My body flares and I'm mortified by my reaction to his words. But can I really hold myself responsible when I'm so wound up a breeze could set me off?

"What are you doing here?" My voice comes out breathy and God—just fucking kill me.

"I live here."

I realize quickly I won't be winning this exchange and begin to clamber out of the chair until his hand lands on my shoulder and I freeze.

"You could have just asked, you know," his voice dripping with lewd intent.

His fingers have time to slide up my neck and into my hair before I push him away. He fists my hair and my head jerks up, mouth opening in a gasp. And to my absolute disgust, my clit throbs in response.

I'm burning up.

I'm on fucking fire.

"What?" It's almost a whisper but I know he's heard me.

"If you wanted to come, darling, you could have just asked. " His voice is low, like we're both unconsciously trying not to disturb the silence surrounding us. His face is too close, much too close. My eyes flit back and forth trying to figure out if he's being serious, but the night is too dark to make out much of anything.

Except the heat of his body near mine.

Finally, he lets go. He smooths out his suit jacket, opens it up and sits down on the deck chair beside me. He pulls a joint out of thin air and flicks his silver zippo open. The flames dance against his irises, watching me. After a long drag, he smiles, and the smoke curls around him like an apparition. His whole demeanor is so arrogant, I hate him on the spot. Or at least I try.

It's not a hard sentiment to conjure up most days.

"Isn't that what a husband is for? To satisfy his wife's needs," he drawls.

"Are you finished?" I bite out.

"Did you?"

I scoff and he chuckles. "If you think I'm going to sit here and feel embarrassed that you caught me masturbating, you'll be waiting a long time,"

He falls silent, taking another drag, his other hand slicking a few errant strands of his black hair back in place. Nothing good comes from Connor being this quiet.

"I've come up with another condition for you being under my protection."

I look over, mentally readying myself to strangle him to death. But, I'm also morbidly curious to hear what's about to come out his mouth.

"Your orgasms," he points at me with the two fingers holding his joint and then jerks his thumb back to him, "are now *mine.*"

I sit stunned for a beat, thinking I might have just gone out of my goddamn mind. And then finally, I laugh. Still, it doesn't quite cut the tension between us. "You must be joking. That's your condition? Sexual coercion?"

Connor's hand smooths over his mustache like he's trying to hide a smile before answering. "Don't sit there, lying to me and tell me that this whole thing doesn't turn you on, Lenix." He sends a haughty wink my way. "I remember what you like."

Heat pools low in my stomach and I would rather suffer an aneurysm than to admit that this shmuck is having any effect on me.

"You do realize that's a hard rule to enforce, right?"

He hums, tapping his finger on his chin as if musing on something. "But now every time you want to slide your fingers into your wet little cunt, you'll be thinking of me, won't you?" he says so deliberately, it feels like every word was carefully chosen to insight a reaction out of me. It's working. "I'll be controlling your orgasms even when I'm not in the room."

The God complex on this guy.

"Why don't I finish what you started, darling? We can both pretend you didn't want it afterwards. What do you say?"

He smiles, and it's pure sex and darkness as he leans forward, his forearms on his knees waiting for my answer. My heart slams in my chest, and I swallow hard, my throat tight in anticipation. My mind is muddled, positively addled by the constant throbbing between my legs. I can't tear my eyes away from him while I chew the inside of my cheek, trying to think clearly but failing spectacularly.

It's inevitable.

I know it.

He knows it.

"Fine," I spit out.

"A deal then?"

I nod.

Silence falls between us. The soft chirp of a cricket nearby is the only soul brave enough to make a sound right now. Connor slowly stands up, stepping towards me, leaning down close to my face.

"No kissing."

He chuckles darkly. "Not my intention, darling."

He doesn't say another word, taking a long drag instead, his thumb curling around my chin pulling my mouth slightly open. His lips are so close to mine, I can feel the tickle of his mustache on my skin. Then he exhales and I taste the marijuana smoke filling my mouth. My eyes fall closed, inhaling deeply, the intimacy of what he just did leaving me somewhat lightheaded. My body tingles with the high making its way down my body, still feeling his breath fanning across my cheek.

He looms over me like a dark entity trying to possess me when I feel his hand find my inner thighs. I try not to dwell on how easily I open my legs for him. His fingers push aside my thong and I swallow back a moan, unwilling to give him the satisfaction. He finds me wanton, my clit already so sensitive and swollen that my eyes roll back in pleasure and I hope—no pray—that Connor doesn't see me do so.

His voice finds the shell of my ear, piercing the silence already so heady between us.

"Tell me you hate me."

I focus back on his face, his black eyes staring at me.

"I hate you." The last word falls sharply out of my mouth followed by a hard gasp, as two fingers slide deep inside me at the very same time.

"*Fuck*," he groans and my legs widen at the sound. "Look how wet my wife is for me."

A flash of frustration slices through me hearing him use that word so freely but it's simultaneously paired with a heat that burns so hot I think I might suffocate.

"Shut up and make me come," I breathe out. I was already so close before he caught me that I know this won't take long. He chuckles devilishly, slowly resting on his haunches, his fingers curling inside of me and I can't help but to moan out loud.

Connor's other hand wraps around my throat, his fingers splayed around my jaw.

"Look at me," he growls, and my eyes slam into his.

The fire I find in his gaze, paired with his thumb circling my clit just hard enough to feel greater than anything on this godforsaken earth, effectively unravels me. I grind myself on him, faster and faster, chasing what I now realize might be the best climax I've ever had. The devious curl of his lips lets me know how much he's enjoying seeing me realize just that.

"Look at you, so sublime, fucking my hand," he whispers, his gaze never leaving mine. "That's it, Lenix. Come all over my fingers."

My eyes widen in what I can only describe as pure shock, my pussy clenching around his fingers while my entire body detonates.

My mouth falls open on a near-silent whimper and the satisfaction in Connor's eyes somehow makes me come even harder, his fingers pumping in and out of me, following me through the aftershock of what he just did to my body. What he just *said* to me.

Everything about this feels wrong.

But also, nothing has ever felt this *good.*

As my soul settles back into my body, I quickly try to break the spell of whatever the hell just happened between us. I need the upper hand before I lose myself entirely. Pushing his arm away, I stand up, and distance myself from Connor. He does the same, his hands falling back to his sides, where they belong. Still, I feel the ghost of his touch on me and something tells me it will linger on my skin long after I storm out of here.

"Move," I say while smoothing out my dress.

Connor says nothing, but steps back, closer to the pool. His smirk never leaves his lips.

And I'm suddenly growing heated for very different reasons.

"See what happens when you behave?" he drawls.

It only takes one hard shove for him to fall backwards into the water. I don't wait around to watch him struggle. I hear splashes and heated curses but I don't look back, storming into the kitchen, sliding and locking the patio door behind me.

# 25

## Connor

My socks squelch with every step I take up the stairs. I got rid of my shoes somewhere between here and the kitchen window I had to shimmy into. I'm dripping wet, my thousand dollar suit stinking of pool water but I can't seem to wipe this fucking grin off my face. Being forcefully plunged into a body of water should have had the same effect as getting my balls dunked into a vat of ice cubes, but I'm as hard as ever.

Seeing Lenix's face twist in anger was almost as gratifying as watching her come undone while having my fingers deep inside her pretty little cunt.

Almost.

I tilt my head to the left when I reach the top of the stairs, water still sluicing down my body and onto the floor. I make a mental note to leave a hefty tip for my housekeeper tomorrow. Lenix's door is closed.

I could find my way inside.

There's a master key tucked inside one of the locked drawers of my desk. It would be so easy to force my way in.

To punish her.

The fiend rattling inside of me knows she would fight too. And I grin even wider. I would find a way. In any case I'd hate fuck her into supplicating my name like I was threatening to possess her soul.

Fuck.

Hearing her mouth out *I hate you* while I pushed my fingers inside of her, her pupils blown so wide I could have easily peered into the very depths of her, was an absolute delicacy. My depraved soul sang for her spite. And now that I've had a small taste again, I need more. I want to eat at the table of Mrs. Connor Maxwell until I've had my fill. And right now? I'm insatiable.

But it'll have to wait.

I stroll into my room and close the door. I peel the clothes off my damp skin and head for the shower. Something tells me Lenix is expecting me to react. After all, I'm not known for my impulse control. But this is one instance when my control will come with a reward later. I just know it will. I don't need instant gratification if I know the delayed treat will be even better—tastier.

I turn on the hot water and wait for the steam to rise

before stepping in. My cock aches, throbbing like it's agreeing with my plan. I fist it hard, my other hand braced against the wall near one of the shower heads. It's easy to envision Lenix on her knees in front of me, her full lips open, her eyes shining and eager to swallow what I give her. I don't last a fucking minute. My neck cords with tension as I keep the image of her behind my closed eyelids while I come hard and fast.

Maybe the sane part of me should worry that this little arrangement between us has already turned sexual and it's barely been a week. Luckily, I'm not on friendly terms with sanity. That would just be boring. Most of the time, it just gets in the way of doing business. I file away all the deviant plans I'm coming up with at lightning speed for later, and climb into bed.

I sleep like a fucking baby.

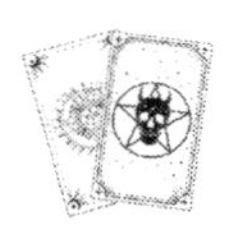

It's early the next morning, I'm in my study, busy answering emails and looking through a few documents Bastian sent over for me to read before the meeting in half an hour. Lenix is still somewhere in the house, somehow I can feel her around. I would rather ignore why I sense her presence in this way. Nothing good can come of it. Nothing good ever comes from me peering into the darkness staring back at me. It's risky. And I don't have the patience for it anyway. My head jolts up, hearing a faint jingling like the sound of bells chiming over a door. I take a deep breath and dismiss it, looking back down at the screen—there are no bells in my entire fucking house.

Speak of the devil… or in this case, speak of Lilith and she appears.

Lenix prances in like she fucking owns the place. Her black hair is straightened and pulled up high into a ponytail, large gold hoop earrings adorning her face, her makeup seeming to accentuate her already flawless eyes and skin. My jaw clenches hard in irritation.

Or, what I think is irritation.

"Have a nice swim?" she says instead of a good morning. Her tone is laced with so much insolence that I decide on the spot that twelve hours is long enough to begin retaliation. An idea quickly etches itself so perfectly in my mind, it's like Michelangelo himself took a paintbrush to the image.

I erase all evil delight off my face and stare her down.

"I didn't invite you in here, Lenny."

She gives me a mock pout, her pink babydoll dress swishing against her thighs while she struts over to my desk, her index finger trailing over the mahogany wood. "What's wrong Connie baby? I thought what was mine is yours—in this case what's yours is mine."

Her ponytail falls to the side brushing against her shoulder as she tilts her head, her ass now resting against my desk and my attention zeroes in on the small dent the hard corner makes against her supple body.

She's mocking me. She's *taunting* me on my own turf and I'm too busy staring at her ass.

Fucking Christ. *Get yourself together.* Am I getting bewitched or some shit? I clear my throat and stretch, locking my palms together behind my head, slowly swiveling my chair towards her. I don't miss the small dip of her gaze towards my widening legs and that's just enough for me to regain my composure and step up to the bat. I don't say a single word—just watch her watching me. She's losing her resolve by the second. When she realizes I'm not about to take the bait, she rolls her eyes and pushes herself off the desk.

"I just needed you to sign off on a few things for the event in April. Figured since we live under the same roof, I'd just hand deliver them for you to have a look before I leave for the office." Her face has fallen serious, bored and slightly irked, almost as if this whole charade was one giant act.

How so *fucking* surprising.

It makes me want to toy with her even more. The urge is curling itself around my spine demanding to be heard. It grips my nerve endings, threatening to lobotomize me if I don't comply. And quick.

"Oh?" I say, my tone swimming in mockery just like hers was. "Off to finally tell your best friend whose cock you're warming at night?"

She glares at me with so much venom that I salivate at the sight. "That would be a lie now wouldn't it?"

"For now."

"Forever, asshole."

My laugh is near damn diabolical.

"Keep telling yourself that."

She narrows her gaze, giving me another one of her classic eye rolls, and turns to leave but I reach over the desk and snatch her wrist.

"Not so fast, darling," I drawl.

She tries to fight me, but my fingers dig into her skin the harder she attempts to shake me free. "What the hell do you want now?" she says through gritted teeth.

"I need you to stay for the meeting." I let go of her arm and my dick twitches when she keeps still, listening for once, looking back at me quizzically. I make a show of checking my watch. "Should start any minute now actually."

"Why?" Is all she manages to say. She's smart enough to know there's a catch and I smile bright and wide while I let her stew in the anxiety of the unknown for a little while longer.

"The crew hasn't met my wife yet. Perfect time for an introduction."

Fire flashes behind her eyes. "This isn't a cotillion, I don't need to be introduced like some fucking prized cattle." Her words are packed with such malice that I'm quite literally being reborn while bathing in the sound of it.

I decide to taunt her even further. "A prized toy, more like."

I can see the insults take form in the curl of her tongue and the rise of her chest, but we're interrupted by Steven and Diego walking into the study before I have the pleasure to hear them come out of her mouth. Both our heads snap to the door.

The two stutter to a stop, their eyes quickly assessing the situation and more specifically my facial expressions. When they don't find a hint of me promising them a swift death if they don't get the hell out, they move further into the room.

"Hey boss," Diego says, heading towards the fireplace and leaning his elbow atop of the mantle. I give him a quick nod but nothing else. He still has some lingering bruises on his face from when I snapped on him a couple weeks ago.

I lack the empathy to care.

Steven follows behind and stands close to him while a few more of my men walk into the room.

Lenix's eyes are now back on mine. I can tell she's quickly realizing she's trapped. She knows who I am—what

I do. I might allow her push-backs when we're alone but she knows she can't pull that kind of shit in front of my crew. The power dynamics have suddenly shifted in my favor and she looks like a wild animal being cornered. And I'm about to take full fucking advantage.

My lips curl in what is most likely a feral grin and reach my hand out to her, leading Lilith straight to hell. From the corner of my eyes, I can tell the room is filling up and most of the people meant to be here have arrived—including Byzantine. I feel his eyes bore into me.

I ignore him. Especially when Lenix gently places her hand in mine and I coax her to approach the chair where I'm still sitting. Her eyes promise sweet retribution.

But for now, she's all fucking mine.

"Everyone," I say, my eyes still locked to hers. "This is Lenix." With a hard tug of her arm, I knock her off balance and she lands on my lap with a small oomph. "My wife."

I can feel the shock crackle around the room and I'm deranged enough to revel in it. I finally turn my gaze to Byzantine, and find his brows furrowed. He knows I'm full of shit, but he wouldn't dream of saying anything in front of everyone. I give him a smirk and a wink.

"Byzantine. You can man the meeting today."

For a few seconds, he stays silent, presumably taking in the whole near-mirage of me and Lenix in front of him. Finally, he shrugs his shoulders, stepping into the role of my second-in-command effortlessly, positioning himself close to the door.

When he begins to speak, all of the attention turns to him, away from us. Lenix hasn't moved an inch since I placed her where I wanted her. But then her lips begin to creep closer to my ear, and I fight a full body shiver when I feel her hot breath on my skin as she says in a seething tone, "I'm going to kill you Connor."

I don't think I've ever been this hard in my goddamn life. Should it be slightly alarming that what got me here was Lenix threatening to kill me? Not really.

My movements are slow, trying to deter any unwanted attention from what I plan on doing to her. Right here, right now. My hand smooths up her thigh, my chest rumbling with a near-silent chuckle. "You can try," I whisper, my fingers now sliding under her dress, "but I'll make your pussy weep in front of all these people before you even have the chance."

Ever so slowly, I roll the chair as close I can get to the large desk in front of us, keeping most of us hidden. My hand hasn't stopped moving up her thigh, her long nails digging into my forearm as I do so. When my fingers find her hip, my eyebrows rise in surprise when all I find is silky smooth skin.

I look up into her glimmering eyes and she quirks a mischievous smile.

"Two can play this game," she whispers back.

Her hand lands on my crotch at the same time as my own finds out how fucking wet she is. No panties in sight.

My lips graze her neck before I let out a small hum near her ear. "My filthy little wife can't help but to play dirty, can she?"

I watch her lick her lips, pulling the bottom one in between her teeth. She's staring straight ahead like she's busy listening into the meeting happening around us. But I know where her attention is when I feel the zipper of my own slacks being pulled down. And in a maneuver that leaves me questioning if she has an actual degree in stealth fucking, she pulls my cock out and slides up my lap, her dress billowing around us, effectively hiding the fact she just slid my dick inside her.

*Shit.*

Her small smirk tells me this might have been her checkmate move this whole time. My cock throbs, her pussy so fucking tight and warm. When I feel the slight sheen of sweat appearing on my forehead, I suddenly consider I may have miscalculated some of my own moves. It's taking every muscle in me not to slam even deeper inside of her or fuck Lenix on the desk in front of everyone—including my father's portrait glaring disapprovingly from above the fireplace.

"What's wrong, Mr. Maxwell?" she says, the innocent tone making my balls tighten while she leans back into my chest, wrapping one arm around my shoulders like she's just settling into my embrace and not currently choking me with her *perfect* fucking cunt.

And of course, this is exactly the moment where the conversation stops and Byzantine looks over, waiting for a reply as if I've heard even one single goddamn word out of his mouth. I grip Lenix's thigh and shift her on my lap but regret my decision immediately when that only makes her slide up and down my shaft.

It might be the few decades shared between us but he seems to realize almost instantly that I wasn't paying attention and reiterates the question. I grunt out an answer, scowling at everyone in the room.

The meeting drags on, every fucking second excruciating long, trying to sit still while Lenix periodically squeezes her pussy around my cock like she's at the gym doing reps. Eventually, I manage to find a sliver of control and lean over to press against her back, my hand snaking around and up under her dress.

I whisper threateningly in the shell of her ear, "You thought you could walk around my men with *this* out." My thumb lands firmly on her clit. "And there would be no consequences?" I feel her body try to contain a small jolt, so I press even harder, circling her tight bud while she clenches even tighter around me. My voice is low and deadly when I speak again. "Let's see how silent you can be as you come all over my lap, shall we?"

"You wouldn't dare," she hisses through her teeth.

"Watch me."

I know this is a suicide mission. I'm halfway there myself. What she doesn't know is the meeting is about to wrap up and as soon as we're alone again, she's going to rue the day she thought she could one up me at my own fucking game. I bask in her fear for a little while longer, that I might force her to come like this, my thumb still administering small smooth circles over her clit.

Just as I thought, Byzantine closes the meeting a few minutes later and everyone slowly files out of the study. The majority barely glance my way, most likely because my new wife is sitting on my lap. The room falls unbearably silent when the only person left to leave is Byzantine himself.

He looks over to us and squints in disbelief. And maybe a little disgust.

"I don't know what the fuck is going on here, and I honestly couldn't care less."

He stalks to the door but before he crosses the threshold, Lenix calls out to him.

"Wait!" she squeaks.

He stops and tilts his head back towards her.

"Just — just don't tell Sunny okay? I need to tell her myself...please?"

He stares down at the floor for a few seconds, looking

like he's debating something but then nods and leaves, closing the door behind him.

As soon as we're alone Lenix tries to stand up but my arm is a steel bar around her waist.

"Where the fuck do you think you're going?"

She huffs loudly trying to wiggle her way off me, and it's definitely not having the desired effect when I groan and she freezes. "I'm not fucking you, Connor," she says flatly.

"Darling — you're currently sitting on my dick."

My other hand travels back up under her dress and I find her as drenched as ever, her clit swollen and begging to be stroked.

"Tell me you don't want this," I say, my voice low and heated.

Her breath catches in her throat, "I don't." But oh, is her body not an instrument demanding to be played. Even as she mouths those two words, her legs part for me and I take full advantage. Pinching her clit, I use the arm already wrapped around her waist to pull her up and then down, my hips pitching upwards as I slam her down on my hard cock.

A gasp, followed by a moan slips out of her mouth and at that very moment, I could kill every other undeserving soul who's ever heard that sound other than *me*.

I can feel her resolve slip. She might hate me but her pussy is fucking drenched and that's the only thing that matters right now.

I know my window for her to willingly give up control is small. And *fuck* does it taste sweeter than honey when she does. Suddenly, I'm on my feet, my arms wrapped tight around her hips. Swiftly turning her around, I drop her on the desk and thrust hard into her. Her legs wrap around my waist, followed immediately by a loud *crack*. My face swivels to the side, my cheek hot and burning, the taste of copper bursting on my tongue.

She just fucking slapped me.

Slowly, I look back over and it's not fear I find in her irises but blown out pupils and absolute indignation.

I smile, tonguing my cheek. "Do it again," I growl.

She only hesitates for a second and when I feel her hand strike my cheek once more, I slam into her to the hilt. Clenching around me, her mouth falls open, her eyes locking onto mine, while both our chest heave in sync. Our bodies have gone perfectly still. The *tick tick tick* of the grandfather clock in the corner mirroring the sound of our heartbeats. Without breaking eye contact, my hand reaches over to where her tits are spilling out of her dress. I circle her hard nipple through her lace bra before my hand trails over the swell of her breast and then up to the smooth column of her throat. The pads of my fingers find the strong pulse of her heart drumming against her throat.

While my hand closes around her neck, I slowly slide my cock out, only keeping the head inside.

"Are you done?" I say, my voice hoarse.

She's so fucking wet, I can hardly think straight.

Her eyes are wide and I can see the moment she decides to let go. It's so fucking beautiful to watch I nearly come at the sight.

And then I plunge all the way back inside.

"Fuck, *Lenix*," I groan out, my fingers tightening around her throat while her hands are trying to gain access to my back, hurriedly pulling my shirt out of my pants, her nails finally and deliciously bitting into my skin. My vision blurs with the sensation of her cunt wrapping around my dick so goddamn perfectly that the only word I can muster up in my feverish mind is *wife*. I thrust into her over and over and over, the word on repeat in my head.

"You feel so *fucking* good," I rasp, my hand traveling down to her chest. "Look how well you're taking me, you're such a good gi—"

"Don't you dare finish that sentence."

I grin at her, my hair falling into my eyes, my hips pumping harder into her. The vision of Lenix right now on my desk, her tits threatening to fall out with every thrust is an image I will remember forever.

"What do you want me to call you then?" I say, a little out of breath.

Her eyes darken, our gaze locked and I nearly turn fucking feral when I realize what I see being reflecting back to me.

Suddenly, I'm pulling her into my arms and turning us over. I sit on the desk, her knees landing wide beside my thighs, straddling me. Her face is so close to mine, I could just lean over and kiss her. But I don't.

"Now," I pump my hips up and she answers back by sitting all the way down on me, my hand snaking between us, finding her greedy clit. "Why don't you be a good little *wife* and come all over your husband's cock."

Her body's reaction to the word is instantaneous.

*Fuck. Fuck. Fuck.*

I don't know what dangerous game we're playing at but right now I couldn't care any less. Lenix is bouncing on top of me, her head falling backwards with my fucking *name* on her lips. Her pussy clamps around my cock as she comes. I follow immediately after. My teeth find purchase on her bare shoulder, spilling inside of her as she continues to squeeze and squeeze and squeeze, grinding down hard on me chasing what's left of her climax.

Our heavy pants are the only sound between us as we fall still, coming down from the absolute fucking fever dream that just happened.

When I feel Lenix tense up, I know the moment is over.

And maybe it's for the best.

I don't even know what to make of what just happened between us.

Still holding on to her, I stand up and set her down. Her palms land on my chest, shoving me back. "This never happened," she says hastily before adjusting her dress and heading for the door.

I let her go.

But not before getting the last word in.

I scoff, making her glance over her shoulder. I lazily trail my eyes up her long legs and say, "My cum is still dripping down your thighs, darling."

# 26

## Lenix

"Shit, shit, shit, shit, shit, shit!" I hiss out, slamming the wheel with every expletive out of my mouth. I'm still parked outside Connor's house, cursing to the high heavens and it's taking everything in me not to slam the horn and scream.

Hands shaking, I jerk my keys into the ignition and start the car. I turn down the driveway and head for the yawning gates. In between leaving Connor's study and running out of the house, I made sure to wash away the evidence—not my proudest moment.

Thank God I have an IUD—still, how could I have been so reckless? Shame, guilt, and mortification trickles down my spine, threatening to overthrow every other emotion existing in my body and take root forever.

What the *fuck* was that?

Clearly, I'm suffering a momentary lapse in sanity. I went in to get Connor to sign some paperwork and ended up fucking him.

I lean over and turn the radio on, leaving it on a random station that I don't even like, too busy hating myself to notice. My shoulders are up to my ears while I drive through Garden Heights.

I can feel the fracture taking form inside of me. It leads into an alternate reality that I no longer recognize. One where I am controlled and seen as nothing but a possession. Too similar to the one I escaped from when I was sixteen. And somehow, what just happened between Connor and I in his office is threatening to pierce the veil and tear a hole into *this* reality. The one I've diligently, if not somewhat fearfully, constructed for the past thirteen years. It threatens to let in memories; of gendered roles, expected behaviors and a docile temperament that I've run away from ever since.

But why?

Why did fucking Connor feel so similar?

It definitely didn't at the time. Or maybe it did—the shame of it all burning me up and curling low in my stomach instead of lust. It was shame that made me come so hard, and I don't think I'll ever be the same again.

Every single touch felt wrong and I've never been so turned on in my life.

Somehow, it was simpler to rationalize what happened near the pool. Nefarious actions done under dark skies. It was easier to pretend, it never happened. That it was all one bizarre dream and forget about it by morning.

It doesn't explain me sauntering into his office, ready to bait him *sans* underwear.

I made that choice.

Yep—I'm definitely losing it. There's no other plausible explanation, other than temporary possession. I refuse to own up to anything out loud. Let's call it a healthy, and well-rounded behavior. I groan out loud trying to forget, but end up *remembering* how he guessed my basest urge and called me his wife. What the hell is wrong with me?

And why was is it so *fucking* hot?

I've always been physically attracted to him, that's not new. But God… it's never been like this. Never this intense. The way he looked at me, in all his fucked up glory from over the desk, his black hair falling into his eyes, a ruthless glint to his blacked out pupils. Connor disheveled is a masterpiece, a perfect rendition of what it means to sell my soul to the devil. I'm drinking at the well of depravity, and it only leaves me wanting more.

Absolutely *not.*

This can never happen again.

I nearly die on the spot recalling the look Byzantine gave us before he left the study. It was obvious he knew exactly what was going on. To have him anywhere near while Connor's dick was inside of me is enough to make me keel over and never wake up.

"Good fucking job, Lenix. You really did it this time," I grumble out loud, now driving downtown, the same radio station droning on about the Noxport traffic. I can barely see in front of me. I'm on auto-pilot, going through the motions in a goddamn trance.

Every single thought swirling inside my head is heightened by the fact that I'm heading to the office about to tell Sunny everything.

*Everything* being the cover story to which is just another of my many lies.

And unsurprisingly, that very thought spirals me deeper into the pit of misery I'm drowning in. The guilt blooming behind my ribs at the thought of lying to Sunny—yet again—is competing with everything else currently exploding in my mind. My insides are a battlefield and the war has only just begun.

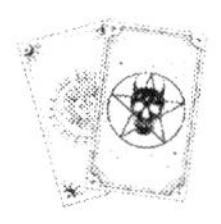

"Hiya, babes!" I internally cringe at the tone of my voice but power through it. Sunny's expression turns bright, her eyes snapping up from the computer screen she was squinting at.

"There you are," she says with a smile and I immediately hate myself even more but somehow keep it together. I head over to her desk and give her a quick kiss on the cheek. "Feels like I haven't seen you in ages," she adds before I turn towards my desk and sit down.

Despite everything, I let out a genuine laugh. "It's only been like, four days."

Sunny lets out a small protesting huff, her attention back on the lit up screen, a smirk curving her lips. "Well it *felt* long to me. So what's new? Fill me in."

I stare at her blankly, not knowing what to say.

*Oh you know, just married and living in the house of the man I've openly hated for the past two years. Not to mention that my brother, who's the leader of a cult mind you, has threatened to drag me back there.*

Instead, I open my mouth and say, "hmm, not much really. Just super busy with Connor's event." *When I'm not too busy getting plowed by him on his desk.*

I swallow down my groan, including everything else crawling up my throat.

This is a nightmare.

I power up my desktop and distractedly clack my nails on the desk while I wait. I need to tell her right now—just use my words and spill. But I'm a coward. Instead, I listen to Sunny fill me in on her weekend and whatever work related stuff I've missed at the office. I nod, and laugh at the right moments, but my mind is churning out every insult imaginable, all directed at me and my inability to just confess.

What if our relationship can't survive this? What if she'll never forgive me?

I don't want her to see me differently…

*That's it.*

I just need to do it. Rip off the band-aid and blurt it out. But it's as hard as finding the courage to nosedive off a cliff.

"Connor and I are married!" I blurt out the words like a screaming banshee, cutting Sunny off mid-sentence. *Great, well done.*

At first, I think she didn't hear me. But that's wishful thinking. She's stopped talking and is now eyeing me from across our desks as I've hit pause on a movie.

I can taste the dread trickle down my throat, bitter and cold.

"What?" she finally says. Her voice is quiet and laced with disbelief because, why wouldn't it be?

I nervously play with my hair. "Connor and I are in love, and… and we eloped over the weekend." The sudden guilt from realizing Sunny might be hurt that I didn't even tell her beforehand stings, even if all of this is one big fabricated lie.

"Connor," Sunny mutters, still staring me down like I'm full of shit—because I am. "And you," she adds, but then falls silent. Starting to sweat, I try to swallow the massive lump stuck in my throat, attempting to conjure up a smile fit for a newlywed. I'm clearly failing because Sunny's eyes narrow and I'm seconds away from running out of the office.

"What's wrong?" she says, her eyes boring a hole straight into my soul.

"Nothing… just some happy news, no?" My smile is cracking under the weight of her hazel eyes, assessing me like I'm about to confess a crime.

She's not buying it. What a shocking turn of events.

I swivel on my computer chair, the small crick of the mechanism now the only sound in the office. We continue to lock eyes and I continue to sweat. We stay like this for what feels like an eternity until finally, I crack.

"Ok fine! That was a lie. We're not in love, but… we *are* married," I say with a slight wince.

"Len, what the hell is going on?" she asks, clearly worried.

I groan, my face landing hard into the palm of my hands. "Please don't hate me," I mumble through my fingers, too embarrassed to even look at her. I hear her stand up and walk over me but I still don't look up. Her fingers curl around my forearm and she gives me a small tug.

"Come. Let's sit on the couch," she says.

Sheepishly, I let her pull me up from my seat and lead me to the couch near the door. We sit and I avoid eye contact until I can't any longer. But instead of finding judgment glaring back at me, I only find worry and I'm hit with such an intense wave of feelings, my eyes sting.

Sunny takes my hand in hers, placing it on her lap and squeezes.

"I would *never* hate you. Just please tell me what's actually going on."

I close my eyes while breathing in deeply, filling up my lungs and then exhaling loudly.

"I don't even know where to start," I say, eyes still closed.

"Start anywhere."

My shoulders slump, my lids finally fluttering back open.

"So… umm…" *Just out with it.* "I have this ex-fiancé…" The next lie forming on my lips slips out so easily, I'm almost impressed—if I wasn't so busy cursing myself for it. "It was from before we met, and well… he was really abusive. I managed to run, and I thought I was done with him. I thought it was all over—until he showed up in town last week, threatening me."

Sunny's hand covers her mouth in shock and I feel downright horrible. Irredeemable. The worst friend someone could possibly have.

"The only thing I thought of doing at the time was ask Connor for protection."

"Why not Byzantine?" Sunny asks and I can hear a

small twinge of hurt in her voice. "I thought you hated Connor?"

"I did! I do… but… there's more," I say tentatively.

I place my hand on top of hers, trying to keep her as close as possible.

"But before I tell you, I need you to know how sorry I am that I've kept this from you and that I love you and… and just—just please try not to judge me."

Because I'm doing enough of that for the both of us.

Sunny's eyes soften before she says, "I promise, Lenix."

"So… the reason I hate Connor is that… well, we ended up getting married on a dare when we were partying in Vegas together two years ago." I scoff, suddenly feeling foolish. "And he's refused to sign the divorce papers ever since."

Her eyes widen, then harden and I can't really make out the emotion behind it or who it's aimed at. "Why?"

"Why what?"

"Why is he refusing to get divorced?" she asks, confused.

I look at her, with a *you know how Connor is* look and answer, "Because he thinks it's one big joke and not *actually* something serious or legally binding."

Sunny just sits there stunned. "That's insane," she finally says.

"Yeah, well… *Connor* is insane."

She blinks a few times, seemingly trying to find the words to respond to the bomb I just threw at her feet. "This is all starting to make a lot of sense," she mutters almost to herself. Her gaze then refocuses on me. "So what does being married to Connor have to do with hiding from your ex-fiancé?"

I squirm in my seat before answering, "I sort of called

Connor and led my ex straight to him. I used us being married to my advantage. And told him that Connor was my husband and to leave me alone—or else."

"Wow…"

I squeeze her hand. "There's more…"

And before she can even synthesize all the information I've already flung on her, I tell her all about our agreement and how it led me to move into Connor's house. I successfully leave out the fact that he now owns my orgasms as a condition of the agreement, and how we've already had sex, after less than a week. That little tidbit of a detail is wrapped tightly into a bundle of shame. And I'll leave it to fester in some dark corner of my mind, desperately hoping her boyfriend won't recount every dirty detail of the meeting this morning.

Sunny suddenly springs up to her feet, her nostrils flaring. "I can't believe him! What a psychopath." She turns to me, hope but also pity in her eyes. "You don't need to do this, Lenix. Byzantine can help you. *I* can help you. You don't have to do this," she says worriedly.

I look up at her with all the love and affection I have for her. Of course she would say that. Of course she'd want to help. But I've done enough harm. I've lied enough to last me a lifetime.

"I know you would, babes," I say slightly defeated, watching her fall back on the couch. "But I don't want you involved in this." She opens her mouth to protest but I raise my hand to silence her and continue, "I need you as far away as possible from all of this. Connor didn't even want me to tell you the real story in the first place."

"Why the hell not?" she replies in a perplexed tone.

"According to him, it would make the lie more believable," I grumble.

I watch Sunny rifle through every single emotion under the sun before finally slumping against the couch in defeat and resignation.

"Please tell me if or when anything new happens, I'll be worrying about you day and night."

"As much as I can, babes," I answer with a small smile.

I lean over to hug her, and still, I'm fighting back tears. I should feel relieved that I've told Sunny but it's making me feel worse. These half-truths are killing me and one of these days I'll wake up to realize they've finally suffocated me to death. Successfully ending the new life I've tried to create after snuffing out the one I left behind.

# 27

## Connor

The wheels of my private plane hit the tarmac with a jerk. We've just landed at the Ukiah Municipal Airport in Mendocino County, a two hour flight up the coast. I check my watch distractedly as I wait for the plane to come to a full stop. I try to fly up here at least once a month to check up on business and visit the sprawling weed farms we own near the Mendocino National Park.

Just another way to hide illegal deals behind the legitimacy of a legal business. My father barely had any legit dealings, favoring the illicit trade of guns and drugs. But this? This is all me. Hiding in plain sight is my favorite activity. With the help of Byzantine and Bastian and the many legal and illicit fronts we own since my father's death, we've made the Sin Eaters stronger than ever before.

A car waits for me when I deboard and soon we're heading towards the farm about an hour away from the airport. I try to focus on answering emails on my phone but I find myself just staring at the screen, my mind stuck in Noxport.

It's only been a day since Lenix and I fucked for the first time in two years. I stayed out most of the night just to avoid her. And this coincidental trip up the coast has me feeling like a teenager who can't manage his fucking feelings. No, not *feelings*, just an uncomfortable tightness in my chest that I can't seem to shake.

I want to keep the memory of Lenix blissfully coming on top of me while I ached with my own release untouched until it's ultimately ruined by reality. I know she'll be avoiding me. So I'm avoiding her right back. This feels so fucking childish, and it makes me want to set myself on fire but I can't help it. So I left the city under the guise of a business trip.

I usually try to stay overnight to make traveling worthwhile since I own a house up here. But leaving Lenix unprotected for more than twenty-four hours has me uneasy. Even if she's the bane of my existence most of the time, I'm still a man of my word. So, I asked Bastian to install a few more cameras around the house—including the guest bedroom.

He raised a brow when I told him this morning.

"For her protection, yeah?" he said.

I gave him a curt nod in response. "What the fuck else would they be for?"

"And who will be in charge of watching the feeds?"

"Give me access and no one else," I spat out.

And so, without much protest and an indolent shrug of his shoulder he installed the cameras and gave me access through an app on my phone.

Before the flight, I even typed out a short message to Lenix telling her I'd be out of town till Friday afternoon. My jaw ticked when I sent it, appalled that I was doing something so fucking domestic as telling her about my whereabouts.

She never replied.

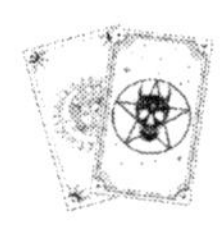

I MANAGE NOT to check the camera feeds all day. Not like I had much free time anyway. And knowing Lenix was most likely at the office all day dampened the urge considerably.

But now the itch is crawling up my spine, my fingers twitching around the sweating glass of mezcal I'm holding. Sitting in the dark kitchen in my beach house, I scowl at the shadows dancing on the wall facing me. My phone is burning in my palm, and there's a smoldering fire in my chest that I'm trying to ignore with my entire existence. Abhorrently, it's connected to the fact that Lenix never replied to my text. It shouldn't bother me. She ignored me for two years before this. Or tried at the very least.

But something's shifted ever since she moved in, a wisp of possessive heat stings my skin, and it's growing hotter by the day. *Especially*, when she's ignoring me like she is now. And so, instead of flinging the glass against the wall, I down the smokey alcohol in one long gulp and head for the bedroom. Changing into a pair of gray sweats, I leave my chest bare and sit on the bed, my back against the pillows lining the headboard. My phone hasn't left my side. I swipe my hand through my hair, then down my face and mustache, finally doing what I've been itching to do all fucking day.

I open the app and after clicking a few buttons, the video feed pops up on the screen, split into six squares for the different cameras. At first, I can't find her anywhere, but finally I detect movement in one of the feeds, realizing that I'm looking at *my* bedroom, not hers. I grin so wide you'd think I've just won the fucking lottery. I click on the video, enlarging it.

Maybe I should feel something other than a thrilling lust at finding her exactly where she's not supposed to be, but instead I settle in like I'm about to watch the best movie ever made. She's wearing a short pink satin robe, her hair falling in natural curls, a rare sight, looking fresh out the shower. From the vantage point of the camera, she's facing away and to my disappointment, I can't see what's hiding underneath. She seems aimless, not looking like she's searching for something in particular. Her fingers trail atop my dresser and that same small tingle I've felt before pings through me.

Then I get an idea.

I reach over to grab my laptop, having the app installed on there too and pull up the video, hitting the full screen. Lenix reappears, not having stopped her slow perusal of my room. This leaves me the freedom to use my phone without losing the image of Lenix where she's not supposed to be.

**Me:** Miss me?

I watch Lenix jump. She looks down at her phone but just as I thought, she ignores my text. So I up the ante.

**Me:** Or maybe it's your cunt that misses me?

Without waiting for a reply that might never come, I send another.

**Me:** Have you been thinking about my cock while you're all alone in that big house?

**Me:** Are you dying to fuck your fingers while thinking of me? Don't forget darling, your orgasms are mine.

She looks down at the phone again, and I watch her make what looks like a small huff of irritation. She heads for the bed and sits down on the edge before typing.

**Lenix:** Hard pass.

By the time my eyes are back on the laptop, she's slid up the bed and is now resting her head on the pillows, her curls splayed around her face. My dick jerks awake at the sight, her spread out in *my* bed.

*The fuck is she doing?*

Her robe has now fallen open, revealing a small pair of white shorts and a tank top underneath. I lick my lips in anticipation. Now with the vision of her on my bed, I ache to push my taunts even further.

**Me:** Try telling me that next time you're so full of me, you can't help but beg for more.

I nearly go blind when I see her hand disappear under those barely there shorts, her head falling deeper into the pillows, phone still clutched in her other hand. My own phone pings with a text.

**Lenix:** There won't be a next time.

I smirk, about to text back but the image is too distracting. Jesus fucking *Christ.* She drops the phone beside her and wiggles her shorts down her legs, her thighs falling open. One hand now squeezing one of her tits and the other back where it belongs.

I palm my cock roughly through my sweats, eyes glued to the screen. I'm so fucking hard that I forget about anything else, not when Lenix is splayed open on my sheets, her fingers circling her clit. Hardly believing this is happening, I curse the grainy feed, the urge to see Lenix as clear as possible overtaking all my goddamn senses. Her hips pitch slightly upwards as her fingers slip into her cunt and *fuck*, it's the most alluring thing I've ever seen.

I suddenly regret being hours away. The need to fuck her senseless, on my bed no less, is so intense my balls tighten at the very thought. But then again… this wouldn't be happening if I was back in Noxport. So I thank the universe as I pull my dick out, spitting into my palm and stroking it hard enough for a groan to spill out of me between my clenched teeth.

I watch Lenix's back arch, one of her hands falling to the sheets, fisting them. Her eyes are closed, eyebrows furrowed like she's angry she's even doing this, her mouth falling open into a small o-shaped expression.

As I continue to fuck my fist at the sight of her, I have a passing thought.

*I shouldn't be doing this.*

But I never claimed to be good… and this?

*This* is exactly what she would expect of me if she knew about the cameras. Something about that spurs me further into the blinding lust I've tumbled into.

The camera in my room isn't even from the new ones I asked Bastian to install—the irony isn't lost on me, but I'm also cursing that this specific one has no sound. The desire to hear Lenix's soft moans is setting me aflame. Thankfully, it still allows me to witness the very moment she does come, her teeth biting her lower lip and an expression of complete rapture painted on her perfect face.

Hot spurts of cum land on my tightening stomach as I do the same. It hits me like a freight train and I let myself be bulldozed by it, the moment now seared into my brain and soul.

I clean up quickly and grab my phone again, eager to send one last text before she runs out of my room like a petty little thief up to no good.

**Me:** That was quite the show, darling. Good thing I was recording this time.

# 28

# Lenix

I'm walking aimlessly down the deserted boardwalk, my mind far away somewhere in the middle of the Pacific ocean. It's dark and gloomy out today but I relish the cold bite in the air while I put one foot in front of the other.

It's been a week since I heard from my brother or my ex-fiancé for that matter. It's grating on my nerves. I can never seem to fully relax, always looking behind my shoulder as if the ghosts of my past will spring out of the shadows like a nightmarish jack-in-a-box ready to drag me back.

There's an eerie calm attached to the waiting like water slowly receding far out from the shore, only to come back as a hundred foot wave destroying everything in its path. What will I do when it comes for me? Will I fight? Or simply drown.

I've been done with work for over an hour but I question if I really want to go back to Connor's right now. Especially after last night, and the *incident* in his bed.

A heady mixture of heat laced with shame shoots up my spine.

The asshole had been watching me. He ignored my calls after his last text. The fucker. I can't say I'm shocked that there's cameras around the house. He probably doesn't see how wrong that is. The bastard lives outside the confines of society, broken out of those chains a long time ago. The guilt will roll off his back like water on a duck. I just know he'll give me one of his slanted cocky smiles and won't bother trying to justify his actions.

Not to mention the added irritation that he caught me in his bed of all places.

I'm such an idiot.

I should have known better—should have picked up on the sheer coincidence of his messages while I was in his room. Instead, I played right into his hand.

I don't even know why I ended up there, my feet just carried me to the end of the hall and I simply walked in. Was I even looking for anything in particular? I don't think so. Or maybe I was unconsciously looking for some small clues that Connor is human and not this larger than life version of himself he parades around in.

A vulnerable hint of humanity. Not to take advantage of but more to understand him better. Not sure why I would even want to know him better that way, it's not like we're close. Never in my life have I misconstrued sex with emotional connection. And I'm not about to start now.

Although I can't deny our sexual chemistry, I would rather swallow glass than to think this is more than what it is. But something about blurring the lines of our arrangement is a powerful aphrodisiac. I have a hard time controlling myself around him, I can at least admit that.

My eyes rove over the sprawling ocean, my mind still restless and without purpose, when I'm suddenly reminded of a legend my father used to tell my sisters and I. Of a young and frivolous girl named Rose who loved to dance. One night, during festivities, a stranger appeared at her family house, and Rose danced with him till the stroke of midnight.

It was then revealed that she had been dancing with the devil.

There's many versions of this story. In some the devil gifts her his own necklace, binding her to him, then dragging the girl back to hell. Then there's one version where the local priest intervenes and saves her. She ends up joining a convent and dying a few years later.

Not sure which ending is worse.

All I know is that I've danced with the devil before and I know I will dance with him again. Especially when he's dressed in infuriatingly dapper suits, with eyes so dark I could lose my way by simply staring back into their bottomless depths, and be led straight down to hell.

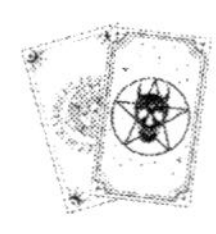

*I'm trapped in my father's office. There is no door for me to escape and his blood is everywhere. Like water running out of a faucet, the room fills and fills and fills. The blood soaks my white dress, rising up my ankles, my knees, my thighs. I can no longer see my father's lifeless body but I know it's still here somewhere.*

*I've killed him.*

*And now I am bound to suffer God's wrath.*

*I will drown in this room. I will die with my father's blood filling my lungs.*

*A sordid baptism fit for a sinner.*

*I claw at the walls, desperate to find a way out, the blood now up to my chest.*

*I won't survive this.*

*I bang on the wall with my fists and scream. I scream so loud it hurts my ears, but I don't stop. I can't stop.*

I jolt awake in bed, frantically sitting up and gasping for air. Fighting at the shadows, terror freezing my veins. I feel hands holding my arms and I'm filled with a blind primal need to defend myself.

"Lenix!" Connor growls, "It's me. You're safe. It's okay, you're okay, it was just a dream."

My mind is still stuck in the room full of my father's blood as I continue to fight against his grasp, my heart slamming hard against my chest.

"Listen to my voice." His tone is much softer now, his hands stroking my arms up and down. "Breathe, Lenix, just breathe."

His words finally cut through the daze, and I fall still,

but my chest continues to rise quickly up and down, my breath ragged and harsh.

"Connor?" I rasp.

My eyes finally adjust to the dark as I try to calm down. His hands are still wrapped tightly around my arms, his body hovering close to me, bare chested and on his knees almost straddling me but not quite.

"You're okay, my darling," he murmurs softly.

The vulnerability of the moment slaps me in the face so hard that I'm suddenly choking on it.

I try to shake myself out of his hold but he just digs his fingers harder into my arms, his eyes never leaving my own.

"Can you not?" I bite out, but he's obviously not deterred in the slightest, never loosening his grip. "It was just a dream, I'm fine." My voice cracks and I flinch at my tone.

"Didn't sound like just a dream to me," he says darkly. "I've heard screams like yours before. And I've usually been the cause of it."

He finally lets go of my arms but leans closer while I try to skitter away, hitting the headboard behind me. His touch is surprisingly gentle and it rattles me almost as much as the nightmare I just crawled out of.

His thumb glides over my cheek right under my eye, fingers sliding into my hair, his warm palm slowly cradling my face. The silence coils around us like a familiar presence, centering me back into my body and far away from the demons nipping at my heels.

His eyes are hard, but the corners soften when he finally speaks. "I know you're hiding something from me. And I know it's bigger than just your piece of shit ex." His other hand lands on my hip, pushing me into the mattress and holding me there. I swallow hard. "I don't care how long it takes. But I will find out. And when I do?" he growls low, his eyes shining purposely in the dark. "I'll kill them all, darling."

He's gone before I even have time to blink, like a wraith slipping back into the ether. I'm left alone with my thoughts, his last words still ringing loudly in my ears.

# 29

## Connor

Hidden in a dark corner of The Chelsea, I glare at nothing in particular, hand wrapped around my drink on the table. Bastian sits next to me in the large booth, laptop open, the light of the screen accentuating his blank features. He's barely said a word in over an hour, simply grunting or nodding whenever I even bother to speak to him. Typical.

"Remember that girl we saw in a wedding dress at that diner we used to go to before Martha died?" I say pensively.

Bastian gives me an odd look and settles back into his seat, closing his computer.

"Yeah..."

"I wonder what happened to her."

"Why?"

My annoyance spikes. "Fucking Christ, I don't know. I'm just saying."

He continues to stare at me as if it's bizarre that I'm bringing this up out of the blue. Hell, I don't fucking know why my thoughts wandered over to that night in particular. They just did.

"Anyway..." he says, clearly uninterested in furthering this conversation. "I've got some news on your missus."

Irritated, I readjust my coat jacket and smooth out my mustache before speaking. "Don't call her that."

"Well, that's what she is, isn't she?"

I shoot him a glaring look, but don't bother responding.

Just the mention of Lenix makes my jaw clench. It's been almost a week since I've truly spoken to her. Not since I woke her up from a nightmare in the middle of the night and saw what kind of fear she hides under all that glitter. The need to eviscerate whoever instilled that fear in her was so strong I could barely hold it together. I left before I did something I'd regret, like hold her to my chest so she could fall back asleep in the safety of my arms. I was mostly convinced she'd push me off the bed anyway.

She's been subdued since then, keeping to herself and I've kept my distance in turn. The only reason I know she's home most nights is because of the camera still installed in her room. I thought she'd have found and removed it by now. But it's still there. And I still watch.

Bastian doesn't bother pretending he's even slightly affected by my death glare, his face stays impassive as he just stares right back. Finally the fucker speaks. "I didn't find any evidence that Lenix even *has* an ex-fiancé."

My eyebrows shoot up in surprise. "What about the license plate I gave you?"

Bastian shakes his head. "Rented under a fake name from what I can tell. I even scanned his face in every database I could think of but nothing came up. It's like the dude lives off-grid or something."

I can't help but feel vindicated. I knew she was lying. Now it's just a matter of finding out why and most importantly *what.*

"There's more," Bastian says while signaling to the server for another round. When he looks back at me, I find a small glint in his eyes. Finding dirt on people has always been his favorite pastime. "Lenix Taylor only started appearing on record around twelve years ago. I couldn't find anything about her beforehand. And considering how little I *did* find, looks to me like she's deliberately keeping a low profile." He pauses, taking the drink the server hands him and I lean over to take mine. He takes a small sip, a hint of a smile on his face before he adds, "Your wife is hiding something alright, but whatever it is, it's much bigger than just a sleazy ex."

I stay silent for a beat, my mind churning out possibilities while I bring the glass to my lips. "He called her Penelope," I muse. Bastian looks over and raises an eyebrow. "Her ex-fiancé, he called her Penelope. When I asked her about it later she told me Lenix was her middle name."

"She was lying."

"I got that much," I reply with a scowl.

Shrugging his shoulders, he starts packing his shit and

stands up. "I'll look into it, but I can't promise you anything." And with barely a goodbye, he strolls out of the bar.

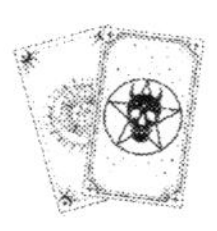

It's late in the evening when I get back home. From the foyer, I notice some light filtering from the kitchen and follow it. I find Lenix at the kitchen island, laptop open and binders full of fabric piled beside her, a glass of rosé clutched in her hand. Her long legs are uncovered, her bare feet perched on the stool. She has a loose oversized t-shirt on, looking like she's wearing just that and nothing else. Her shoulders lift in surprise when she hears me walk in but says nothing, taking a sip of wine instead.

"Working?" I ask.

"Barely," she mutters, closing her computer with a sigh. She lifts her arms over her shoulder and stretches, the hem of her shirt riding up her thigh. My eyes track the movement, now wondering if there *is* something under that cotton shirt.

I stand on the other side of the island and suddenly don't know what to say.

*Fucking hell.*

Feels like I can only find the right words when I'm taunting her—or fucking her. I turn my back and open the fridge just to have something to do. "Hungry?" I ask from behind the door.

She laughs. "Connor Maxwell knows how to cook?"

My mood sours instantly, glad my back is facing her so I can hide the small wince that off-handed comment just elicited. My mother was a great cook, all my favorite memories of her were in this very kitchen. I used to try to help, even at five years old, barely reaching the counter. But then she left. Disappeared out of my life. And the kitchen became unbearably empty and quiet.

Before closing the fridge, I shake off the unwanted memory and grab a few containers off the top shelf. I turn back to face Lenix, a smirk now firmly placed on my face. "I have a delivery service that comes every week," I say while laying out some kind of fancy mushroom risotto and green salad between us on the counter. "Who has time for meal prep anyway?"

She lets out a small chuckle and scans the island as if assessing what I just took out from the fridge.

"Good enough for you, darling?" I tease.

Her eyes slide back over to mine, a smile curling her lips and *shit*, she's so fucking beautiful when her guard is down.

"Sure," she says, settling back into the small stool backrest, pushing her work shit off to the side and taking another sip of her wine.

Waiting for the oven to heat up, I take off my suit jacket and place it on the stool next to Lenix. I unbutton my wrist cuffs, and roll up my sleeves. All the while, she watches me as I do so. Her attention makes me hyper-aware of my actions, and I'm suddenly forgetting how to just move around in my own body. *Great.*

Shaking off my unwanted nerves, I reach over for the bottle of mezcal, uncorking it and pouring a healthy amount into a tumbler. Lenix is quiet, still observing me while I take a burning sip and settle back into my cocksure attitude.

"Why the Sin Eaters?" she finally says.

"Why what?"

She rolls her eyes as if her question was painfully

obvious and I'm the idiot here. "Like, is there any meaning behind it?"

I place my palms wide on the counter, leaning into them and tilt my head with a grin. "Trying to get to know me, are you?"

"Oh my God, nevermind," she huffs, crossing her arms over her chest. "Just trying to make conversation."

I continue to stare at her, not bothering to acknowledge the small squeeze behind my chest from Lenix asking me a personal detail about my life.

"I'll tell you what," I say as I lean even closer, almost conspiratorially. "I'll answer your question, if you answer one of mine."

"You're truly unbearable," she bites out, her eyebrows dipping with a glare. Her walls are back up, doors shut and triple locked. "Why does everything have to be a negotiation with you?"

She's irritated. *Good.*

This was getting uncomfortable anyway. At least this Lenix, I can handle. Knowing I won't get anything out of her now—or she'll just feed me another lie instead of the truth—I answer anyway.

"Sin Eaters were common back in the seventeenth century. Mostly in Wales." I take a sip before continuing. "My father's mother was Welsh, it's where he got the name. They were social pariahs, shunned and most importantly, feared. They were only called upon for funerals, where they would consume the food left for them on the dead body."

Lenix wrinkles her nose. "Ew."

I chuckle softly. "It was meant to represent the sins of the deceased, the Sin Eater would eat the food and by doing so, absorb their sins and absolve their souls. They basically carried the sins of the dead inside of them, and because of it, were damned to spend eternity in hell with no chance of redemption."

She blinks, a slight glint of fascination in her eyes, but there's also something else there I can't quite put my finger on.

"Sounds kind of… noble," she finally says.

I laugh, grabbing the foil container and sliding it into the oven before turning back to face her. "Or they were irredeemable even before they ever became the local Sin Eater." I wink, giving her a crooked grin. "Just like me, darling."

# 30

## Lenix

It's early morning. I'm slicing into green onions on the cutting board, getting ready to whisk up a quick omelet before heading to the office. Ewan wounds around my legs, purring loudly and letting out a small meow announcing his presence in case I forgot he was there. I've been letting him out of my bedroom lately and Connor hasn't said anything, so I'm taking advantage.

My eyes are fixed on the cutting board but my mind is anywhere but here.

I've been unsettled.

Not feeling like myself. Well, not feeling like Lenix Taylor that is. Who knows if that's even who I am. Or just another guise for me not to look too closely at the decaying mask I've fastened overtop my real identity. Either way, I feel like I'm fading. Going through the motions, pretending everything is fine when it's not.

The dream I had about my father's death rattled me to the bone. I haven't come close to feeling any kind of normal since.

Living here under Connor's protection isn't sustainable. I can't pretend to be his wife forever. I should be relieved that it's been two weeks since I've heard from my brother—but the silence feels intentional, like a shark swimming in the shallow depths before the fatal strike. As if I have a giant invisible countdown over my head, I can hear the ticking of the seconds but I can't see how long I have—and it's driving me nuts. It makes me wonder if I'll survive any of it

I don't hear Connor enter the kitchen and I startle when he speaks. "Is my wife making me breakfast? How thoughtful," he drawls.

I shoot him a searing look. "In your dreams, assho—" My words die in my throat when I look down and find the kitchen knife I'm holding is covered in blood. It clangs on the black marble counter after I let it slip out of my hand, a shocked breath squeaking out of me. I quickly glance up to Connor who's staring at me quizzically and by the time my eyes find the knife again on the counter, it's back to normal. No blood in sight.

In a blink, I'm suddenly reminded of the daydreams I would slip in and out of when I was a child. They had faded and eventually disappeared after I ran away.

*That's it. I'm losing it.* I'm seeing things now?

What might be the most startling thing of all, is this *feeling*. This deep rooted awareness, an all-encompassing knowing that this has happened before. This nonsensical, however baseless, belief that I've stood in front of Connor just like this.

*His* blood staining my hands.

But the feeling dissipates almost as fast as it came, and I am left breathless.

"What the hell was that?" Connor asks with a small frown.

My heart rate triples as I try to suck in a breath and laugh it off like I didn't just hallucinate something close to his death. It's the stress. It *must* be the stress. My mind is playing tricks on me. That's all. I quickly bring my index finger up to my mouth, sucking on it and then look at it pretending to find an invisible cut. "You just startled me. Thought I cut myself," I answer, my voice weaker than usual, and my smile looking more like a grimace, I'm sure.

I know Connor isn't buying it. His eyes narrow and I start to sweat. Rounding the corner of the island, his dark eyes don't leave mine. I refuse to break eye contact and admit defeat. Trying to contain the tremble in my hands, I place them on the counter behind me and manage a forced casual pose before he invades the space right in front of me.

Slowly, he places a hand beside mine, his pinky finger gently grazing my thumb and lightning sparks up my arm just by that soft touch alone. He hasn't stopped staring, as if he can make me confess just by his forceful gaze.

It almost works.

But then he speaks. "Liars get caught, darling."

His hips are now pressing against mine, pushing me into the island behind us. His other hand finds the curve of my shoulder, his fingers trailing up my neck and then curling around my chin, holding me there. Pressing against my bottom lip with his thumb, he pulls it down slightly.

I should be pushing him off. I should sneer, or talk back, or *something*. But I don't. Maybe it's because I'm still too unnerved by what just happened. Or maybe I'm just too tired to fight this morning so I let him. And I'm sure he's noticing by the devilish curl of his full lips, watching me.

"I need you to buy a dress," he finally says, a dash of amusement in his baritone voice.

"What?" I say in a hushed tone, feeling slightly whiplashed by the change in topic.

He releases me and takes a step back, sliding his hands into his plaid slacks. His shoulder leans on a cupboard near the fridge, one foot over the other, casual, elegant and downright infuriating.

"The mayor is having a fundraiser for the upcoming election on Thursday. His uncle, Governor Morrissey will be attending. As will we."

"I can buy my own, just let me know what colo—"

"You can't afford the kind I want you to wear."

"Okay, well fuck you too then." I turn to leave, but he grabs my wrist barking a laugh and that only annoys me even further. My nostrils flare and my chest grows tight by the time I glare back at him.

"That's not what I meant," he says with a cocky smile. "I just need you looking a specific kind of rich. I need you dripping in wealth, not just a pretty dress, but an *expensive* one. I need you stealing everyone's attention, especially the governor's."

Ewan chooses this exact moment to jump onto the counter next to me and I watch Connor's body jolt before taking a large step back.

I laugh in disbelief. "Wait. Are you scared of cats?"

His eyes narrow as he stares the cat down before dragging his gaze back to mine.

"I don't trust it."

"I'm sure the feeling's mutual," I say in jest, scratching my cat behind the ears.

He pulls out a black Amex and holds it between two fingers, handing it to me. I roll my eyes at the gesture. "Is that supposed to impress me?"

"I just need you to buy a gown, Lenix. It's not that deep," he says, his tone dripping with boredom.

I hold in the urge to karate chop him in the vocal cords and snatch the card from his hand instead. "Fine. But I won't stop at just the dress."

He gives me a lazy shrug, turning his back to me and starts to make his way out of the kitchen. But before turning the corner and disappearing from sight, he gets the last word in from over his shoulder. "Spend my money all you want, darling. It turns me on."

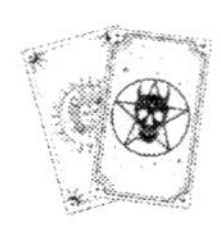

I'M AIMLESS AGAIN. It's my lunch break and I've managed to wander back down to the pier. I can't get the image of the bloody knife out of my head. And the strange impending guilt I felt towards Connor in the aftermath. I must be projecting… shifting emotions that should be aimed towards my father to him instead.

Doesn't explain the bloody knife. And the bizarre fear attached to it, as if I shouldn't be trusted with a knife around Connor.

Yep. Definitely losing it.

Looking up, I focus my bleary gaze on my surroundings and realize I'm standing in front of the palm reader's tent.

Maybe not so aimless after all.

I don't bother questioning it. Pushing the flap open, I walk inside. I'm struck by the same smell of incense as the first time and it pulls at my memories of Connor and I, three weeks ago. The interior is quiet, a soft hum of instrumental music playing from somewhere in the back. While I wait for the psychic to appear from wherever she's hiding, I realize with sudden clarity that my weird hallucinations—if you can call them that—started after that day.

I let loose some of the anger I've been collecting and cross my arms, now ready to confront the palm reader about it. Finally, she appears, smiling like she was expecting me which only makes the tension inside of me flare.

"Come. Sit," she says softly.

Annoyed, I still heed her gentle order and settle into the chair very slowly while I shoot her a suspicious stare. This time, instead of taking my hand, she pulls a deck of tarot cards from a red velvet pouch and starts to shuffle, the same peaceful smile on her face.

"You did something to me," I finally state.

"Oh?" she simply says, still shuffling. The hushed whispering sound of the cards sliding against each other feels almost threatening to my ear. "And what do you think I did?"

She pulls a card out of the deck and places it to face me, tapping it gently before resuming her shuffling.

The Hanged Man, it reads.

I know nothing about tarot, and she doesn't supply an explanation, so I roll my eyes and answer her instead. "I've been seeing things—troubling things. And it all started after you told Connor that we were connected. That somehow my *life line*," I air quote the words as insolently as possible, "is written in his palm—or whatever. This can't be a coincidence."

She hums, looking almost pleased with what I just told her as she pulls another card out of the deck, The Moon this time, placing it right next to the first card.

"A coincidence? Or synchronicity?"

I blink. "Isn't that the same thing?"

Her eyes twinkle when her gaze flits from the cards to me. "One holds the magic of the universe at the very center of it—the other one does not."

"Okay..." I drag out the word while trying to make sense of all the thoughts clambering in my head. "So, why is the universe making me think I'm about to stab Connor to death?" I blurt out, annoyed with this cryptic back and forth.

She pulls a final card from the deck as the last word spills out of my lips. My heart squeezes when I see the image depicted on it. A person who appears to be bleeding to death, lying face down, ten swords jutting out of their back.

*Great. This bodes well.*

"This isn't a forewarning, my dear," she says, waving her hand over the cards as evidence of what she just said. "This has already come to pass... but you are only *now* making amends for it."

Sudden and intense fear overtakes me with such shocking speed, that I'm left trying to choke in air and failing. Still, I attempt to keep my outward demeanor blank. "What the hell is that supposed to mean?" I hiss, getting more annoyed by the second. "A forewarning? It's already come to pass? None of this shit makes any sense."

"Karmic ties never do. But one thing is certain, you and

the other were always bound to meet like this. Whether you remember all the other times you spent connected to him is irrelevant. "

The more she speaks, the more I want to break everything in this place.

I refuse to hear anymore of this fucking bullshit.

I stand up and knock the chair over in the process. "I don't know why I even came here," I scoff, crossing my arms tightly over my chest. I can't believe I tried to take her seriously, but obviously she's just some common hack. What did I expect? Still, I begrudgingly pull out a twenty and throw it over the cards still laid out on the table.

"For your lies," I say coldly before walking out.

# 31

## Lenix

It's Thursday night and I'm dripping in wealth just as Connor demanded. The gown is gold and encrusted with diamonds. I didn't bother looking at the price. My only criteria was to look drop-dead gorgeous. And I've definitely succeeded. The halter top wraps snuggly around my neck, the cleavage so low that it ends just above my navel, the bottom half flaring dramatically, covering my legs all the way down to my heels. I bought a diamond bracelet to go along with the look and matching earrings just for the hell of it.

I'm making last minute touches to my makeup in the guest room ensuite when Connor strolls in unannounced. I shoot him a look through the mirror.

"Ever heard of privacy?"

"Considering you haven't bothered taking down the camera in your bedroom, I'd say this little attitude of yours is all for show," he quips.

I sigh. Loudly.

I know I don't have a valid reason for why I haven't hunted that thing down. Unwilling to acknowledge the small part of me that likes being watched by Connor. Saying nothing in response, I swivel around and face him.

His eyes rove down my dress, and then up again, gaze darkening while he slowly smooths his hand over his mustache. "You're breathtaking," he says under his breath.

"I know."

He flashes me a quick little side grin, before catching my left hand in his. Without breaking eye contact I feel him slide something over my ring finger. Looking down, I realize it's an engagement ring—a two stone diamond ring, one a princess cut, the other pear.

"What the hell is that?" I say in slight disbelief.

His lips curl, flashing his teeth while pressing us against the bathroom counter. "Just keeping up pretenses, *wife*."

The last word trickles feverishly down my spine, my stomach dipping low when my eyes fall to his hand, finding a gold band on his ring finger.

Last time we hadn't worn any, blaming it on our haste to elope. People had found it oddly romantic. But now—enough time has passed for us to have bought the damn things. Rationally, I know this is just part of the charade we're playing. But the weight of the diamonds on my finger feels remarkably real and I swallow hard, finding myself sinking deeper into the quicksand of this arrangement.

Letting go of my hand, his fingers caress over my hips, while his own press even closer, trapping me between him and the counter.

He's been doing that a lot lately.

"You seem wound tight, darling," he says in a low tone, while beginning to hike up the heavy fabric of my dress, inch by slow inch. "Have you been keeping your hands to yourself?"

The feel of the hem rising higher and higher against my legs makes goosebumps erupt all over my skin, but I try to hide my body's reaction by giving him a hard glare. "You tell me. You're the one watching me day and night."

Unbothered, Connor runs his tongue over his teeth like he's preparing for the best meal of his life and then smiles. He laughs, low and dark, smoothing over my skin like silk. My core clenches and I lick my lips in response. It's getting harder to pretend I'm not unbelievably turned on by this man simply existing.

"My… my… sounds like I need to repent then," he muses, dark eyes hooded and glinting with vice. "Maybe I should fall to my knees and ask my wife for forgiveness. Would that please her?"

Before I can even breathe out a *yes*, he lowers himself in front of me, and I can practically see his eyes dilate into black obsidian the lower he gets. His knees finally hit the floor and I've never seen something so beautiful.

It's intoxicating.

His eyes are burning into me, searing so deep I can't look away. Not even when I hitch my gown higher, and place my stiletto-clad foot in front of him. I don't say a single word, only tilting my head towards my heel as my only command.

The smile he flashes in response is enough for me to let my free hand rest back on the counter behind me just to have something to hold. I watch as Connor delicately picks up my foot, his eyes never leaving mine and gently presses his lips to my skin.

I'm near-drunk with power.

But I'd be a fool to think Connor isn't in control—even now, on his knees. I revel in the feeling nonetheless—swallowing it long and deep as it warms my stomach like a glass full of bourbon.

He carefully places my foot down, and then cradles the other one. This time his fingers caress up my calf, moving higher and higher up my thigh. My knees nearly buckle underneath me.

"Tell me, my darling. Do you still hate me now?" he says before burning another kiss at the top of my foot.

I try hiding the hard swallow and the fact that I think I've lost the ability to speak, especially when one of his hands is coming dangerously close to where I want him most.

He raises an eyebrow and it almost feels like a taunt.

He's waiting for me to answer his question.

I take a slow inhale before speaking, trying to center myself back into a space of control. "Ask again after you've made me come."

I pull my foot out of his grasp and turn around.

"Unzip me."

His fingers whisper across my skin before I feel the tug, the dress loosening around me. Delicately, I step out of it, and carry it into the bedroom, laying it on the vanity chair before walking out into the hall. For a fleeting second, I think he won't follow, but then I hear his steady steps as I enter his bedroom, strutting in with nothing but my black stilettos and adorning diamonds.

I sit at the edge of his bed, and watch him lean against the door, studying me. His gaze is serious, like this is the most important thing he'll ever witness and I slowly open my legs wide. With a feral curl of his lips, he pushes off the door, and stalks towards the bed.

I point to the carpeted floor in front of me.

"Kneel."

Connor's feet stagger, it's so quick I would've missed it if I wasn't already seeking a reaction out of him. His smile is devious as he closes in, kneeling in front of me for the second time tonight.

I could get used to this feeling.

His black eyes light me up, never leaving mine as he slides his hands over my open thighs, his thumbs digging into my flesh.

But before he can get any further, I squeeze my thighs closed and give him a taunting chide.

"It'll cost you."

Connor's dark chuckle is like an opioid threatening to pull me under.

"Your orgasms are mine, remember?"

He tries to lunge, but I pull back, propping one stiletto on his chest and tut.

"At a price, Mr. Maxwell," I drawl.

His gaze dips between my legs and then back up again. My heart is pounding behind my ribs but I force an expression of arrogant ennui on my face, removing my foot from his torso, waiting for him to react. His face is serious, hooded eyes of the purest black. He rests back on his heels, his hand disappearing into his coat jacket and pulling out his wallet. His heated gaze never leaves mine. Slowly, he slides out a hundred dollar bill and flicks it at my feet.

"Enough?"

Lust engulfs my senses but I keep my demeanor calm. My lips twitch mischievously, the shake of my head infinitesimal before slowly unfurling my palm in front of him.

The low growl rumbling through his chest tells me he's as equally affected while he pulls out another hundred dollar bill, his eyes still locked in and burning, placing it into my hand.

Then another.

And another.

I swallow hard, my core clenching while he finally places the last one atop the rest. My fingers barely have time to close around it when Connor's hands grip my thighs once more, dragging me close to the edge of the bed.

"Now let me taste what I've paid for," he groans.

And *God* that shouldn't sound so good. He pulls my left leg over his shoulder. The one with the faded scars that speak of a different time, a different name. His lips trail over them but says nothing and I wonder suddenly if he's ever noticed or has never dared to ask.

My errant thoughts quickly skitter out of my mind when his wet tongue swipes at my sensitive skin while the harsher bristle of his mustache tickles the same spot. The dual sensation makes me fall back on my elbows, discarding the money beside me and closing my eyes on a sigh.

His teeth rake my inner thigh, pulling my other leg up onto his shoulder and I link my ankles together against his back, pulling him forward. I feel his hot breath against my pussy before the thrill of his flat tongue drags against my seam and then slowly up to my clit. It throbs under his touch and I let out a long moan that only spurs him further.

"Jesus Christ *Lenix*, I've fucking missed this," he breathes against my skin, and somehow my name on his lips sounds more intimate than any other name he's ever called me. My heart stutters and heat envelops me so absolutely that I find myself wanting to burn at the stake if it means feeling the high of having Connor between my thighs like this forever.

He laps, and bites and *teases*—and I am undone.

His tongue swirls around my entrance and it takes me every morsel of my dwindling self-control not to tell Connor to fuck me right now. To fuck me in nothing but ill-gotten diamonds. *Fuck*. I could come at just the thought.

"You taste exactly how my filthy little wife should taste," he moans, sucking my clit into his mouth, a small mewl escaping me with the sensation.

"And how's that?" I say breathlessly.

I look at him then, his lips and mustache glossy with my own desire, his eyes pitch black and I'm fucking *burning*.

He pauses, meeting my gaze, giving me one last lick with his hot tongue, then shaking his head before saying, "Like irredeemable sin."

Two of his fingers slide deep inside of me, my back arching underneath me, thighs tightening around his neck. I'm so close that it only takes Connor another long, tight flick of his tongue against my sensitive bud for me to unravel.

I hold his head against my center, the diamond ring on my finger glinting against the light while my body seizes in such intense pleasure that I'm not even sure how to make sense of it. It pulls me in every direction, bright light bursting against my vision until I finally sag back on the bed, sated and out of breath.

The silence that follows is a living, breathing thing curling around us and leaving me speechless. Eventually, Connor is the first to break the spell.

Standing back up to his full height, he smooths out his suit jacket and fixes his cufflinks like a bored aristocrat. "Do you still hate me now, darling?" he asks, an amused smirk on his beautiful, wicked lips.

I sit up, back straight, naked with one leg primly crossed over the other. I extend my left hand out in front of me, cocking my head to the side and studying my ring with the same bored mannerism he just used. Finally, I look over and give him a smirk of my own.

"More than ever."

# 32

## Connor

The Noxport Yacht Club is already swarming with people when we arrive at the mayor's electoral fundraiser. Given, we are arriving fashionably late after the small detour we took in my bedroom.

You couldn't tell Lenix is freshly fucked just by looking at her.

She glints, glitters and glistens with every step she takes around this wretched place, even the light can't help but be pulled into her orbit. I would be lying if I said we didn't look like a power couple tonight. Noticing a collection of eyes trained on us, I puff out my chest like a goddamn neanderthal while slipping my arm around her waist. It's an irritating possessiveness that I can't seem to tame whenever I'm around Lenix lately. I pull her into my side, challenging anyone to see what fucking happens if they let their gaze linger on my wife for too long.

Even if the urge to find a bathroom and have Lenix screaming my name while I pump my cock into her is taking most of the real estate in my head, I can't forget the goal tonight. It's also considered gauche to be sporting a hard-on at these types of things, I hear. I audibly clear my throat. Lilith in question gives me a strange look but I turn my attention to the faces filling the ballroom instead, mentally tallying who'll be worth my time tonight.

I spot Mayor Hawkins in the far corner, his usual entourage milling around and affording him the attention they're paid to give him. My eyes assess the crowd as I lead Lenix to the bar, my hand gently placed on the small curve of her back. On our way there, she surreptitiously reaches behind and wraps her hand around my arm, her thumb digging into the soft skin of my inner wrist. She attempts to pull my hand away but I'm stronger and don't budge. Trying to yank it away one last time, she eventually gives up and lets out a small huff.

"What's the problem, darling?" I whisper by her ear. "Can't bear your husband's touch in public?"

A forbidden thought pops into my head. I stop us in our tracks and use the same arm already around her to pull Lenix into my embrace. A small gasp escapes her perfect pouty lips as I hold her body tightly against mine, my other hand finding the smooth skin of her neck, cradling her face in my palm.

"What are you doing?" she hisses low, subtly struggling against my grasp. "People are watching."

I smile, my eyes flicking over her face, enjoying having her trapped like this far too much.

"Exactly," I rasp before catching her lips with mine. I swallow her protests and deepen the kiss knowing she'll be fuming about this later and it only makes me want to kiss her even harder. My tongue slips into her mouth and I can feel her giving in an infinitesimal amount. Her hands slide up my chest, clutching at my lapels while her tongue finds mine and I taste her all over again. I find myself craving every single one of her tastes, desperate to savor her in every lewd way possible.

*Fuck.*

Why does this feel so good? And why do I already want to kiss her again when her lips are still pressed against mine. This was clearly a dangerous impulse, because now my cock is suddenly swelling against my trousers. I grip Lenix even harder, losing track of where we are and who's watching.

But she doesn't.

She pushes against my chest with just enough force that our lips part and I crash back to reality, causing my hold on her to slacken.

Her breath hitches slightly when she looks at me, stepping away from my arms. "You fucking twat," she growls through a smile—still trying to keep up appearances. But there's a lot less heat to her words than I expected.

"What?" I goad, swiping my hand down my mustache, effectively hiding my smirk. "I felt like kissing my wife. What's wrong with that?"

She stares at me like I'm an imbecile.

"I hope you enjoyed that because you're not about to do that again any time soon," she replies, through a forced smile, turning her back to me and heading towards the bar.

"Care to wager, darling?" I tease.

I watch her shoulders rise, and her steps falter but resume quickly without acknowledging what I just said. I chuckle low, following right behind and slip beside her when we reach the bar. Lenix ignores me, flagging the bartender and ordering a Patrón on ice, and I order a mezcal neat. While we wait, I lean my weight on my elbow, assuming a casual pose while I do another sweep of the room. My eyes finally catch on Governor Morrissey.

Tall and lithe, a perfect picture of health for sixty-six. He looks nothing like his nephew, who oddly looks older than him while being in his early fifties. The governor's salt and pepper hair is cut short and swept to the side, a neatly trimmed dark beard adorning his face, blue eyes sparkling as he greets his constituents with hearty handshakes. A small crowd is forming around him and my attention lands on Mayor Hawkins standing behind the governor. I nearly burst out laughing when I notice jealousy written clear across Hawkins face. He looks like a spoiled son standing in his father's shadow.

The bartender returns with our order and I turn to Lenix to tell her we're headed over there. I'm immediately distracted by her taking a quick sip, a small drop of alcohol slipping over her bottom lip, her tongue darting out to catch it. I groan.

*Jesus fucking Christ.*

"Stop that," I bite out.

She rolls her eyes. "I didn't do anything, Connor. I'm just standing here."

Annoyed, I wave my hand in the air as if to dismiss

what just happened. I take Lenix by the hand and surprisingly I feel her fingers coil around mine. "It's time to play, darling. Let's go dazzle the governor with your beauty, shall we? I hear he loves pretty young things," I say with an arrogant bite.

"I'm not *that* young," I hear Lenix grumble behind me as if that's the point worth debating while the crowds part for us with ease. We weave through bodies, pretentious cologne and old lady perfume clinging to my clothes, my eyes nearly water at the intensity of it all. Finally, we reach the other side of the room, making my presence known to the mayor first. He seems pleased to see me, at least one bastard is paying attention to him at his own event.

"Connor, my boy!" he bellows.

Fucking hell, I hate when he calls me that. I accept his brandished hand anyway, while his other hand lands on my shoulder practically shaking me where I stand.

"Always a pleasure, Henry," I answer with a tight smile. "You remember my wife Lenix."

His eyes sweep over to her, and I grind my teeth as I watch him drink her in, like she's something to be enjoyed by anyone other than *me*.

"Of course! How could I forget that face?" He winks at her, and my entire body tightens. He then smiles back at me conspiratorially. "And how can I forget such a whirlwind love story? Still in your honeymoon phase I hope?"

"More than ever," Lenix answers for us with such delicate grace, I almost believe her.

"Enjoy it while it lasts, kids."

He winks *again*. My jaw ticks but I keep the rest of my face relaxed. You'd think he'd know better than to call the leader of the Sin Eaters, *kid*. But I afford him the slight, tallying it up and adding it to all the other stupid shit he's ever told me over the years, biding my time. I have no doubt I'll end up killing him one day. I let my frustration filter into that locked vault until I need to use it—and paste on a permanent smile.

"We sure are," I reply, my arm finding Lenix's waist like a magnetized puzzle piece.

The mayor's eyes look over my shoulder and his face falls for a split second before fixing the fakest fucking smile I've seen tonight. I don't need to turn my head to know who's approaching us from behind. Governor Morrissey is finally coming our way.

# 33

## Lenix

"There you are Henry," Governor Morrissey says.

I watch Mayor Hawkins' eyebrows dip but smooth out quickly. "Been here the whole time Josiah," he answers tight-lipped.

"And who do we have here?" Morrissey asks, looking Connor up and down, barely affording a glance my way.

*Great, one of those.*

"Connor Maxwell, sir. Pleasure to meet you. And this is

my wife Lenix." He exchanges a hard handshake with him and still, the old man barely looks at me.

"Pleasure is all mine." He smiles too wide, too bright. "Always lovely to meet supporters of my nephew."

Hawkins bristles at the word nephew, clearly peeved that his uncle didn't use his official title. I hide my amused smile behind my drink, sipping it slowly while observing this massive pissing contest between the two of them.

Connor doesn't seem interested in partaking in any of it which, annoyingly, sends a small thrill down my spine. They're just a bunch a fucking gazelles prancing about compared to him. I don't *hate* the idea of being connected to such power. Especially, when I had that same power making me see the entire galaxy not even an hour ago.

The conversation shifts onto a subject I'm—with no surprise—already bored with. I lean into Connor's hard body and whisper, "I'm going to freshen up".

His grasp on me tightens, his smoldering eyes find mine and he kisses me softly on the lips. "Hurry back, darling," he replies with a grin.

*Fuck.*

Why do I keep letting him kiss me tonight? Well, *let* might be a stretch, considering I can't push him away when everyone here believes we're happy newlyweds — I wish I wasn't enjoying it this much either.

Connor's skilled lips are maddening and I'd be loath to say I didn't want to taste them again before this evening ends. None of it is real anyway, so why not enjoy it for what it is?

Delectable, undeniable and *hot.*

I excuse myself and navigate through the crowd, heading towards the large ornamental doors that lead out into a quiet corridor, the bathrooms located at the very end.

My heels barely make a sound as I walk along the long hallway runner, digging through my clutch to find my phone for a quick mindless distraction.

Inside, the bathrooms are as opulent as everything else in this place. Intricate gold trims to match the faucets, white marble sinks and a cloying potpourri scent that makes my nose wrinkle. Nothing is more humbling than having to pee in a diamond gown, but I make do. I then check my reflection in one of the mirrors, adding a touch of gloss to my lips and finally, fix a small flyaway back into my updo. I give myself a small satisfied smile through the mirror and head for the door.

I don't have time to reach for the handle before the door swings open, and I jolt backwards in surprise.

"Hello, Mrs. Maxwell," Governor Morrissey drawls, locking the door behind him.

My blood runs cold.

He's still wearing the same smile from before and I'm suddenly, and horrifyingly, reminded of where I've seen such a smile before—Sacro Nuntio—and the next words out of his mouth solidifies it.

"Or should I call you Penelope?" His voice is hard but still, he smiles like a true politician.

The room shrinks, spins, sinks and does everything but sit still. My past slams into my present like two atoms colliding into each other at the speed of light. I see my life flash before my eyes in the span of one slow time-bending second, forgetting everything about who I am, who I was, or *might be*. My given name spoken out loud like a curse poisoning me from the inside out.

Still, I try to hide the slow deterioration of my very existence and smile. "Governor," my voice comes out thin but oddly steady. "You're mistaken, my name is Lenix, not

Penelope." I let out a small polite laugh. "If you will excuse me."

I try to side-step around him and reach for the door, my hands cold and clammy. It was a fool's gamble, and all it does is bring me closer to his body. He grabs my wrist, spinning me around and slams my back into the door, knocking the wind out of me.

"You disgusting little heathen," he sneers, venom imbued in every single word out of his thin lips. "Look at you." His face finally morphs into an appalled grimace fit for his real nature. "How dare you shame your father's memories like this."

My mind scrambles further. The paralyzing fear I've let slumber all these years, suddenly let loose, rushing into my veins and freezing my body against the door.

"Wh–who are you?"

His grimace turns into a disturbing smile, his hand still wrapped tight around my wrist. "Your brother's influence reaches heights you couldn't even begin to imagine, Penelope. You thought you were safe chaining yourself to the devil? What a repulsive little *whore* you've become."

I swallow hard, my thoughts still reeling, making it almost impossible to react.

*What is happening?*

"You've slain a messenger of *God*. Do you know what that makes you?" He slams me into the door once more, my head bouncing with the force but my words are non-existent, I can barely keep it together as it is. "Do you?" he hisses.

"Eternally damned," I finally manage to croak out.

He releases me then, stepping back. I stay glued to the door, trying not to lose myself in the fear clawing through me.

"That's right," he says, changing back into his role as the Governor of California.

How the fuck did this even happen? How is *he* a part of Sacro Nuntio, when I've never seen his face before? He must have somehow been planted—put into power so the commune could have sway politically. Which explains how they've always avoided persecution all these years. I know I'm not the first to run away. Someone must have tried to reveal their vile secrets before. I'm left with so many unanswered questions, but I keep my mouth shut, eyeing him wearily.

"You must pay for your sins, Penelope. As long as you're alive, your soul belongs to us." His cold, beady eyes drag back to mine. "The only reason we've yet to take you by force is because your brother wants you pliant and submissive. An offering, if you will. However," he growls, his face turning into a snarl, "if you do not return by choice? Then the fate of your youngest sister might be dire indeed. Either way, your little dalliance with the devil is over, *child*."

*Lucy.*

"Wha—what would you do to her?" I stutter, my voice cracking.

"Are you heedless enough to find out?" he spits out.

He gives me one last disdained sneer, muttering under his breath like an afterthought, "By his touch, we live." And swiftly unlocks the door, opening it with me still trembling against it. I stumble forward, shock suffocating my senses and let him walk out, the threat he just spat hanging over my head like a deadly guillotine.

I swallow hard, and then swallow again, taking a few steps towards the mirror to catch my breath and will my heart to beat a little slower. I place my shaky palms on the sink and lean forward, my head dropping between my shoulders, eyelids fluttering closed. I stay as still as a statue until I'm certain I can control my emotions, which must have been *too* long because as soon as I walk out, I find Connor leaning against the opposite wall.

My heart skips a beat, breath catching in my throat.

"Stalk much?" I say a bit too hotheadedly, thankfully, with no quiver in my voice.

He grins, clearly amused, but his face falls serious once his gaze has had time to linger on me.

"Everything okay, darling?"

*Shit.*

He can't know what just happened. Not when I still don't know what my next move is.

I clear my throat, and force a smile, tucking my clutch under my arm. "Of course, why wouldn't I be?"

His eyes continue to peruse me up and down. I'm about to break into a nervous sweat when finally, he just hums and pushes off the wall, leading us back to the ballroom.

The rest of the evening is a blur of pleasantries. My mind splintered into a millions pieces, trying to avoid looking at the wrecking ball that just smashed into my perfectly constructed life of lies. I answer when spoken too. I laugh when appropriate. Shake hands. Clink glasses. Eat hors d'oeuvres and pretend they don't taste like ash. I smile at Connor when his eyes find mine. And even let him kiss me once or twice more before the night is over.

This time, I feel nothing.

I'm locked behind a wall of terror.

And by the time I find myself alone in Connor's guest room again.

I know what I need to do.

# 34

## Connor

There's a tickle on my cheek, and I swat it away half-asleep. My eyes are closed but I can tell it's morning. I flop on my back, the sheets tangled around my hips and the tickle returns accompanied by something wet nudging my face.

"The fuck!" I yell out, yanking my eyes open and sitting up, ready to kill whatever just made its way onto my bed. What I find staring back is *that thing* making itself comfortable on my imported duvet—not before butting its orange furry head against my thigh like it's trying to tell me something.

"The hell you want, demon?"

I try to shoo it away but it just sits there, unbothered. I swear it's glaring at me and I inadvertently fall into a staring contest with the damn thing.

After a few loaded seconds, now less sleep-groggy, I come back to my senses and I realize how dumb I must look. But then a shiver of foreboding trickles down my spine, and I'm out of bed before I can even understand the feeling.

I pad down the hallway towards Lenix's room. The strange feeling heightens with every step I take, especially when I realize her door is wide open. Nothing looks out of place, but somehow it feels unbearably empty when I step inside. The cat follows me in, and I nearly trip over the animal while it meows profusely.

"Can you shut the fuck up?" I snap, but it just meows even louder.

My gut feeling solidifies when I find the closet empty.

An indefinable feeling overtakes me and I become deathly still. It's followed by an emotion I know intimately: anger. I slam the closet door closed and stalk back into my room, swiping my phone from the bedside table and pulling up the camera feeds.

I knew she was acting strange last night, from the moment she came back from the bathroom. She put on a good show, but I could tell. She was too placid, her eyes vacant.

But I know Lenix. She'd shut down and lie if I'd even come close to forcing the truth out of her. So I let her be, and planned on teasing it out of her over the next few days.

But then I discover her bedroom empty?

I finally land on what I've been searching for after a few minutes of rewinding the recording. It only confirms what I already know. Lenix is trying to run. Suddenly, all this anger built up inside me is redirected back at myself because *something happened last night.*

Someone must have gotten to her, and I just stood there and watched her unravel.

She asked me to protect her—and I did nothing.

I rewatch the footage, grinding my teeth and realize the timestamp is only from an hour ago. She might still be in the city. I dial Bastian's number and bark through the phone when he answers. "Did you ever put that tracker on Lenix's car?"

There's silence across the line and I want to reach through the phone and rip out his fucking throat when he finally sighs heavily, "Of course, I did."

"Ping me her location right the fuck now."

Hanging up, I throw a white shirt and black jeans on and run out the door.

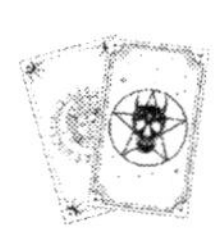

TWENTY MINUTES LATER, I'm banging on Lenix's apartment door, having bullied someone into letting me into the building. I question if she's left her car in the parking lot but pound the door some more until I finally hear the lock turn.

"What the hell is wrong with you," she hisses, grabbing my arm and pulling me inside.

"I could ask you the same question." I leer at her, curling my lip in disdain. "You know the whole running away, works better when you actually *leave*."

"You didn't even give me the fucking chance!"

"So you were trying to run then..." I say with more vulnerability than intended.

She crosses her arms and gives me one of her looks that typically amuses me but right now all I can muster up is resentment.

"Leave me alone, Connor."

Resentment turns to rage.

"It's a little too late for that, darling," I growl.

I stalk towards her, but then something catches my attention, my eyes landing on the diamond ring still on her finger. Her gaze follows mine and she quickly hides it behind her other hand.

I chuckle darkly, swiping my thumb against my bottom lip when I realize that her little escape was a feeble attempt at best. Some half-hearted bullshit. Or maybe all these little missteps were her subconscious screaming to be heard. Especially when something else dawns on me.

"You were gonna leave without your stupid cat?"

Her eyes well up, growing ever so wide, and she suddenly looks painfully innocent. Like she was never meant for this life. Like one day she just took a wrong turn and ended up here—with me.

"I didn't know what else to do." Her voice is so low, I barely hear her.

I watch as a single tear falls and travels down her cheek.

Two long strides and I'm pulling Lenix into me, her lips trembling as both my hands cradle her face. I force her to look at me, eyes still swimming in a torrent of sadness and I can barely contain the murderous rage building inside of me.

"You can trust me, Lenix. Tell me who to kill and I will." I drag in a deep breath before speaking again. "I can't protect you if you keep lying to me. I just want to keep you safe."

More tears spill down her cheeks, but she keeps eye contact and *God* she's so fucking beautiful it hurts.

"You're going to hate me," she whispers.

I smile, gently kissing her forehead before fixing my gaze back on hers.

"My darling, I already do." Her smirk is genuine but weak, at least it's something. "Are you going to tell me the truth this time?" Her eyes widen in what feels like fear but nods, her face still cradled in my palms. "That's my good girl."

Her body slackens and she huffs out a long sigh, rolling her eyes. I let go of her face and take a step back, laughing softly.

"You couldn't help yourself, could you?" she says.

"Felt like the right moment," I reply with a shrug. "Now come." I take her by the hand and lead her to her god-awful pink couch, sitting down at opposite ends.

The way she's nervously glancing at me, you'd think she was on trial for murder.

"My childhood wasn't normal. I didn't realize it until—until…" she trails off, her eyes up to the ceiling, blinking back tears and presumably trying to find the right words. "I didn't have access to the outside world. I was beyond sheltered. Led to believe we were the chosen few and the prophet was a god amongst mortals."

Her gaze lands back on me, while I'm trying to make sense of what she's saying.

Taking a large inhale, she squirms in her seat and finally says, "I grew up in Sacro Nuntio… ever heard of them?"

My eyebrows raise in surprise. *Shit.* Not what I

expected. "Yeah, they own a bunch of land near Redwood forest."

She nods before looking down, wringing her hands and inhaling deeply. "My real name is Penelope Lincoln," she says, swallowing loudly, swinging her eyes back up. "I was one of the prophet's many daughters. Polygamy was encouraged, and one of his many sister wives was my mother." She pauses, seemingly looking for her words. "His name was Jasper Lincoln. He claimed to be the reincarnation of the archangel Raphael." She laughs softly in disbelief after saying it. "I *thought* I was happy living there, it wasn't until much later I realized how fucked up the entire thing was. I—I thought I was happy until my father called me into his office, the day of my wedding—I was barely sixteen."

"*What?*" Is all I manage to choke out. Rage tastes like bile in my throat as I try to contain my reaction and let Lenix finish her story. I sit in horror as she recounts what happened inside those four walls that day. Of what her father tried to do to her. I try to keep my face blank but the fury I feel inside is indescribable.

"I didn't mean to kill him… I just wanted him to stop," Lenix says in a wobbly whisper. "Or maybe deep down I did… 'cause next thing I knew, I was hitting him across the head—and then he fell. His head hit the table and before I realized what I had done, it was too late."

Her hand raises up to her mouth, her eyes even wider than before. She looks frighten, as if she's scared of how I'm going to react—like I would feel anything but pride for what she fucking did. Warring emotions battle inside of me, the urge to kill so strong it's hard to sit still, but the urge to hold and protect her is as heady in my chest. I try to breathe through the shock and anger, knowing Lenix had to live through this fucking nightmare with no one there to help her.

"I didn't know what to do..." Her voice sounds so small, not like my usual Lenix. Almost like she's back in that sick cult, sixteen and much too innocent, eyes still shining with sorrow. "So I ran away with just the clothes on my back." She lets out a small humorless laugh as if remembering something. "It just so happened to be a wedding dress. I ran for what felt like hours... I didn't even know where I was heading. I just knew I had to keep running..."

The image of her in a wedding dress, running for her life, knocks the wind out of me as my awareness heightens. It yanks old memories into the forefront of my mind, the same feeling of protection I felt then, surging through my veins.

Of a diner in the middle of nowhere.

Of Martha, and boysenberry pies.

And a girl in a wedding dress.

# 35

I feel sick.

I don't know what to think. What to do. What to say. Connor is staring at me from across the couch with an expression I can't make out and *fuck* I wish I knew what he was thinking. I'm trying not to cry but I'm struggling. It's all so difficult. I don't want to remember. It hurts too much. I've been pushed into a corner like an injured animal with nowhere to escape.

The shame is so thick in my body, it feels like I'm about

to combust from the inside out. Shame is so insidious, it's hard to describe in words. The feeling is so acute and painful, that I'll do just about anything not to ever feel it again.

Lie.

Run.

Pretend.

Betray.

Anything. Just not *this*.

I would burn it all to the ground if given the chance. My body is trembling and I think I might be in shock. That can't be right. Nothing has even happened. But it's like I never gave myself the chance to mourn and now everything is slithering back out to collect what's due.

My soul.

"Lenix?"

Connor says my name like he's trying not to spook me.

My eyes swivel to him, stifling a sniffle, hating myself. "Yeah?"

"Where did you run to when you escaped?"

I give him a questioning look, not sure why he's asking nor why it matters.

"I found a diner in the middle of nowhere…" I trail off when I see his face morph into pure shock, but he tries to hide it quickly. Not quick enough.

I sit up straight. Nerves buzzing through me. "What?"

His mouth falls slightly open, his eyes dancing between each of mine, slowly assessing as if he's taking me in for the very first time. The unease starts to curl around my throat, tightening my airway. "Connor…"

"I was there that night," he says almost distractedly, as if even his voice isn't sure how to form the words to emote what he's trying to sound out.

There's a latch door inside of me that opens, and my heart free falls.

The depth of those five words are infinite. They can mean anything, to anyone. But to me. To us? They can only mean one thing.

We've met before.

Although I've understood the full weight of what he just revealed, my brain latches on to nothing. Reaching for thoughts that are thin as air, all I manage is to repeat myself. "What?"

Connor's hand moves slowly over his face, shock still etched deeply into the grooves of his skin. "Me, Byzantine and Bastian… we were all there that night."

The image of the diner is so hazy, like someone recounted the memory back to me so many times I've managed to reconstruct a blurry image of it in my mind. Only remembering the wide strokes of the night Penelope faded away and I became Lenix.

But I do remember three men. Ungodly men. The first I had ever seen.

And now, the one with the blackest of eyes, the unholiest of them all, watches me with such intensity I can barely breathe.

"I don't know what to say…" I utter quietly.

Connor taps his finger on the couch as if mulling something over, his eyebrows knitted, almost angry. "I just left you there," he finally says, his gaze avoiding mine, his voice drenched in defeat.

The gut-wrenching response my body slips into is almost too much to bear. I'm not built for these kinds of emotions, I'm aching to shut it all down. So I do the only thing I *can* do and change the subject before I start sobbing in front of him, and never stop.

"That day in the parking lot, it really was my ex-fiancé you saw. He was there on behalf of my brother." Almost too nervous to find his gaze from across the couch. His eyes are stone-cold when I finally peer over to him. He doesn't say anything, waiting for me to elaborate. Taking a deep breath, I continue, "He's now the leader of Sacro Nuntio, I don't know how but he found me. He threatened to drag me back so I could repent for killing our father. That's when I came to you." I bite the inside of my cheek, my heart thudding hard against my chest. The same guilt and shame as always shackling me into this painful reality. "I was still trying to figure out what to do when—" I take a deep inhale, wanting to get my statement out as fast as possible. "When last night happened."

"*What* happened?" he growls, his fingers in a tight fist, knuckles turning white.

"The governor cornered me in the bathrooms."

"Morrissey?" Connor says incredulously and I nod.

"I—I don't even know how it's possible, but he's a part of Sacro Nuntio. He threatened me… slammed me into the door. Said they would hurt my sister if I didn't come back willingly. So—so I decided to go back. You intercepted me, and here we are." My voice cracks and Connor's jaw clenches.

"You were going to give yourself up?" he says, his voice boiling with anger. I can't tell if it's directed towards me or them.

"What else was I supposed to do Connor?"

He stands up, the rage coming off him like waves of noxious fumes.

"I told you I was going to protect you didn't I?"

He paces in front of the couch, body wound tight, neck

and arms corded, prowling like the predator I've always known him to be.

"But what about my sister?" I choke out.

"I'll take care of it."

"How?"

He clenches his jaw, sliding back onto the couch. "I'll figure it out. Just trust me, okay?"

I fall silent.

Could this work?

Could Connor truly help me out of this mess?

Breathing out deeply, I concede, too bone-tired to continue this fight alone, and nod.

"Good. And in the meantime I'm going to rip Morrisey's fucking heart out of his chest," he growls.

"You can't just kill the Governor of California," I say half-heartedly.

His eyes darken into something lethal—powerful.

"He was a dead man walking the moment he touched my fucking wife," he rasps.

His words hold such intensity that in that very moment I choose to believe him. Even if there's a million hurdles left to overcome, I allow a small bubble of hope to take up residence inside my chest.

"Okay," I simply say.

Because what else *can* I say?

He pulls me into his arms and I let him. Silence surrounds us, both of us now lost in our own thoughts. I find comfort in his calming scent of cedarwood and orange blossom, sinking even deeper into his embrace. I listen to the beat of his heart, strong and steady while my eyelids eventually grow too heavy to stay open. I fall asleep in Connor's arms like it's the most natural thing in the world.

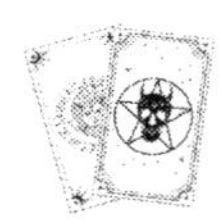

I DON'T KNOW how long I sleep for but when I wake up, Connor is still sitting close by, watching me. My heart pinches at the sight but I try to ignore it.

"Please tell me you weren't watching me this whole time—that'd be creepy, even for you," I say, mostly in an effort to break the tension between us.

He laughs, low and soft and it feels like silk on my sleep-warm skin.

"No… just thinking, that's all."

"About?"

His eyes soften, his gaze still fixed on me. He swipes his hand through his hair, smoothing back a few errant strands out of his face. His movements feel intentional, like he's biding his time while considering something quietly behind his hard facade.

"I still can't believe it was you in that diner, Lenix."

My eyes close at the tone of his voice, unwilling to see what emotion is attached to those words. When I reopen them, I stare at my hands and let out a single dry chuckle.

"Yeah me neither…"

Suddenly, I'm on my feet, feeling too raw—too broken open, eager to have something to do and not have to succumb to Connor's longing stare. I head to the kitchen and pull out a half empty bottle of tequila and pour us each a glass, not even bothering to ask if he wants one—I know he will.

"I don't even know why I've kept it all these years…" The words stumble out of my lips like an afterthought.

"Kept what?"

Taking a deep breath, I slink back to the couch and hand him one of the glasses.

"My wedding dress…" I laugh dejectedly. "Ironic, if you think about it… The one day I wish I could forget and I'm holding on to the most fucked up part of it. "

I expect him to laugh. To return this awkward sentiment. But his eyes darken instead, licking his lips and then his mouth twitches like he's readying for a kill.

"Put it on," he says. His tone is serious—deadly.

"Excuse me?" I blink. He must be joking. "Why the hell would I do that?"

His eyes grow even darker, his thumb smoothing over his bottom lip while incinerating me with his stare. "I want to corrupt my filthy little wife while she wears it. Because you should have never been wearing a white dress for anyone but me. "

*Oh.*

He's not joking.

I stifle a nervous laugh, but I can't ignore the burning hot fire that his words just ignited inside of me. Still, I say, "There's nothing hot about that dress, Connor. It's a puritanical nightmare."

He hasn't moved an inch. "That's not the point of this, now is it?" He holds his hand out to me, teeth flashing into a wide smile.

An invitation. A summoning.

And I take it.

He pulls me with more force than I expect and I fall into his body, catching me by wrapping a strong arm around my waist. He almost looks giddy and I can't help but laugh.

"You're psychotic, you know that?" I say while pushing off of him, heading to the bedroom.

"And what does that make you, darling?"

I don't bother answering, because—well, he has a point.

He sits on my bed while I disappear into my closet, knowing exactly where the damned thing is even if I've avoided looking at it for years now. I find it tucked at the very bottom of a box in a forgotten dark corner high up on a shelf. My heart pinches when I pull it out, remembering how I tried to wash it by hand as if the stains were a metaphor for all the sins I had recently committed. I never did get all the stains out.

The air around me seems to electrify, crackling from everything left unspoken or omitted from that day. I take off my clothes and slip the dress on, the skin on my arms breaking out into goosebumps as I slide into the sleeves and pull the soft fabric up my shoulders. It's impossible for me to button up the back without someone's help so I leave it undone. The hushed swish of the fabric against my feet makes me freeze and I'm suddenly back in my mother's bedroom, facing the mirror beaming at my reflection.

I don't know how long I stand there for. It's long enough for Connor to find me motionless in my closet, lost in a waking dream.

I land back into my body with a jolt when I feel his finger graze my spine. From the open back, both hands find my shoulder blades and then slide down to my ribs, slipping underneath the dress and around the front.

He closes in, his chest pressing into me, his palms finding my breasts, toying with my nipples and then squeezing. I let my head fall on his shoulder, his lips brushing the sensitive skin near my ear and I let out a small sigh. The moment is so delicate. Especially for us.

Such an undisturbed kind of quiet that I don't expect what comes next.

His hands leave my body and the next thing I know, he's thrown me over his shoulder and is walking out of the closet.

I yelp in surprise, but don't have time to struggle against his hold before I'm landing on the mattress with a bounce.

I glare at him as he looms over me, but then I'm suddenly struck with how breathtaking he looks. In a simple t-shirt and jeans, he still exudes such power, it's hard not to respond to it.

There's madness in his eyes, and my core clenches at the sight.

"Let go," he says softly.

Like an incantation.

And again, I'm lost in all the different meanings these two words can mean.

Let go of this memory haunting you.

Let go of this piece of you.

Let go of your control.

I sit up straight, my hands clasped almost demurely in my lap, my head tilted back, looking up. His pupils dilate at the sight and I lean into this moment even more, smiling with all the naive innocence I still have tucked away somewhere inside and nod.

I watch Connor's throat bob as he swallows, the rest of him motionless. The seconds stretch slowly between us. Then he smiles and I fall head first into the abyss.

He grabs me by the back of my neck, his fingers threading through my hair, tugging my head further back. His tongue is a scorching brand on my skin, tracing a proprietorial path up my neck, all the way up to my flushed cheek. Connor's lips slam into mine, tasting like the darkest of nights and the cure to all my shameful secrets. I'm left gasping and breathless, when he finally pulls away. Not before biting and sucking my bottom lip into his mouth, tugging and then releasing it with a wet pop. He straightens back up while grinning.

"On your knees, darling." His head tilting slightly toward the floor as he says it.

The part of me that would usually balk at his order is quiet today.

Instead, I'm aflame.

A desperate need ravages my senses as I slide down to the floor. Connor is already tugging on his zipper, the hard curve of his erection pushing against his jeans. I can't resist joining his hurried fingers at his waist, needing to see, to touch, to taste.

I've never seen a more perfect cock in my life. I've always thought so. But I've never dared tell Connor that, unwilling to stroke his ego with a *compliment* no less. But I find myself telling him just that while my hand strokes his thick shaft, his broad head already glistening with precum. It's a hasty whisper of adoration and his answering groan winds me up so tight, I can barely think. So, I just *do*.

I give the underside of his cock, one long broad lick before wrapping my lips around it and I feel his hips hitch in response.

"*Fuck*," he says under his breath.

I relax my throat, hollowing my cheeks, swallowing him down until his cock fills me completely. His hands grab my hair, keeping me there while I choke on him, my eyes watering. Pushing his jeans further down, my palms find his ass clenching under my touch.

He loosens his grasp and I release him from my mouth, taking in a much needed breath. I look up from under my eyelashes, and let my tongue fall flat. He taps the tip on it, staring at me with unadulterated intensity while alternating between stroking himself and thrusting into my mouth.

"Look at you," he drawls, his cock throbbing against my tongue, swallowing him down to the hilt once more. "What a pretty little wife I own."

This should incense me—instead I moan around him like I've never heard something so fucking hot in my life. His lewd chuckle tells me he knows exactly what that just did to me.

"Come here," he growls, my mouth suddenly achingly empty as he pulls me up on my feet and throws me on the bed once again. With the same wicked grin adorning his face, his eyes rove down my body, the white dress still covering most of me. He reaches down, picking up the bottom hem and with a speed my brain can't even register, rips the fabric in half, uncovering my naked body up to my waist.

He reaches behind and pulls his t-shirt over his head in one practiced swoop, his arms and torso flexing deliciously as he does. His jeans are off shortly after and the sight of him naked sends me tumbling down even further into the yawning abyss. A part of me hopes I'll never find the bottom, if it means seeing Connor just like this.

The devil unchaining me from my shackles, freeing me from the very hell I've been warned against.

I notice his eyes lingering on the faded scars on my thigh.

Maybe he has noticed them before after all.

He seems enraptured by the sight, his brows creased, chest rising rapidly, torso wound tight, and biceps bulging while his hands are in tight fists.

"Connor," I say softly. His eyes flit quickly to mine, but his expression doesn't change. It takes a few more seconds for him to calm down from wherever his thoughts took him. What I find now is a promise—unsaid but not unseen. A promise of blood and chaos, and revenge. A small thrill racks through me, unencumbered by the usual feelings of guilt and shame—but only of retribution.

Finally, he prowls towards me onto the bed, and I move back up closer to the headboard. He brings both of his hands to my face and with a tenderness I wasn't expecting, gently presses his lips to my forehead, my eyelids fluttering shut at the sensation.

Then his mouth finds mine. The kiss starts slow until it eventually builds into a fiery blaze, razing to the ground any lingering memories that aren't about us. Here. Now.

His cock lays heavy on my stomach, his body edging closer, deepening our kiss and I suddenly feel that same desperation as before. An urge building and building, propelling me into this heightened need for one thing only. I don't want his fingers, or tongue or anything else that's not the fullness and force of Connor thrusting inside of me.

I reach between us, and wrap my hand around the hardness of him—throbbing against my palm, and so fucking perfect. He breaks away and pushes me down onto the mattress, throwing my left leg over his shoulder. His lips trail across my scars, his soft gaze relaying the words left unspoken while his hand slides up my thigh with such territorial intention that a small moan escapes me and his eyes close on an inhale at the sound.

And by the time his eyes are back open, he has one hand around his shaft and the other flat on my stomach, fisting the tattered shreds of the dress as he drags the head of his cock against my slit, my head falling into the pillows at the heightening sensation.

"So fucking wet for me," he says, his voice low and rough.

My nails dig into his forearms, my gaze finding his and the intensity pulsating off him while he watches me makes my head swim. He doesn't break eye contact when he finally pushes into me and I clench around him in bliss.

"*Fuck*," I say around a moan. "You feel so good."

He thrusts hard into me, his lips kissing my leg still up on his shoulder, biting the soft skin near my knee and my back arches off the bed.

"Better remember this feeling, darling," he growls, his hips snapping into mine, his fist still tight around my dress. "'Cause only your husband can fuck you this good."

He lets my leg drop, his cock still throbbing so deep inside me that I can't speak, can't think, the sensation so vibrant that I forget everything but Connor fucking me.

His hand finds my mouth, three fingers curling over my bottom lip, sliding inside and my skin *burns*. I can taste him on my tongue and I reach blindly down to my clit, finding it swollen and achingly sensitive. With his hand still holding my mouth open, his thrusts still forceful and rhythmic, he leans over to the bedside table and grabs the glass of tequila he left there.

I'm hypnotized by the vision of him above me, his darkness rolling off of him in waves, his tattooed body gleaming with sweat and I think I'm going to come just by watching him. He takes a leisurely sip of his drink as if he's not currently fucking me to absolute oblivion.

His heated eyes are so full of desire and intent when he slams the glass back where it belongs, leaning back over me. He takes the same fingers that were just splayed over my yearning tongue and squeezes my cheeks, spitting the tequila into my gaping mouth. My body flares and I eagerly swallow, the alcohol burning down my throat while his hips still piston into me.

I'm on fire.

I'm on fucking *fire.*

His eyes track small droplets that have escaped down my face, his hand moving down to wrap firmly over my throat, and licks me clean.

His lips ghost over my own and I'm gasping for more, pushing my head up to catch his mouth with mine. I'm so eager to taste him again, swallow him down as my orgasm builds and builds and builds that I can't do anything other than beg Connor to please—*please, don't fucking stop.*

"Tell me who owns you, Lenix," he says through clenched teeth.

But he doesn't even let me answer before ripping the rest of the dress up the middle. A heady sense of freedom ignites bright in my chest at the sight, watching the ruins of the dress still clinging to me while he palms my tits with his hands like he's always been meant to do just that. Like we've been here before and we'll be here again and again.

My pussy clenches hard around him as my climax finally crests over me, the feelings so fierce and profound that I lose all sense of self for those few blissful moments. With both hands around my face, Connor kisses me with every smoldering part of him—I'm lost but then immediately found again.

He pulls out, stroking himself above me. His jaw clenches hard, his eyes black, hooded and with a groan, he comes all over my chest and neck, his head falling back while he spills and spills. Hot, dirty, and *fucking* perfect.

I can't stop watching him like this—black hair falling into his face, chest heaving with exertion, spent, satisfied and I wonder if this is becoming an obsession.

He leans over, dragging a finger in his own release, and grins like he's the devil himself. "Look at you. So beautiful covered in your husband's cum." His gaze slices up to me, his smirk widening. "Would you follow me to hell for a necklace like this?"

His expression is darkness personified and I'm already yearning for more of him.

Then he's off the bed, still naked—*still* fucking glorious.

"Don't move," he says while walking up to the shelving unit near the window, strolling up to it as if he knows exactly what he's looking for.

"What are you doing?" I ask slightly suspicious.

"Creating new memories."

When he turns back to face me, I realize he's holding my polaroid camera in his hands.

I blink in disbelief. "You can't be serious."

"Deadly." He raises the camera to his face and snaps a picture of me still breathless and splayed out on the bed. "And it's mine to keep," he says with a smile.

The whir of the small machine fills the silence between us, the polaroid slowly sliding out from the bottom. He pulls it out and gives it a little shake before placing it on the bedside table. He slips back beside me and pulls at the sleeves of the wedding dress, the only part of it still clinging to me, and I let him fully undress me. I watch in rapt attention as he uses the ripped fabric to clean me up. His touch is tender, caring and my heart nearly burst out of my chest.

"Let's go home," he says softly and my mind is so fried that I just nod.

Unable to really understand the weight of what he just said or what it might mean.

# 36

## Connor

We wash off before leaving Lenix's place. Her shower is really only meant for one, but we squeeze in together anyway. I'm having trouble letting her out of my sight. There's too many emotions churning uncomfortably inside me. I don't know what to do with myself, so I pin her to the shower wall and kiss her. She seems to have resigned herself to the idea of us kissing, and now I can't get enough. Her skin is smooth and slick with water and it would just be so easy to fuck her again but instead I swallow one last of her moans and pull away.

Dragging my hand over her wet hair, I cradle her cheek. My thumb swipes over her kiss-swollen lips and she offers me a sad smile and my chest fucking *aches*.

Why does it hurt to look at her?

These past three weeks have been a giant head-fuck. It's getting hard not to see Lenix as exactly what she is.

My wife.

I can't find the humor in any of it anymore. Not when she looks at me like this, water clinging to her long eyelashes, her gaze missing the familiar hardness from the armor she usually hides behind. Especially not when I finally pieced together what those scars on her thigh might have originated from. I might not know the exact way she got them, but it still fills me with such murderous rage that it's hard to keep my face relaxed, even here in the shower.

The itch to kill is getting more difficult to ignore, but I push it down for now.

It's not time.

Not when I can hold Lenix like this and let the pretenses fall for a while. I kiss her one last time before turning off the shower, and we step out. I'm half-convinced this was all just a figment of my imagination. And we'll fall back to our old ways before our skin even dries from the water still clinging to our naked bodies. Maybe that's exactly what will happen.

But one thing did change.

She's mine now.

And I'll burn the whole fucking city down in my wife's name.

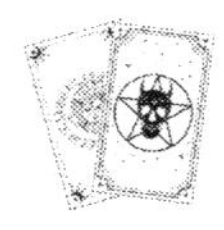

WE'RE BACK HOME.

I know what I just said. And I fucking mean it.

Lenix took the day off, napping in the guest room. Little does she know this is the last time she'll be sleeping in there. She belongs in my bed from now on. Knowing her, she'll probably dig in her heels and tell me I'm crazy, but I couldn't give two fucks about it.

Let her.

She can act like she's mad, fuck me like she hates me, and pretend she's not as obsessed with me as I am with her. I don't care. As long as she leaves the impression of her warm body in the sheets beside me every morning.

I'm pacing back and forth near the wide window in the study, waiting for Byzantine and Bastian to arrive. The polaroid picture I took of her this morning weighs heavy in the inside pocket of my suit jacket, but I force myself not to pull it out and look at it again. Or else I'd be glued to the damn thing all day. I've never seen something so beautiful in my goddamn fucking life. And I know I'll be replaying what we just did on loop until I can get my hands on her again.

"You good brother?" Byzantine says while he walks in, Bastian following right behind. There's an edge to his casual question, as if he's already picked up on something by just a quick glance my way. It wouldn't be the first time.

I roll my shoulders, trying to release some of the tension to no avail. I walk over to the leather couch near the fireplace and sit while the guys find seats of their own. I ignore his question and jump straight to why I called them here.

"I'm killing Governor Morrissey. Figured I should let you two know," I say casually.

Byzantine eyebrows shoot up, then frowns, smoothing his hand over the tattoo on his neck that hides the scar from when he almost died. It's an unconscious tick, and it usually means he's lost in thought or piecing something together. Today, I'm guessing it's the latter.

"Care to elaborate?" he says.

"You finally discovered what your wife was hiding," Bastian cuts in.

Byzantine gives him an odd glance, most likely because of how casually my cousin keeps referring to Lenix as my wife. But I refuse to acknowledge either of their statements and focus on what's important—eviscerating Josiah Morrissey.

I place an ankle over my knee, leaning into the cushions of the couch behind me. Pressing my hand over my mustache, I fall silent for a beat.

I try to keep my voice as even as possible when I finally speak. "Remember that girl we saw running into Martha's diner in a wedding dress years ago?"

"Why do you keep bringing that up?" Bastian remarks.

"Jesus fucking Christ," I bite out, glaring at him. "Can you answer the fucking question?"

He gives me his classic impassive look and crosses his arms, I'm seconds from pummeling his face with the butt of my gun. I take a deep breath, my jaw ticking and continue, "The girl was Lenix."

"What?" Byzantine says incredulously. "How—"

"I pieced it together when she told me she ran away from Sacro Nuntio when she was sixteen with nothing but a wedding dress on."

"Lenix grew up in a cult?" he adds, still confused.

"Look," I break out in a sigh. "You'll have all your answers when she decides you can know. Not even Sunny knows, so keep this shit to yourself." I fix Byzantine with a hardened stare. "What's important right now is that Morrissey is part of that fucked up cult and not only threatened Lenix physically but blackmailed her into returning so they can do God know's what to her."

I can see Byzantine chewing on his unanswered questions but I don't have the patience for any of it right now. I know he can tell and luckily keeps his mouth shut.

"I understand we had more long-term plans involving the Governor but none of that matters anymore. Informing you two is simply a courtesy." I adjust my cufflinks and roll my shoulders like I'm already mentally preparing for a fight. "I'm killing him no matter what. You don't need to get involved if you don't want to. This is personal, not business." I slide my gaze to Bastian. "Find his weakness and routines. I want to know when to strike and it better be soon."

He nods, stands up and leaves.

Byzantine stays silent until we're left alone, his eyes hard and serious. But then an evil smile slowly appears on his face.

"Let the fun begin," he says.

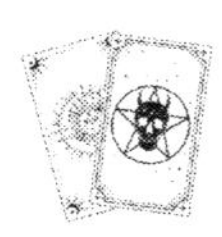

It's past midnight, and I find Lenix outside near the pool, staring at the stars. I changed into nothing but gray sweatpants before seeking her out. The moon is full tonight, illuminating her striking features. Her hair is curly, looking fresh out of the shower, a large black hoodie swallowing her up whole. There's just enough light for me to see her size me up, her eyes lingering on my bare feet before fixing her gaze back up to the sky.

My first instinct is to crack a joke—a jab about her watching porn out here like last time, but something stops me. I just sit next to her instead, waiting for her to break the silence.

"Do you believe in God?" she asks, her knees curled up to her chest, arms wrapped tight around them. She presses her cheek against her legs, turning to me, waiting for an answer.

I'm still fighting the urge to cut the tension by laughing but stay serious.

"A sinner like me can't believe in God, darling."

"Why not?" The innocence I hear in her tone slices into me. And I'm rendered speechless. "You believe that Byzantine and Sunny's souls are somehow connected, don't you?"

"What does that have to do with God?" I answer.

The moonlight dances in her eyes, her gaze studying me before finally looking back up to the sky on a long exhale.

"I guess you're right," she mutters.

I know she's circling around the point and I bite my cheek mulling over what to say before breaking the silence.

"You grew up in a fucked up cult, with fucked up beliefs, where your father tried to rape you in the name of your *fucked up* God." My voice cracks, that same rage as before feeding into my veins, but I clear my throat and continue, "You protected yourself, Lenix. You saved yourself when no one else ever bothered to. Your soul doesn't belong to God."

The urge to tell her it belongs to *me* burns my tongue but instead I say, "It belongs to you. No one else."

Guilt has never been an emotion I ever really paid

attention to, but it damn near swallows me whole knowing she was stuck in that place.

There was no way for me to know. How could I?

But the guilt doesn't lessen. It only fuels the fire burning in my chest. The promise that now that I *do* know… well, those fuckers are going to wish their fucking God would smite them where they stand, instead of suffering through what's coming to them by my hand.

I stand up, but she doesn't move, her eyebrows slightly creased looking like she's still busy wondering if her soul is eternally damned or not. But finally, her fingers curl inside my palm and I pull her up, kissing her on the forehead before heading inside.

She follows me silently up the stairs but when she turns to head for the guest room, I snatch her wrist, and tilt my head towards her.

"That's not where you belong." The words from earlier echo behind the intent of what I just said. "You sleep in my bed now."

"You've got to be kidding me." She tries to yank her wrist away but I don't let go. Some of her usual fight comes back and my balls tighten at the sight. *There she is.* "You fuck me in a wedding dress *once* and you suddenly think we're blissfully married?"

My chuckle rumbles low as I pull at her arm and drag her with me down the hallway. "Not in the slightest, Lenny. You're still as irritating as ever, but it doesn't change that I want you in my bed."

By the time we've entered the bedroom, she's sighing overdramatically, grumbling in defeat. "Fine, I'll stay."

As if she had a choice.

Eyeing me warily, she approaches the left side of the bed. She takes off the oversized hoodie, an equally large t-shirt hiding underneath and slides under the covers, her gaze still studying me suspiciously. I don't bother entertaining her leering and act as if having her in my bed isn't messing with my head more than it already is. I step out of my sweats, leaving myself in nothing but black briefs and climb in.

She's lingering at the very end of the mattress, so after turning off the lights, I catch her by the waist and pull her into me. Her body stiffens for half a second before she lets out another small sigh. "You really are the devil," she mutters softly while curling into my chest.

She falls asleep not long after, and I find it hard not to stay up all night just to count her slumbering breaths while I plot out my next kill.

# 37

The morning sun shining through the open curtains wakes me up. When my consciousness gradually floats back to me, I nearly jolt out of bed when I sense a hard, warm body next to me. Then I remember it's Connor. And I'm in his bed.

*Great.*

This isn't complicating things now is it?

I was too tired to push back last night, and if I'm being perfectly honest… not so sure I can find the strength to care this morning either. Not when there's more pressing matters taking up most of the space in my head.

I feel overloaded. It's as if thinking too much about all of it has the same effect as not thinking about it at all. My mind goes blank, and the usual nerves wash over my body.

Connor rouses beside me, most likely woken up by the sheer weight and density of my thoughts. His eyes are still closed, his messy hair falling onto his sleep softened features while his wide palm finds my stomach, lazily searching for the hem of my shirt. When he does find it, his fingers smooth over my skin, up my ribs and graze the swell of my breast. He groans long and low, and my body lights up, my thoughts skittering somewhere quiet in my mind.

But they're quickly replaced by different thoughts when his hips press against mine, his erection practically burning into me.

*What the hell are we even doing?*

Does it matter?

Not when his lips feel so soft against my skin. Or when he removes his hand from under my shirt and traces a possessive path up my arm, his strong fingers wrapping around my jaw and throat.

His eyes snap open then, a curl of a smile on his lips still heavy with sleep. His beauty wholly captivates me and my mind effectively blanks out for good.

*Fuck it.*

Hastily, I take my panties off before pushing Connor on his back and straddling him. He chuckles, the delicious tone of it alighting my skin. Grasping my ass in both palms, his fingers dig into my flesh as I pull my shirt over my head.

"Fuck Lenix… You're so perfect. And all fucking *mine*," he growls.

I desperately try to ignore how his words make me feel,

but a small mewl escapes my lips while I grind myself against him.

"Just eat me out already," I say breathlessly while leaning forward, grabbing onto the headboard, and placing my knees on either side of his head. His eyes turn into the deepest black as his gaze fixates on my open thighs, my pussy just inches from his face.

"Sit," he commands, pulling me hard on top of him. My back arches, mouth falling into a silent gasp as his tongue finds me already wet and wanting, the slight brushes of his mustache on such sensitive skin somehow so erotic that I can't seem to catch my breath. His grasp digs even deeper into my skin, lavishing my clit with such precision that all I can do is grind myself even harder into his face.

"That's it," I whimper, "just like that."

My soft praise seems to spur him on, fucking me with his tongue, his palms splaying wide over my ass, then up my hips and back.

Keeping one hand on the headboard for balance, I lean backwards and slide my hand into his boxers to find what I'm aching for most. He groans, the reverberations traveling deep into my core. I clench my thighs around his face while moaning loudly. His hands leave my body for a split second, just long enough to yank his boxers down his thighs, and I give him a hard stroke the moment he does.

I put my weight back onto my knees and push off his face. Connor eyes me like a feral animal defending his kill. I tsk, and he settles as I slide my fingers down my slit and into my pussy, slicking my hand with my own arousal.

"*Fuck,*" Connor says under his breath, and I can feel his body tighten underneath me as if he's holding himself back. The tension slackens when his mouth latches onto my clit once more and I lean backwards again, my palm now sliding down his shaft with ease. He lets out another groan and his hips hitch upwards, chasing his pleasure into my tight fist.

The room fills with our harsh gasps, and breathless moans. Lost and mindless. I can feel my orgasm building. I must have said it out loud because suddenly Connor pulls me off him, flipping me onto my back and thrusting into me with such force that I'm left gasping with that same desperate need as before.

"I needed to feel you," he says in a feverish haste. "I needed you just like this, Lenix." And *fuck*, why are his words feeling as good as his cock throbbing inside me, hitting me in just the right spot, making me feel senseless, weightless, *fucking* untethered.

His hand collars my throat and I swallow hard against his palm, his eyes burning me with his stare. "Tell me, darling," he says between punishing, blissful thrusts. "How does it feel to be fucked by the devil?" My eyes nearly roll into the back of my head just by watching him embody such arrogant grace, such raw display of power. His presence is all-encompassing and I'm so close, *so fucking close*. "How does it feel to know he owns you—*mind, body, and soul?*"

My eyes lock onto his while I shatter into a million little pieces. Connor falls on top of me, kissing me harshly, my moans bursting on his tongues while he fucks me harder and harder until I feel him swell, spilling deep inside of me. He mutters a curse into my neck, whispering promises of the world into my ear and my mind is splintered. Ash in the wind.

Our skin sticks together as he trails kisses up my throat, finding my lips again while he slowly pulls out of me, feeling his release coat my inner-thigh. There's an intensity to the way I'm feeling that suddenly makes me panic, and I stiffen under his warm weight.

Connor straightens and peers down at me—studying me.

"This doesn't need to mean anything," he says softly.

"I didn't say a word," I stammer out.

"You didn't have to," he answers with a grin. "You're easier to read than you like to think."

I roll my eyes and he snickers, pulling away and climbing out of bed. I watch him stroll into the ensuite, all chiseled back and perfect fucking ass. He comes back with a wet towel and hands it to me. "I'd take the pleasure of cleaning you myself, but I don't think you'll let me," he quips with a wink.

I nearly chuck the damn thing in his face. Instead, I surprise him, and maybe even myself when I say, "Fine. Do it then." Handing him back the warm, wet towel.

I try to keep my limbs loose as he kneels close to me on the mattress. Glancing up, his eyes darken, his tongue swiping over his bottom lip. Before I know it, he's leaning down and giving me one long, broad lick from asshole to clit before straightening back up. I fist the sheets, my mouth opening on a silent gasp, my gaze slamming into his.

But his eyes are trained on my body, face relaxed like he didn't just do anything that garnered any type of reaction. The towel now between my thighs, his touch tender and I immediately regret my decision. As if he's playing *emotional chicken* with me and I'm clearly losing by the way he's watching me squirm under his stare. I evade his gaze and my eyes land on his chest. Not an inch of skin isn't covered by black and gray tattoos. Suddenly, a thought lands with a thud at the front of my mind.

"You never answered her question that day," I say, almost to myself.

Connor plops the towel on the bedside table and sits on his heels, facing me.

"What question?"

"Did you have a birthmark over your heart before all of these tattoos?"

His eyes shutter, I know I've hit a nerve, but he answers anyway.

"I did."

# 38

## Connor

It only takes me a few days to plan out exactly what to do with Josiah Morrissey. How I'll make him suffer. From the perfect location to kidnap him, to the method I would use to watch him take his last sorry breath. Like an artist conspiring with the universe to find inspiration for their masterpiece, I listened to the darkest of muses as they whispered how to execute my magnum opus.

Byzantine and I break into Morrisey's mistress' condo while he's visiting her in the city.

In a way, it feels like poetic justice taking him from there. How he considers himself high and holy when he's warming his withered dick in a girl fresh out of high school. She doesn't seem all that bothered to watch him be dragged out of her bedroom, especially after the considerable amount of hush money I push into her palm before we leave.

We then interrogate him on the most pressing matters: are there any more cult plants in the government? Would the cult survive without Lenix's brother? It takes a few hours of Byzantine torturing the Governor of California for him to finally answer yes to both. We pocket that information for later.

The final step is to let him marinate.

I don't know what possesses me to have this kind of patience. The willpower to wait and not jump for instant gratification—but every single cell in my body knows the wait will be worth it.

Two days later, he's ready for me. And seeing him now. It certainly *was* worth it.

I step off the porch and into the yard, Byzantine on my heels. We're at one of our safe houses, miles out of Noxport and away from civilization. I craved the freedom to hear Morrissey scream his penance into the very air I breathe.

He's naked, on his knees, a chain wrapped around his neck connected to a cement pillar, arms tied behind his back. We've left him out in the scorching sun this whole time. Even from here I can see his skin is red and tender. Ripe for what's to come.

I was feeling somewhat nostalgic for this kill. So I chose to flay him. Skinning people alive used to be a common method of torture during the medieval times. They'd typically boil the victim in hot water or leave them out in the sun for a few days to make the skin easier to peel off their body.

Morrissey's head jerks upwards from where it was lolling between his sagged shoulders as we approach. His eyes are swollen from the sun burning his face, he squints, trying to peer at who's walking up to him. But he knows it's me. I'm his entire world now.

"You're going to burn in hell for this," he hisses, his voice hoarse from disuse and dehydration.

"Save me a seat," I drawl.

My fist tightens around the handle of the knife I'm holding. The blade is wide and curved. Perfect for skinning a deer. Or the Governor of California.

Byzantine stays silent, keeping his distance. He knows this part is for me and me alone. Having no interest entertaining a long-winded conversation about good versus evil with this piece of shit, I decide that scalping him first might shut him the fuck up.

It doesn't.

But his gargled screams could make an angel sing. A symphony of howls, moans, and wails while I hum to the melody of his tortured pain.

By the time I peel the skin off of his face, he's gone silent. Most likely in shock, but he's still conscious. I know he won't survive getting his entire body flayed, so I relish these lasting moments where he's holding on to his conviction, praying to false idols when he should be praying at my feet.

When he finally goes unconscious, he falls slightly forward, the chains still restraining him. I shove him backwards, his body hitting the ground already soiled with his blood.

I could end it. I could just kill him now.

But I don't. Because this fucking cult thinks they know who the devil is but they haven't met me yet. And Morrissey's body is the perfect canvas for a proper introduction.

As time passes, my muscles grow sore from crouching for so long.

"Help me carry him," I grunt to Byzantine, nodding towards the table near the shed.

Without a word, he grabs his feet while I take his arms and we haul him over there. After a while, the repetitive motions grow tedious and my mind starts to wander. It eventually finds its way back to Lenix—lingering on memories of the first night she slept next to me a week ago, and how amazing she looked sitting on top of me the next morning. My thoughts finally stumble onto the question she asked while I was cleaning her up.

"So, how does reincarnation even work?"

When Byzantine doesn't answer my question, I look over to where he's sitting. He's found a random lawn chair, now lounging a few feet away from the shed, phone in hand. I know he's heard me. The curious look on his face is a dead giveaway.

Annoyed, I coax him further. "Well?"

"Hell would I know?" he mutters.

Irritation races hot through me, but I bite my tongue. I turn back to the unconscious body on the table—pulling and cutting, pulling and cutting.

"You're the one who claims to remember his past lives, for fuck sakes," I eventually say while gritting my teeth, the sun beating hard on my shoulders, sweat pouring down my back.

"What's this about?"

I consider not answering just to antagonize him but I breathe hard through my nostrils and decide to open Pandora's box.

"A few weeks ago, this palm reader told Lenix and I that we were connected."

I cut a large piece of skin off Morrissey's stomach letting it flop to the ground, before looking back to Byzantine. "Like you and little miss sunshine."

"You got your palms read?" he says in disbelief.

"*Jesus Christ.* Can you stop answering everything I say with a question?"

He raises his hands in surrender.

I start on the governor's lower half while I mull over my thoughts.

"She asked if I had a birthmark over my heart."

Confusion etches across his features. "Well, you do."

"I know that. But how did *she* know?"

"You didn't bother to ask?"

"I pulled a gun on her instead and left," I mutter with a crooked smile.

He laughs but then falls solemn, leaving the silence hanging between us for a stretch of time while I continue with the task at hand.

"I wouldn't leave it unanswered if I were you," he finally says.

"So you *do* believe in all that shit?" I spit out, feeling half insane just having this conversation in the first place.

He shrugs. "Nothing surprises me anymore."

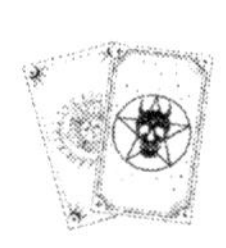

A FEW HOURS LATER, I'm back in the city, showered and smelling a hell of a lot better than when Byzantine dropped me off an hour ago. I'm currently standing in front of the palm reader's tent, wearing a plain black t-shirt and jeans, hoping it will help me blend into the crowd. I've been rooted to the boardwalk for the past five minutes. The thought of pulling out my gun from the back of my jeans and shooting myself in the head sounds preferable right now than going in there. Anything to evade the feeling racketing behind my chest.

Feeling *ridiculous* doesn't even begin to cover it. Mortified feels a lot closer to the truth.

I force myself to finally snap out of it. I just flayed the Governor of California, I think I can handle some half-pint witch lady. Squaring my shoulders and straightening my spine, I walk in.

This place is as hokey as I remember. No surprise there. Still, I nearly jump out of my skin when the woman appears out of what feels like thin air.

"*Fucking Christ*," I mutter under my breath, eyeing her up and down with derision.

She smiles and tells me to sit.

So I stay standing.

"As you wish," she says softly and places her clasped hands on the counter separating us.

We stare at each other for what feels like an eternity until I crack and speak. "You remember me, don't you?"

"I do." She observes me, her face open and inviting before continuing, "Are you ready for the answer to your question?"

"Is there one?"

"Perhaps," she answers and I feel my patience dwindling rapidly.

"Hurry the fuck up," I bite out, rubbing my hand over the back of my neck. "I don't have time for this shit."

She sighs as if dealing with a difficult child and I can't comprehend how I'm still standing here entertaining this bullshit.

"When you die a violent death, it leaves an imprint on your soul. From one life to the next you carry that wound," she says while placing a palm over her heart. "Birthmarks are believed to be clues left behind from another life."

My mind goes blank. I don't know if I should laugh or storm out of here. But I can't deny the pinch in my chest when I hear the words slip past her lips.

I clammer to find something, *anything* to say. "What the hell does this have to do with me and Lenix being connected?"

She smiles, looking like she knows something I don't. My blood boils but I manage to keep calm because, somehow, I need to hear what she's about to say.

"You should ask the one who's life line you have etched in the palm of your hand."

# 39

The ocean breeze is a small comfort against my cheek. The sweet scent of spring lingers in the air as I close my eyes, trying to enjoy this quiet moment. But it won't last. Even this is an illusion. It's been over a week since I told Connor everything. It felt freeing at the time but now I just feel raw. Splayed open with my insides seeping out.

I hate it.

I haven't told Sunny yet—and it just doesn't feel right for Connor to know and not her. Which explains why I'm avoiding her when I can. I can't bear the reminder that our friendship is a sham. She has no idea who her friend is, and the longer I wait to tell her, the more I dig my grave even deeper.

Which is why I'm on my lunch break alone again. I made up an excuse about having to run some errands, but all I really wanted to do was *run*. I let out a slow breath and open my eyes. My gaze finds the ocean again and I allow myself this minute fracture of peace, if only for just this fleeting moment.

I'm trapped in limbo. In a liminal space where I'm knitting a web of false security around myself while the threat is still out there. Telling Connor about the commune simply quelled the smallest of aches. I know my brother won't give up. I'm the perfect sacrifice for his mission towards Godliness.

I might have been out of the fold for thirteen years but I still remember how it felt to think you knew in the deepest parts of your soul that you had the answer. That God would protect us all, if only we complied. Thinking of Lucy still ensnared inside Sacro Nuntio, being subjugated to God knows what makes me sick. I've suppressed the thought of her for years, and the guilt of leaving her there is excruciating.

I watch the waves roll onto shore, biting my lip to try to quell my nerves. My phone pings in my purse on the bench beside me. Needing a better distraction than just my own brooding thoughts, I dig it out. It's a notification from my news app. I almost dismiss it, until my eyes land on a name and a chill travels down my spine. With clammy palms, I quickly unlock the screen and pull up the article.

*Holy fucking shit.*

My eyes rove over the words on the screen but I can barely process them.

Governor Morrissey is dead.

Flayed and found crucified on an upside-down cross in front of the *fucking* California State Capitol.

No leads, and no clear evidence. They're calling it a senseless murder.

But I know.

Connor looked me square in the eyes and brazenly promised me his death.

But not like this.

I can't breathe. I can't fucking *breathe.*

I stand up on shaky legs, turning back towards the office. After forcing down the near-paralyzing shock of what I just read, I find my bearings again and dial Connor's number. It rings and rings, and all I want to do is smash my phone on the sidewalk. Hearing his haughty tone over voicemail doesn't help me calm down in the slightest. When it finally beeps for me to leave a message, I whisper-yell into the phone, "Connor *fucking* Maxwell, what the *hell* did you do?"

I'm distracted, not paying attention to where I'm going, my feet dragging me back to the office on auto-pilot. Ending the call, I sharply turn a corner, and slam face first into a hard body.

"Oh my God, I'm so sorry…" I splutter, looking up at the person I just body-checked. My words catch in my throat, thickening with fear when I realize I'm staring straight at my ex-fiancé.

"Patrick?" It's barely a whisper.

I don't have time to run before someone's arm circles my throat from the back, a cloth covering my mouth and nose. I can't help but to breathe in a sharp gasp, trying to feed air into my lungs. It's a mistake. I watch Patrick's lips move but I can't hear anything, his face slowly blurring before everything fades to black.

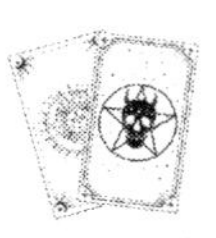

*Lucy and I are on our knees, trying not to squirm in the last row of pews. It is where the children gather when our father gives a sermon. We are told to stay kneeling for most of the service. It is stuffy inside the church today. Quiet. A few stilted coughs. Babies are not allowed in here when he speaks. Our father does not allow interruption. Only adoration.*

*Sweat trickles down my spine, under the weight of my stifling cotton dress. My legs hurt and all I want is to stand up and stretch. Slowly, I reach for my sister's hand and entwine my fingers in hers. I incline my head the tiniest of amounts to look at her, and she does the same. She is five years younger than me and I can not imagine a life without her.*

*Her smile is my favorite thing on earth. I grin back and squeeze her hand three times. A private signal meant for just us two. Stay strong. Make our father proud. And do not move until he is done.*

*Our hands stay tightly clasped until finally, our father calls the end of the morning service. We unbend our sore knees and smooth out our dresses. Mother gives us a look and a small nod.*

*Our smiles are wide while we weave through the mass of adults milling about, and our hands rejoin as soon as the fresh air fills our lungs, breaking into a run. We are still young enough not to have any afternoon duties. We head to our favorite place. The open field behind our house, our giggles trailing us all the way there.*

*When we are deep into the high grass, Lucy turns to me, letting go of my hand and falling onto her back. I do the same, the grass tickling my face while we both try to catch our breaths. After a few seconds, she turns on her stomach, her feet kicking softly in the air, playing with a small flower nearby, looking lost in thought.*

*"Faith's wedding is next week," she finally says.*

*She is our oldest sister. Different mother but same father.*

*I stay on my back, watching the spongy clouds drift across the sky. "I know."*

*Then I let out a pleased hum. "I cannot wait to get married."*

*When she falls silent for a time, I turn to look at her. Lucy's face is serious and I suddenly miss her smile.*

*"Do you ever worry who Father will choose for you?" she asks.*

*Her question surprises me. But I answer truthfully.*

*"There is nothing to worry about Lucy," I say, reaching for her hand through the blades of grass. "The choice was never ours to make. It is divinely chosen, there is no mistake—only our destiny."*

*She stays silent, but then responds with a radiant smile, beautiful and innocent. Flopping on her back, we watch the clouds for a little while longer.*

*"I cannot imagine living in a house without you," she says, with a laugh. "Promise we will build our houses next to each other?"*

*I smile. "I promise."*

# 40

## Connor

While walking out from a meeting at The Chelsea, I reach for my phone inside my coat pocket. As usual, my screen is full of missed calls, texts and unanswered emails. I find a voicemail from Lenix hiding in the mix, my thumb hovers over it but I don't have time to press it before receiving an incoming call.

It's from Sunny.

She never calls me.

I fight the foreboding chill crawling up my scalp and answer. "Yeah?"

She skips over all formalities, her voice carrying a worried lilt that puts me on edge. "Have you seen Lenix today?"

"Not since this morning. Why? What's wrong?" I say hurriedly.

Staying silent for far too long, my patience almost snaps before she speaks again. "She didn't come back from lunch, and her phone is going straight to voicemail, but her car is still parked outside the office."

"*Fuck*," I hiss, my mind already miles deep into the worst case scenario.

"I'm worried, Connor," she says, her voice shaking.

"Call Byzantine, and let him know," I tell her through clenched teeth. "We'll take care of it."

I hang up, practically sprinting to my car. Before I drive off, I pull up Lenix's voicemail, and notice that it was left around the same time Sunny says she saw her last. I slam my phone on the dash and peel out of the parking lot. Her voice floats out of the speaker and I'm having trouble concentrating on the road ahead.

*Where the fuck am I even going?*

Office.

By the tone of her voice, I know she's seen the news. The gory little gift I left on the Capitol steps. Did it have to be so public? No.

But did it thrill me to know that Sacro Nuntio would see one of theirs desecrated across national news? Absolutely.

I knew Lenix wouldn't approve. Her heart isn't as black as mine. Not even close. But I also know in my fucking *bones* that she hasn't run away on her own accord this time. Not to mention she left her car behind. That should be the first glaring clue.

I'm seething, stuck in downtown traffic and this close to driving up the sidewalks, forcing everyone out of my way. I slam the steering wheel with my palm in frustration, saving Lenix's voicemail and dialing Bastian next. He answers on the first ring.

"If this is about your wife, Byzantine already told me. I was about to call. Her phone hasn't moved in hours. East corner of Wilfred and Mullins."

"Can you access the street cameras?"

"Working on it." I hear the fast sounds of his typing while he falls silent.

"Call me the second you do."

He ends the call without saying another word.

I'm only five minutes away from her last known location but time stretches into an infinite moment of stress, impatience, and fear. Before I decide to plow into someone's bumper forcing them to *fucking move*, I give up and park. I run the last block, arriving at the east corner of Wilfred and Mullins with trepidation spiking my adrenaline.

My first sweep of the sidewalk comes up with nothing and I'm about to jump down Bastian's throat when I notice a garbage can a few steps away. Stalking over to it, I peer inside, my heart plummeting into my guts when I find Lenix's phone inside. It looks deliberately smashed, the screen obliterated. The rage spewing up and out of me is pure and unfiltered. I see red, my vision blackening.

Glock in hand, my brain is void of rational thought. Knowing the phone is beyond repair, I empty my bullets into it, clenching my teeth until the fucking thing is in pieces. I'm left empty, lightyears away from any relief. I don't bother placating any wary onlookers and get the fuck out of there, texting both Byzantine and Bastian to meet me at my place.

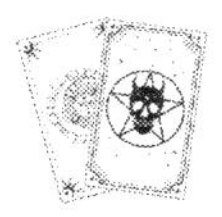

The smoke from the joint I just rolled spills out of my mouth when they finally enter the study. I'd already be three drinks deep if I didn't need to keep some kind of clear head—the weed now a necessity if I plan to survive the day without killing anyone, myself included.

"You got anything?" I bark.

Bastian gives me a look that almost passes for compassion, before saying, "They got her."

I snap.

Losing the last shreds of my control, I swipe my hands across my desk, the contents crashing on the floor. My fist slams into the mahogany wood over and over, swearing loudly, losing myself in these confusing, devouring feelings I can barely describe, until slowly, I claw my way back from the spiral I slipped into.

A few strands of hair have fallen into my eyes, I take a deep breath, smoothing it back. Crouching down, I pick up the joint, my knuckles now swollen and bleeding. I focus on the physical pain while taking a long drag, the smoke weighing me back to earth.

Both Byzantine and Bastian are close to the fireplace, tight-lipped and standing at attention waiting for me to speak.

"Show me," I growl.

Bastian winds back to life, shrugging his bag off his shoulder, pulling out his laptop while approaching me. He places it on the desk, his fingers dancing across the keyboard, until a video pops up on the screen and he taps the spacebar, pressing play.

Seeing Lenix walk down Mullins Street sends a desolate shiver down my spine and I battle the fury trying to take over once again. She's on the phone, her curt movements and hand gestures telling me she's angry.

I glance down at the timestamp and realize I'm watching her leave me the voicemail. I suddenly wish I could reach through the fabric of time and manipulate the past, if only it meant I could have answered the call.

I bite out a few more expletives but keep my eyes glued to the screen. From the camera's vantage point, we can see a man waiting for her just around the corner of a building. Squinting my eyes and examining closer, I finally recognize her ex-fiancé.

Rage engulfs my limbs but I hold back, trying to study the footage instead. "Someone else was following her," I say pointing at the second person. One in front, and one trailing a few feet behind her.

"Yeah…" Bastian trails off, having already seen the inevitable.

Watching it unfold, and knowing I can't do anything about it is pure fucking torture.

She walks right into him, the other guy inevitably putting her into a chokehold and I've never been more blood thirsty in my entire fucking life. Seconds later, a van pulls up and they throw her in the back. Before jumping into the vehicle, her ex-fiancé slams his heel a few times onto her dropped phone, picks it up and throws it in the trash. Then they're gone.

The silence in the study is deafening. I clench and unclench my fists, my eyes still frozen on the now black screen of the laptop. The screen reflects my face back to me and I can't bear to look at myself so I slam the damn thing shut. Bastian glares at me, sliding his computer off the desk but says nothing.

"How the *fuck* did they manage that? Downtown in broad fucking daylight?" I say, my voice cold and deadly.

"Wilfred Street was closed a few blocks down from there. It held up traffic. Waiting at the corner for her was clearly intentional," Bastian answers.

"News about Morrissey just broke today, how were they this fast?" I add incredulously.

I wouldn't have left her out of my sight if I knew it'd put her in any kind of danger.

I fucked up.

And now they have her.

"Looks like they had already planned to kidnap her. You killing the governor was just the perfect reason to hit hard and fast," Byzantine says, still standing by the fireplace.

"So we kill 'em all," I state. "Blow the whole fucking place up. It's not as if we don't know where they're taking her."

I'm crawling out of my fucking skin. This roaring wrath needs an outlet before I turn it all back onto myself.

Byzantine gives me a pained glance and I know he's imagining Sunny in Lenix's place. I can already tell I won't like what he's about to say. "We need a proper plan, brother. We can't risk putting her in danger."

I slam my palm on the desk in irritation, jaw clenched, my lip curling into a snarl. "I'm not going to just leave her there, while we stand around and do nothing." I turn to face the window, staring out but seeing nothing, my hands interlocked behind my head. "God knows what they're doing to her," I say. More to myself than anything.

I turn back around, Byzantine's gaze softening and I would rather he punch me in the face than look at me like that.

"Just let Bastian do what he does best. I promise you, Connor, they'll fucking pay for this."

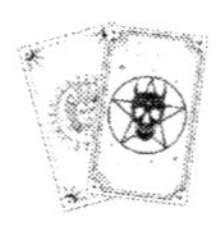

IT'S ALMOST morning and I haven't slept.

How could I?

The bedsheets smell like her. It's an unending torment. But I deserve it.

How could I let this happen?

I failed in doing the one thing she asked me to do—protect her. If I believed in karma, I'd start to think I'm paying penance for all the fucked up things I've done in this life. Good thing I don't. Doesn't lessen the guilt, or the heavy responsibility I'm holding over my head for every single thing she'll suffer at the hands of those fuckers. I cycle through all the gruesome ways I'll kill them. Like a lullaby, I count dead bodies like I'm counting sheep, but still, I can't sleep.

I've spent the past two hours replaying old recordings from the cameras installed around the house. In some of them, I appear with her. There's been a hard knot in my throat since I've noticed the few stolen glances she's given me while I wasn't watching.

It almost looks like affection. Like deep down, she enjoys my company more than she could ever admit. My bones ache not being able to hold her.

I had to turn it off before I smashed everything around

me. Now I'm just staring at the polaroid picture I took of her as if it's the most treasured thing I own.

And well, maybe it is.

I hear a small scratch at the bedroom door, already ajar. It creaks open and I spring upwards, reaching for my gun on the bedside table.

A furry head pokes through and I realize it's Lenix's cat. I leer at it, but I can't find my usual disgust for the animal as I watch it saunter into the room like it fucking owns the place. To my horror, the little demon jumps on the bed.

"What do you think you're doing? Your mom isn't here okay? Get out." I point to the door, but it just watches me.

Ignoring my demands, it creeps even closer to me and I can hear it purr loudly while still eyeing me down.

*Why the fuck is it doing that?*

It curls right next to me, settling into the crook of my arm as if we've cuddled up a million times before, its paw stretching out and resting on my chest.

I'm too fried to find the energy to care that the damn thing is invading my space. Falling back into the pillows behind me, a burst of Lenix's scent wraps around my senses, and I groan in frustration.

I decide to focus on the only thing I have of her right now and tentatively scratch the cat behind its ears. It purrs even louder, causing the sound to reverberate through my body, nudging the back of my hand like it's asking for more. So I comply.

My heart squeezes with an ache I'm still struggling to define, and I exhale roughly. "Don't you worry, little devil," I hear myself say. "We'll get her back."

# 41

## Lenix

I regain consciousness slowly.

I've been in and out, slipping into memories from so long ago, I wonder if I'm dead.

But eventually, my senses slam back into me. One by one, they tell me where I am… and maybe death is the better option if it means not having to face *this*. I keep my eyes closed but the smell of the room threatens to swallow me whole. When I can't bear to pretend any longer, I open them.

I don't think I've ever felt fear so potent before.

Not when I watched my father bleed out in front of me. Or when I hallucinated Connor's blood on my hands.

I clamber out of bed, familiarity mixed with equal shock and disgust at seeing the same beige walls I used to stare at all those years ago.

The paint still cracked. The room still smelling faintly of mold.

My knees buckle underneath me and I crumble to the floor. My hand slaps over my mouth, keeping the shocked gasp from ever leaving my lips.

*This isn't happening.*

I'm dreaming. It's just a dream.

Moments from now, I'll wake up in Connor's bed and sigh in relief.

But even in my terror, I know my hope is futile.

As if these past thirteen years never happened. I'd merely slipped into a catatonic state and finally woke up from the fabricated life I've perfectly crafted in my head.

How else would I have escaped?

I was destined to suffer this fate.

The only thing keeping me grounded in the present are the clothes on my back. I hold on to whatever shred I can while my mind slams against the decaying walls of this jail cell.

It's what it should be called.

It felt like a prison then too. I simply didn't have the words to describe it yet. Left to stare at these walls for days while the men roved freely about, never subjugated to any of the archaic shit the women were put through daily.

My gaze lands on the door and I skitter to my feet. I'm holding on to the smallest sliver of hope, but even that sliver whispers in my ears that it's useless. Either way, I try to open the door. It rattles under my hold, locked and most likely bolted. A pained whimper bursts out of my mouth and I pound my fist against the door.

*Don't cry, Lenix. Don't you dare cry.*

Turning around, I desperately search for something, *anything* that could help me escape. Instead, my eyes snag on my father's portrait still hanging on the wall. I lurch back into the door in horror as if I'm witnessing the rise of the antichrist themself. I'm trying my best to stay calm but I feel so weakened, struggling to draw strength from the person I've become.

Only Penelope exists here.

Jerking my eyes away in disgust, my sight then falls to the *holy* book on the table near the bed. The rage building behind my chest propels me forward. Stomping towards it, I snatch it in my hands. The thin pages rustle as the book cracks open. I grit my teeth, hating that tears are welling up in my eyes but I ignore them and struggle in a deep breath. I stay frozen for a few seconds, staring at the book that was the reason behind all my suffering.

My fingers find the pages and *rip.* I tear the book apart, channeling all of my hate into destroying the lies I'm holding in my hands.

When it's finally laying in tatters at my feet, I stare at it numbly and spit on the torn pages.

I hear the door creak behind me, a small gasp following close behind.

Turning, I nearly fall to my knees.

"Mother?" I say softly.

She's aged but looks the same. Cold yet still so beautiful, big brown eyes like my own, her complexion darker than mine. It's as if thirteen years haven't separated us but only a year or two. My body fights against itself, wanting to move towards her but also run as far away as possible.

Finding horror splashed against her irises at what I've just committed, I know I've lost her. Maybe I never had her at all. Her gaze falls to my feet, then back to my face, and if I had any hope she'd welcome me back, it's answered with the sneer slowly disfiguring her face.

"You are not my daughter," she spits.

I almost smile.

I'm losing grip on reality and nothing even feels real—especially standing here in front of my mother who seems to hate me more than the devil himself.

I glare at her but say nothing. What words could I ever utter to the woman who knowingly and willingly sent her daughter to be raped by her own father?

How is *she* the one with ire in her eyes when I was the sacrificial daughter?

"Put this on," she finally says, placing what I already recognize as the typical dress for women of the commune. Bile rises up my throat as I can feel more of Lenix slowly being stripped away as they try to revert me back into Penelope. She turns to leave and I step forward.

"Wait."

I expect her to ignore me but she stops with her hand on the doorknob.

"What does Frederick plan to do with me?" The worry found between the lulls of that one sentence makes my skin itch.

At the mention of my brother's name, her face softens and I'm sickened at the sight. He's not even her own son, but she preens like a proud mother nonetheless.

"You will sit trial before God," she replies with all the

righteousness of someone whose faith has never been tested.

"Oh?" I say tauntingly. "And how will that work exactly?"

Her face falls. "How dare you mock our Lord and Savior, Penelope."

I roll my eyes, but I'm struggling to keep up my nonchalance. Especially when I am reminded of *her*—the person I once was. She's taking up more and more space inside of me as if this wretched place is giving her strength. Ironic since all I can feel emanating from her ashes is the shame of having fallen so far down. The paralyzing guilt of having lived an immoral life so different from the path I was taught to follow.

But somehow I find the will to stay strong, and stare my mother down, my mouth upturned with a jeering smile.

"Only God can save you now. By his touch, we live," she says, fervent and pious before closing the door behind her.

I shudder when I hear the deadbolt, and I let loose a breath. The bed creaks under me when I sit, refusing to look at the clothes my mother ordered I wear.

Suddenly, I feel a gaping absence.

I look down at my hand and realize they've taken my wedding ring. My heart plummets, and I swallow hard, fighting the wave of emotion threatening to take me under.

It shouldn't matter. It doesn't matter.

It wasn't real. It was never real.

But the tears fall nonetheless.

Laying on my side, I face the wall and curl my knees up to my chest, doing my best to control the shake overtaking my body. The room has no windows, it could be any time of the day, and I wouldn't know. So I close my eyes hoping to just fall asleep and pretend I'm not here, that *this* isn't real.

My thoughts drift, and slowly they find Connor in a safe corner of my mind.

I shouldn't be surprised he's the one I reach for while stuck in this desolate place.

I need to believe he's coming for me.

No. For Lenix.

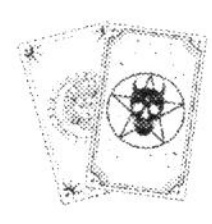

Time passes, but I can't tell how much.

The only thing keeping it from morphing into something non-linear, a black void I'm falling mercy to, is my gnawing hunger between the sporadic meals brought to me. At the very least, the room has a small bathroom with a shower. The smallest of mercies. As much as I would rather set the dress on fire, I finally relent after what feels like days, not wanting to wear my now soiled clothes over and over.

How long has it been? Hours? Days?

Nothing feels real anymore.

Warm tears flow down my cheeks as I gingerly slide on the thin white cotton slip first and then pull the light blue dress over my head, the very act feeling like a betrayal of the person I've fought so hard to become. The cotton fabric falls all the way down to the floor, and I choke back a sob while my arms slip into the long sleeves, teeth clenched but my jaw still wobbles while I clasp button after button up my chest and neck—like a noose around my throat.

I fall on the bed and cry, my shoulders shaking with every sobbing inhale.

Deep down, I always believed I didn't deserve the life I

managed to build for myself in Noxport. And this is just proof that I was never destined to escape my sins. My eyes feel swollen but I can't stop crying. Eventually, I fall asleep, clutching my old clothes to my chest as if it could somehow bring Lenix back from the darkness she is disappearing into.

Hours later, or maybe only minutes, I still can't tell, I hear the door open behind me. I keep my back turned assuming it's just another meal, proof that time is in fact moving forward.

"Penelope."

His voice chills my spine and I freeze, my eyes snapping open.

I can't remember a time when I've ever feared Frederick's voice like this. Not until I heard his voice through the phone over a month ago. It's a bizarre kind of dissonance to navigate. When I can still remember the person he was before he became… *this.*

I turn around slowly, the springs of the mattress digging into my hips but I keep my face blank. I find him leaning against the wall. I force down the rage building inside from seeing him like this, so arrogant in his virtuousness. It makes me want to hurl whatever I can find at his face. Instead, I sit up, my feet firmly planted on the dusty carpeted floor and glare at him.

We never looked alike, having different mothers. His features sharp, his skin so pale, you'd think he's never seen the sun. His thinning brown hair is long, fastened at the nape as if he just stepped out of a period piece. The hate I feel for him is instantaneous and I lean into it with abandon.

"Back in your place, sister."

"Don't call me that," I snarl.

He lets out a small huff through his nose, pushing off the wall and walking towards me. My back straightens, trying my hardest not to move an inch, unwilling to show the abrasive effect he has on me.

His hand strikes my cheek. My head whips to the side, shocking me before it even begins to sting. I can taste the subtle tang of blood in my mouth before turning my face back to him.

"Remember who you are speaking to," he grinds out.

I give him a sinister grin, my hand finding my burning cheek, before spitting blood at his feet.

"How holy of you."

Outrage flashes in his glare, but he blinks it away quickly, settling back into his messianic persona, and smiles.

Our father must be so proud watching over from whatever fucked up place he is now.

"You know, your mother didn't believe me when I told her I had found you. And how you were eating right out of the devil's palm."

His hand grazes my cheek, then my chin, and I feel sick.

"Don't you fucking touch me, you pathological piece of shit," I hastily whisper, pulling my face out of his grasp.

He hums as if I've somehow proved his point, looking down at me.

"How rewarding it will be to break you, Penelope," he says before turning on his heels.

I watch the door close behind him, the slide of the deadbolt like thunder compared to the quietness of this godforsaken room.

I'm suddenly so cold as if Frederick took all the heat with him when he walked out of the room. My bottom lip quivers and I bite it hard enough to stop it, unwilling to acknowledge how much he's left me shaken.

His last words still echo in my ears and fear coats my insides like tar. His threat could mean anything. I sit, unmoving for what feels like hours, my mind coming up with all the possible punishments he believes I deserve.

Eventually, my tired body cries out for sleep and I lay down, crawling under the covers that are anything but comforting. I fall into a restless sleep. This time the image of Connor never comes, as if deep down even my subconscious doesn't believe I deserve to be saved.

# 42

## Lenix

I must have slept longer than I thought. I'm still groggy when the door opens and a voice I don't recognize barks at me, "Come."

I stand up and shuffle to the door to meet the man who's waiting for me. I should feel relieved to be allowed out of this room, but I'd be a fool to think that anything good is waiting for me outside of these doors.

"Where?" I still find myself asking, although I know he won't be answering my question.

Ignoring me, he leads me out of the secluded house, the sun hitting me with such force, I wince. Craning my neck, I glance around, slowly taking in how different the commune looks now. Bigger for one. Like a self-sustaining village hidden away, surrounded by forest.

He leads me down a winding dirt road, and I suddenly realize we haven't passed another soul since we walked out of that horrid place. Foreboding tightens around my throat.

I follow him up to what looks like a theater, newly built by the look of it, and I stutter to a stop. But the man takes my wrist, opens the doors and pushes me inside. I stumble over the hem of my dress, trying to regain my balance.

When I look up, I freeze. The entire community seems to have gathered here to watch my downfall. As they stare, wrath and disgust fill the room with its stink.

I feel myself wilt.

*None of this should matter.*

None of it.

I should be able to stomach their judgment and let it wash over me. But today, I can't find the strength.

The man pushes me between the shoulder blades, forcing me to move along. I heed to his silent order, shuffling all the way up to the stage where my brother waits for me in triumph. The theater's painfully silent and I feel my mind slowly shutting down.

I walk up the short steps leading to him and with it, my dignity fades. Especially when I look into Fredrerick's face, his smile more evil than all the darkness I've ever witnessed, even in myself.

The crowd is so quiet, I can hardly stand it. The uncertainty of what's about to come gnaws at my ability to fight for myself. I'm battling against old ghosts. Of a girl who obeyed and never dared to speak out of turn. I can no longer tell who I am when I finally look my brother in the eyes.

He points to a chair in front of him on stage.

The thought of sitting down and facing the weight of my old community has me clutching at the last bit of resistance I have left.

"No," I say through cracked lips.

I try to turn around, but my arms are pulled backwards and I thrash against whoever is holding me, but I'm too weak. A second pair of hands join the first and the more I fight, the more I feel their grasp tighten, binding my wrists with a rope around my back.

*Don't cry. Don't cry. Don't cry.*

Instead, I reach for what will incense them most. While they drag me to the chair, I curse their God with every vile thing I can think of. The crowd's medley of shocked gasps makes me smile, a deranged looking thing I'm sure but who am I to them now but a wicked, broken thing?

Let them witness it. Let them see.

I'm pushed down and tied to the chair, now forced to look at the faces I've avoided for the last thirteen years. I fight against the urge to close my eyes, I can't stand the thought of showing them any more weakness. I refuse to find the one person I can't bear to see in the crowd, or else I'll crack. So for now I focus on a point at the back of the room and keep my eyes averted.

"For if the woman be not covered, let her also be shorn: but if it be a shame for a woman to be shorn or shaven, let her be covered," my brother says in a commanding tone. A small murmur ripples through the crowd, heads nodding to what Frederick just quoted.

The words rake over my skin and suddenly I know with absolute certainty what's to come. I might have left a long time ago, but an infuriating part of me still remembers most of what I was forced to memorize as a child.

My head is yanked backwards and I hear the snip of the scissors before the first strands of hair drift to the floor. I feel my fortitude fail and can't help but close my eyes. Not when Frederick continues to cut strand after strand of my long black hair.

I'm shaking, but I can't crack now. I can't let him win.

The crowd begins to chant a hymn I recognize from childhood, the words eating through my soul like acid. Eventually, I hear the buzz of the clippers and when I feel the cold, hard glide on my head, my resolve disintegrates. My eyes open, and my gaze sweeps over the sea of faces staring back at me. I find her sitting near the front.

*Lucy*.

My worst fear was to find her sneering with the same vitriol as everyone else. Instead, her face is nearly blank, shut down, but she can't hide the emotions in her eyes. The hurt I find there reaches out to me and I take it. I hold on to it with everything I have, connecting us to one another, everything else fading away.

I don't even realize I've been crying until I feel the tears soak into my dress, but still, I hold on to the hope that my sister isn't lost to me. I hold on to the belief that there's a part of her that still loves me as deeply as I love her even after all these years apart.

While my brother continues to shave my head, something shifts and I'm suddenly filled with hope so powerful that if I still believed in their God I would find awe in this grim moment. I would find purpose in what I'm being subjugated to and know with absolute certainty that I will find my way out of this.

When arms take hold of me again, I don't fight back.

They drag me out of this godforsaken place and I hold on to Lucy's gaze instead until the very last moment.

Back in my room, I'm stuck in a shocked daze, back between the four walls that call out to all of my fears and laughs at my pain. The silence is deafening, the overwhelming fog of the past and present oppressing my future.

Listlessly, I walk into the small bathroom, unbutton my dress and step into the small shower. The water is too hot and not hot enough, it turns my skin raw while I feverishly rinse away as much as I can of what just happened. The steam rises, turning so thick I can barely see in front of me. My shaky hands slide over my shaved head while the tears continue to spill.

It's not the loss of my hair that has me choking back a sob. It's the manner in which it was done. The power Frederick tried to strip away from me as he did so. He wanted me to feel shame. He yearned for my submission.

And I gave it to him.

I let him see my tears, and I grit my teeth at the memory. I slam my palm on the wall and slide down to the floor, the hot water still scalding my skin. I don't know how long I stay huddled like this but I can't move. It's long enough for the water to turn cold, and I invite the feeling. By the time I shut the shower off, I've turned numb.

Before leaving the bathroom, I force myself to look into the small cracked mirror. I can no longer recognize who I find reflected back.

Was Lenix ever real?

I can't tell anymore. Nothing makes any sense.

All I know is that I've been stripped bare. Broken open.

I don't know who I'm supposed to be. Or who I ever was. None of these skins fit.

How am I to discern the truth hidden behind all these lies?

When I finally walk out of the bathroom, I find fresh clothes waiting for me. I don't bother obsessing about the lack of privacy and just slip the dress over my head. I sit on the bed, losing myself in the dire thoughts claiming my sanity, and stare at the wall until my vision blurs. Through the fog, the vision from long ago finds me once again. The same I used to have back when I was Penelope. Of a bloody knife. Of hurt and heartache. And of retribution straight through the heart.

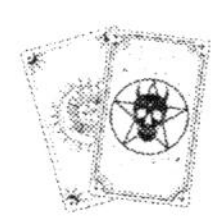

"Penelope?"

I'm so far down in the tunnel of my own thoughts that it takes the voice a few more times repeating my name for me to wake from wherever I was lost to.

"It is me... Lucy." Her voice cracks when she says her name, sounding like a part of her is as lost as I am. Uncertainty lingers in her tone as if I wouldn't remember her after all this time.

How could I ever forget my baby sister?

Having fallen asleep, I roll on my side slowly, terrified she'll morph into all the others who were condemning me today.

Maybe it wasn't even today. Time slips and slides, my grasp on it slowly waning.

"How did you get in here?" I whisper, still only half believing she's really here and not a mirage from my tired mind and lonely imagination.

She holds up the keys in her hand.

"Mother." She quirks a sheepish smile and tears spring to my eyes.

"Lucy," I choke out. "It's really you."

I sit up while she hurries over to the bed, sitting down and taking me into her arms. Her lilac scent is so painfully familiar that I hold her even closer, terrified she'll disappear under my touch.

My tears spill and spill, until I can barely remember a time before this. A time when I wasn't cracking, raw, and vulnerable. I ache with the need to hold her as long as I can. She seems to feel a similar way because her embrace is as hard and long as mine.

I can't let go. Because this moment is perfect, even if life isn't.

Finally, her sniffles grow quiet, as do mine. We let go, pulling away to better see each other. And what a sight she is. The last time I saw her, she was eleven years old.

She's no longer a child—the innocence gone from her eyes, my throat tightens, choking back a sob because I can only imagine the worst.

*I left her here.*

"I did not know you were back until I saw you this morning on stage," she says, her voice still shaking. "If I would have known, I would have come. Please believe me, Penelope."

I stare deeply into her eyes, my lips trembling, the words fighting to come out but also to stay in. "You don't hate me?" I dare ask. "I killed him, Lucy." My hand flies to my mouth. "I killed him."

Again, I cry.

I cry so hard, I don't know if I'll ever recover from it.

But then, she claps her hands over my free one and squeezes it three times. Our private signal. My heart cracks open, bleeding for every second we've been forced apart.

"If he was anything like Frederick then I am glad he is dead," she says with such vehemence that I'm left blinking back at her, wondering if I just hallucinated what she just said. But the resolve on her face says it all and I'm left empty.

"What did he do to you..." I manage to say through the dread.

The tears are still burning my cheeks, the guilt like acid burning my throat.

Because I know. *I know.*

I might have found a way to escape but she didn't.

"I left you here," I choke out through a sob, taking her face into my hands, desperately trying to convey everything I have left inside of me. "I'll never forgive myself, Lucy," my voice quivering and hoarse. "Never."

Her eyes are wide with grief, but then she blinks and the hues of relief blend alongside it, leaning into my touch.

"You are here now, Penelope," she says soothingly, her formal and proper choice of words reminding me of the aching distance between us now.

She smiles, and I don't think my heart can bear it.

"I never lost hope," she says, her voice like a balm on the wounds that won't stop bleeding. Her lips purse, eyebrows cinching, she swallows hard as if trying to keep herself from crying. Still, her eyes glimmer with unshed tears. "I always knew you would come back for me."

# 43

The initial resolve I felt while holding Lucy in my arms slowly withers. She hasn't been back since. Whenever that was. Time is a web, and I'm caught inside of it, captive and struggling but unable to escape.

I find myself staring at the wall most of the time, whether it be with the light switched on or off. It doesn't matter. My hands keep forgetting my hair's gone, repeating small unconscious movements around my head and neck like I've done my whole life. Tucking my hair behind my ear is the most common one. My nostrils flare in irritation whenever I do it as if it's a personal affront that my hands can't remember my head is shaved.

The cold chill at my nape is new. The soft rustling of air that now breezes over my head when I walk or pace around the room is still so foreign, it sends chills down my arms and back whenever I feel the sensation.

I'm finding new ways to soothe instead, however small and benign they are. Like the feel of the buzz cut underneath my palm when I distractedly smooth my hand over my scalp while thinking.

Although. I would rather not think.

But I don't have much choice. It's either succumb to my own thoughts or read the accursed book taunting me on the bedside table. The shredded one was replaced. I would rather gouge my eyes out than read my father's hypocritical lies ever again.

So I've built a small cove in the recesses of my mind. I don't let myself enter often. Only when time has slowed to a stop and I can feel myself sinking, do I enter. It's where I've tucked Connor away. He waits patiently for me there. The sun caressing the striking angles of his face. His eyes glinting with mirth as I approach him. Here, I don't let myself doubt that he will come for me. Here, I have faith.

But it always hurts the most when I leave him behind for the four cracked walls of my punishing reality. Waiting for the torment to continue. Wondering what humiliating punishment my brother has for me next.

When I can't hold it in any longer, my thoughts stray into dangerous territories—like how I could turn the bed sheets into a noose.

But even those morbidly comforting images don't ring true.

I refuse to give up.

I will never let *him* win.

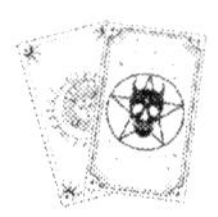

I'M LOST in a daze when I hear the now familiar slide of the deadbolt. My eyes snap to the turning door handle. It could be anyone. It could even be Lucy.

But it isn't. Of course, it isn't.

Instead, it's just another faceless sneering acolyte who I would probably recognize if I gave a shit. I stand up and approach him before he even spits out an order. I'm preserving my strength for more important things than to resist a useless command from a small man.

There's a small shift within my inner turmoil today. The hopelessness feels less palpable. It's slowly being replaced with anger. It cloaks me like chainmail, helping me stand a little taller than before. Instead of a nervous shuffle, my feet move forward in strides, my shoulders high and tight and not curved inwards. Maybe knowing—hoping—Lucy will be nearby is what's giving me strength. I'm not alone, no matter how loudly the loneliness throbs inside me.

I know I'm walking towards more of the same punishment—probably worse. But today, I don't swallow the shame as usual. I imagine myself spitting the putrid feeling at their feet. It belongs to them, not me. It doesn't prevent my limbs from shaking from apprehension, as much as I wish they didn't, I can't control it.

Eventually, we turn the corner into the town square. Or the closest thing the commune has to it. Shops, if you can even call them that, circle the area. The ground is simply dry-packed dirt, and sitting right in the center of it is a large tree, helping with shade.

Like before, people overflow the square, but this time I don't see any children, and somehow that detail sends an ominous shiver burrowing down my spine. At the foot of the crowd, my brother stands. Hatred roils in my stomach at the sight. He sports the same satisfied smile on his face as before while he watches me near him.

"Sister," he says softly as if just for us, tilting his head.

"Fuck you," I respond through clenched teeth.

Humming, his eyes travel down my body and then back up. "I see your will has not yet been broken." He looks over to a small wooden stage that seems hastily built, and my gaze follows. I notice a trough on the raised platform before my eyes jump back to Frederick. "Hopefully, today will rectify that," he says assuredly.

He snaps his fingers and suddenly more than one set of hands are on me, pulling at my dress. I struggle but it's useless, seconds later the dress is over my head and I'm left with just the thin cotton slip covering my heaving body.

I fight the urge to cross my arms around my waist and bare my teeth instead.

"The sins left for you to atone are enumerable, Penelope. Stop fighting it. It will only make it worse. Give in. God is waiting," he commands in a devout tone.

"I'd rather burn in hell," I hiss, and take comfort in the small dismayed gasps rising from the crowd.

He lets out a frustrated sigh as if this was expected of me. "Very well."

Waving to the men still surrounding me, a familiar rope tightens my wrists behind me, my shoulders burning at the strain. But I keep my head tall, my glare latched onto Frederick's repulsive gaze. He nods towards the stage and the men push me up the shoddy stairs, forcing me to kneel in front of the trough full of water—facing the crowd once again.

My mind filters through all the possible humiliating scenarios that could involve what's in front of me but I don't have to wait long. I have just enough time to sweep the crowd for Lucy and find her pushing her way to the front. A small relieved smile ghosts my lips before my entire head is dunked into the frigid water.

I thrash against the hands holding me down, the precious breath I should be holding in lost while I scream. My knees slip against the ragged wood, splintering my skin while my body tries to fight against their tightening grasp, but still, they keep me underwater.

My lungs burn and I choke. And finally, *finally,* I'm lifted back up, my vision blurred from the water and tears. I wheeze and cough trying to regain my breath, but before I can do any such thing, my head is dunked back in. Thankfully, this time, my survival mode kicks in and I keep my mouth closed, fighting to keep in as much air as possible.

They keep me down for as long as the first time and by the third, I've stopped fighting it. I'm near blacking out, water sluicing down my head and throat, gasping for air over and over. Through the ordeal, I lose the wherewithal to find my sister's gaze, but I hold the image of her tightly in my mind.

*She's the only thing that matters.*

But then my body splinters in half. White, blinding pain slices through me and it's so acute that I don't even understand what or where it's coming from. I bellow into the water and continue to wail even when I'm pulled out. Fingertips dig into my shoulders and arms, trying to keep me on my knees but I've lost all mobility.

That's when the stench hits me.

Burning flesh.

My mind is slow, sluggish, but I still manage to blink past the blur and find my brother standing over me, a glowing branding iron in his hands.

I've never felt such all-encompassing hatred until this very moment.

Between the retching, gagging, and incomprehensible agony—I send out a prayer.

Not to God.

No.

To Lenix.

To a future version of her—of myself—who will reclaim her power and fight back.

She will save me. She will enact my revenge.

And when the time comes, she will dance on my brother's grave.

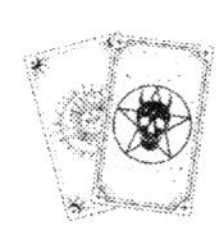

I'm back in the room. I might have lost consciousness, I can't tell. The pain has now localized, the throbbing concentrated on my right hip. I lay on my left side, facing the wall, shivering through the pain. I fall in and out of reality. Like the rising tide, I drift out to sea, back to shore, again and again.

Through the haze, I feel soothing hands stroking over my skin, and I can't help the pained whimper that escapes me, my body sensitive to even the gentlest touch. The wet slip is now dry, sticking to my skin and those same hands lift it, carefully peeling it off my hip where it congealed with the blood. I cry out but find no strength to move.

"I'm so sorry," the voice quivers. The wisps of reality still lingering near me recognize my sister. My lips mouth her name but no sound leaves me. I float in and out of consciousness again while she tends to my wound. Tears fall silently into the musty pillow underneath my heavy head, and I hope she understands my small sighs of gratitude.

Eventually, she kisses me softly on the shoulder and leaves, turning the light off on her way out. I wish she didn't. I wish she could stay and sit with me. Hold my hand while I mourn what didn't survive my brother's wrath.

Maybe that piece of me had already been dying for years, I just couldn't let go of it until now.

That piece was Penelope.

I fall asleep. Hours, maybe, stretch by and I gradually regain my sense of awareness. Slowly, I remember who I am. My body still aches, but I'm finding my way back.

Some time later, I hear a loud crack from outside the bedroom, like something being ripped off the wall. The door slams open, but as usual, I'm facing away from it. I lag to turn around, my limbs protesting, still too sore when I hear him call my name.

My heart stops.

I must be hallucinating.

I'm suddenly too terrified to look and find nothing but heartbreaking disappointment.

But then he says my name again and I am reborn.

# 44

## Connor

"Lenix?" I whisper.

The room is dark, her body huddled on a small single mattress in the corner. I can hear, more than I can see, a rustle on the bed. The terror coursing through my veins is near-paralyzing. Somehow I find my way out of the stupor and quickly palm the wall near the door looking for the light switch. Finally, the bedroom is bathed in light, and my body turns cold.

My eyes quickly assess the suffering, mistreatment and aftermath of me leaving her here for four days—four fucking despairing days, wondering what hell they were doing to her.

She tries to sit up, wincing as she does which finally spurs me to move. Three quick steps to the foot of the bed and I'm crouching down, my gaze leveling with hers, hands cradling her face in aching apology.

"Are you hurt?" I keep my voice steady but I'm seconds from blacking out into a murderous rage. I'm trying to keep it together for Lenix, but when her eyes find mine, everything else dissolves away. My focus zeroes in on her and her alone. She's shaking most likely in shock.

"Connor…" she rasps, her shaky hands trailing a path from my forehead, to my cheeks, ghosting over my mustache and then my lips. There's a stream of tears on her cheeks and I use my thumbs to wipe them away. "You came," she whispers.

A knife to the heart would have the same effect as the words she just uttered. Still holding her face in my hands, I take her in bit by bit. It hurts too much to take her in all at once.

They shaved her head.

I can't even fathom the manner in which it happened. It accentuates her features, her eyes wide and pained. The dark circles under her eyes, evidence of her exhaustion. All she has on is this thin, white dress that barely covers her body. I've never seen her this vulnerable.

Cracked open.

The guilt of leaving her here, even for one fucking second, leaves me hollowed out.

Undeserving.

With it, the overwhelming need to keep her safe is staggering. The weight of it reminiscent of Atlas banished and enslaved to hold up the earth on his shoulders for the rest of eternity. The difference is… for her? I'd do it willingly.

I kiss her softly. Needing to taste, touch—anything, to remind me this is real, that she's back in my arms, however fragile she may look.

"My darling, I will always come for you," I say, my lowered voice choking up.

A small sob tumbles out of her mouth, her body slightly slumping towards me and I feel gutted. My insides spilling out at her feet. Then I see her wince again, and my rage barrels back tenfold. My hands trail down her shoulders, holding her steady.

"What did they do to you?" I say through gritted teeth.

I watch her eyes glaze over, like she can't bear to relive what I'm asking her to recount. Then I track her hand moving over her thigh up to her hip, hovering but never touching.

More tears spill over her face, down her neck and I've never felt so powerless.

"My brother…" she says softly, her voice devoid of emotions. "I couldn't breathe. I was drowning… and then I felt it… it…" she trails off, stumbling over her words. "It burned so badly."

I somehow manage to piece together what she's trying to tell me. And when I do, all logic fades. I have to fight the urge to stalk out of the room and kill every living soul I cross paths with who let this happen to her.

"He branded you?" I hiss, unable to process—only seethe.

Somehow, me saying it out loud snaps her out of the daze she had fallen into. Her eyes clear as she looks at me with hard intent and nods.

She moves to stand and at first, I try to keep her sitting, but she gives me a look that tells me the Lenix I know is not lost underneath the distress written on her face.

Still, she allows me to help her stand up, her knees slightly buckling under her weight.

She steadies herself, shoulders straightening. Just that small movement makes my chest squeeze—I'm in awe of her strength.

I crave to pull her into my arms, hold her and never let go but I take a deep breath instead. Smoothing my hand over my face, I try to regain some semblance of composure when I see her eyes flit to my bloody knuckles.

"How did you know what building I was in?" she asks with innocent curiosity.

"We intercepted the guards at the gate." I hold out my hand in front of me as if this is the first time noticing how mangled it is. "You'll be surprised how quickly people cower when faced with their own mortality."

"We?"

"Sin Eaters. We have the place surrounded."

Lenix's expression is a complexity of feelings. "My sister."

"We'll get her out, I promise." Hoping my assured tone will soothe her somewhat.

She nods, her eyes still vacant. "What time is it?"

For a second I find her question strange until I realize there are no windows in this place and I get incensed all over again.

"Early morning. It's still dark out."

"Good." She nods, lost in thought.

Moving towards the door, her right knee buckles under her weight. I'm by her side in a heartbeat, aching to support her, but she holds up her hand as if to tell me she's fine. She's not fine, but even here in this dire environment, crushed under her brother's heel, she's still fighting for her independence.

In that moment, I know.

As much as I'm itching to kill everyone who ever laid hands on her, tonight I will bear witness instead. I can recognize bloodlust when I see it. And hers burns bright like the fires of hell.

I'm fighting against the searing need to coddle her but instead take a step back. I let her straighten herself, understanding her desire to do this alone. Even if it's just walking out of this room on her own two feet.

She stops near the door and looks down at her bare feet, then over to her shoes. The vulnerability swimming in her expression when her eyes find mine cracks me wide open.

"Could you?" she says in a barely audible whisper, her voice cracking against the vowels.

I'm sinking to my knees before she even manages to finish her sentence. Resting one hand on the wall beside her, she holds out her foot and I slip the shoe on, doing the same with the other. I look up at her, and watch a lone tear fall down her cheek, her tongue swiping out to lick it away when it touches her lips.

"Thank you," she murmurs.

Those two words hold the weight of everything left unsaid.

"Always," I whisper, pressing a kiss on the scars peppering her left thigh before standing back up.

# 45

Connor's men are like wraiths in the night, occupying every corner of the compound. Meanwhile, the men who degraded me, sleep soundly in their beds, dreaming of their righteous *God*, leaving the rest of us to suffer under the weight of their sins.

It's near dawn now and Connor and I are cloaked under the shadows of the Redwood forest. It sits at the edge of the commune's property, there are no houses or buildings here save for one small chapel. It's a humble wooden thing, built by my father's hand, tucked under the canopy of trees near the forest's edge with a large pond flanking it. It's no longer used for community sermons, the size of the commune having outgrown it.

It doesn't mean it's abandoned, however.

There's only one path to reach the chapel and from our position, we're facing it. The weight of Connor's leather jacket on my shoulders is comforting. Having nothing to wear but that same soiled white slip dress, he insisted I wear something of his. It smells like him, earthy but also somehow bright, and it anchors me, reminding me of Lenix. His fingers keep finding my skin while we wait, small soft strokes as if he needs continuous reassurance that I'm real, that I'm here with him, not still lost.

Most of the sky is still an undisturbed expanse of navy blue, but the horizon is yawning awake over the pond. It brightens the edge of the woods, and the rustle of leaves makes it feel like the forest is arising with it.

A branch cracks and my gaze snaps to the people approaching the chapel. I knew I'd find them here. Observing a tradition that precedes even them. Every morning, the inner circle, first of my father's, now Frederick's, meets at the chapel before the morning sermon.

I smile, anticipating what's to come. Connor's warm lips find my nape presumably knowing what feelings are somersaulting inside of me. I look back over to him, my smile widening, it feels almost manic but I don't care. The brand on my hip is still on fire, and I'm aching to finally have an outlet for the rising ire still hot inside of me.

We watch as a few more join the others already inside. I'm not surprised to find the same men who were involved in my punishment here this morning, including Patrick. I was horrified, yet not shocked to learn Lucy had been forced to marry him in my stead after I ran away.

Lucy's now safe. Bastian took her far away from here as we stayed behind. She doesn't know what I'm about to do. I pray she'll forgive me. I would rather live an eternity with her resentment than know she's still trapped here with Patrick and our brother. Nausea rises at the thought of what he most likely did to her, and the anticipation becomes unbearable. I shift my weight from one foot to the other. Connor's hands run up and down my arms, the heat of his body surrounding me.

"Soon, my darling. Just a few more minutes," he whispers in my ear.

Taking a deep breath, I notice a flock of birds against the morning sky while the seconds slowly tick by. Until finally, *finally*, it's time and my adrenaline soars just like the birds above.

I'm out of body.

Hurried steps down to the chapel.

The crunch of gravel underneath my feet.

Hushed breaths out of my mouth.

The old wooden steps leading up to the door creak beneath my weight, the beat of my own pulse thrumming against my eardrum as I look back over to Connor. He grins and winks in reassurance, following me up the stairs like a haunting dream filled with retribution.

For the men inside, I'm their nightmare.

Through the open door, I see them congregating near the back and stride in. Channeling every ounce of courage I can muster into my movements, I rap my knuckles on one of the pews.

"Morning, gentleman," I drawl.

At the sound, my brother's head swivels to the side, his gaze slamming into mine.

"Penelope?" he snarls, shifting his glare behind me, his eyes widening when he sees who's followed me in. He has the nerve to genuinely look surprised. Like he never even considered this outcome. As if his arrogant and callous belief that God would protect him and his sordid plans never allowed for sinners to best him, especially in his own home.

This time, it's my turn to deliver him a serene smile, I don't need to turn around to know Connor is flashing his own malicious grin.

While we stare at each other from across the room, the chapel flickers into darkness, followed by loud banging. Frederick's attention turns to the windows on either side of the room. I can tell the moment he realizes what's happening.

We're trapping them inside. Nailing boards over the windows so that they have no way to escape. Turning this holy building into the prison they forced me to return to.

"What have you done?" he hisses.

"Isn't it obvious," I say cooly, cocking my head to one side, my smile growing even wider. "I'm sending you to hell."

"You *bitch*," Patrick yells out while lurching towards us, trying to attack. I don't even have time to flinch before a switchblade flies through the air and sinks into his eye, jolting him back onto the floor—dead.

I turn to Connor in surprise, his lethal grin ablaze across his face.

"Anyone else?" he quips with that same sinister smile, his handgun now in his hand, scanning the room for his next hit.

Frederick's face morphs into one of pure disgust, his attention snapping to me instead of the heathen holding the gun.

"Filthy harlot," he spits but doesn't move. "I should have slit your throat when I had the chance."

I hear the gunshot before I see his body jerk. He falls to his knees with a loud bellow, his hands cradling his crotch, blood seeping through his fingers, gushing onto the floor.

"You should feel like the luckiest man alive to have your life in my wife's hands," Connor growls, his body vibrating with unadulterated rage. "Because if it was me, I would rip you apart limb by limb and then feed them to you."

When his dark eyes land back on me, they soften and I can't help but to press a chaste kiss against his lips.

I give Frederick a disinterested glance, still writhing on the floor of the chapel, his men cowering beside him, and my damned soul sings.

"I could end your suffering now, and kill you with my own two hands just like I did our Father," I say slowly. My smile is thoughtful while he howls something unintelligible, this strange calmness beginning to flow through me. "But I rather like the idea of you in agony. I guess your God had a plan for me after all."

All I want now is for it to be over.

"Let's go," I tell Connor, his body still tight with anger, but his touch is gentle when he threads his fingers through mine. Side by side, hand in hand, we step out of the church leaving Frederick to his fiery death. Outside, the door slams closed behind us, soon to be nailed shut.

In a way, I've left Penelope trapped inside too, kneeling on a pew, still praying for miracles where there is only tragedy. She's a stranger to me now, one who belongs amongst the ashes of my past.

The smell of gasoline hangs heavy in the air when the devil places a matchbox in my palm. "After you," he says with a barely there smirk.

My heart swells, thirsty for revenge.

I eagerly open the box and strike a match. Flicking it, I watch it soar through the air, until it falls on the ground, igniting the trail of gasoline ablaze. The fire eats a path up to the chapel, flames licking up the outside walls so fast I barely have time to take it all in.

Soon the entire thing is engulfed in flames. It's mesmerizing. The most depraved of masterpieces. Especially when a symphony of loud bangs and screams reaches my ear like an offering to the darkest parts of myself.

The fire warms my frail body, rekindling something inside of me that I thought was dead.

I turn to Connor, the reflection of the burning wreckage glinting in his eyes drawing me in. I pull him into a kiss. A hard, passionate kiss imbued with feelings too big to even describe. I draw them with the stroke of my tongue, he groans into my mouth deepening our embrace. His mouth is as hot as the fire burning my past into ashes. Fisting his jacket I'm wearing, he pulls me closer, his body hard and utterly fucking perfect.

And suddenly I know.

*I know.*

What I feel for Connor is real. All the feelings I've been scared to touch or even acknowledge for the past two years, or maybe even longer, overcome me and it feels like being struck by lightning.

It takes my breath away.

But I don't want this awareness to be forever interwoven with this moment, so I swallow it back down, breathing in Connor like a drug instead.

When we pull away, my eyes find his dark, glorious gaze. My arms slip around his waist, while my head finds the crook of his neck.

We stay silent, watching the chapel burn, the flames dancing over the quiet ripples of the pond. The screams inside eventually die down, and I know in my heart that my brother's end has come.

Breaking the hypnotizing spell, I finally whisper, "Let's go home."

# 46

## Connor

It's late afternoon by the time we get to the house. Home, Lenix called it. Unsurprisingly, I notice Sunny's car waiting for us. Byzantine must have called ahead. She bursts into tears when she sees us pull up. Lenix gingerly steps out of the car, still sore from her branding and Sunny rushes to help her. They hug, cry and Lucy eventually steps out of the car too. Sunny embraces her as if they've known each other for years.

I leave them to their heartfelt reunion, although I would rather take Lenix into my own arms and hold her for the foreseeable future. I don't know how I'll ever let her out of my sight again when I'm still shaking with the fear of her being taken. The guilt is chewing me up but I'll pretend it's not. I'll pretend I'm fine. That I'm still the same Connor I was over a month ago before Lenix carved a hole in my chest and took up residence inside of me.

I walk up the stairs, and head for our room, stripping down to nothing but boxers. I end up sitting on the edge of my bed, lost in thought long enough for Lenix to walk in.

Looking up, I find her leaning in the doorway still wearing that ratty white dress, my leather jacket hanging slightly off one shoulder. All I want to do for the rest of my life is worship at her altar. She is a goddess amongst us sinners.

"Where's your sister?" I rasp.

"Guest room," she answers quietly.

I clear my throat and hold my hand out toward her. She pushes off the door, a small wince paints her face, but she tries to cover it quickly. I keep my expression calm, but inside I ease the snarling monster by imagining shooting her brother's dick off all over again. Fucking worthless piece of shit. I would have done much worse if given the chance. But this was Lenix's moment, not mine. I gladly stood by my wife's side while she burned the whole thing down.

She steps between my open legs, my hands caressing up her thighs while my forehead falls on her stomach, my eyes closing. Her fingers rake through my hair, down to my nape as I savor the small shiver that accompanies it. I pull slightly away in order to look up at her.

"Let me take care of you," I say softly.

Her throat bobs, giving me a small smile, and nods.

Once on my feet, I sweep my arms under her legs, picking her up and into my arms. She lets out a shaky exhale that I can almost convince myself sounds like a small laugh, wrapping herself around my neck while I carry her into the ensuite. Placing her back on her feet near the counter, I move to turn on the shower. At least mine is large enough for two, with a wall-mounted rainfall, and a built-in bench if Lenix needs it.

She looks almost doll-like in this light—carrying that evasive vulnerability she's always so desperate to hide, especially around me.

Something has shifted between us, I'm sure she can feel it too. Still, silence accompanies our movements, as if words can't be used to describe what is smoldering between us.

I push my coat off of her, letting it fall to the floor. My hands find her shoulders, fingers slipping under the small straps of her dress, tugging them down her arms, the material falling quietly, pooling at her feet.

Both our eyes fall on the soiled bandage on her hip covering the branding. I go to try and remove it but she pulls away slightly.

I look up into her eyes, the pain there guts me all over again. She shakes her head as if to say she doesn't want me to see. My face softens, hands cradling her cheeks, my thumbs caressing just under her eyes. My lips press against hers, hoping she understands the feeling I'm trying to relay with each touch.

Nothing else matters other than she's here, safe, with me.

"It needs to be cleaned, my darling," I say with my lips still ghosting her own.

She concedes reluctantly, one silent tear falling over my

thumb still resting on her cheek. I slowly pull away, and with more tenderness than I even knew I possessed, I peel off the bandage, making her hiss.

What I find underneath makes my insides twist and my jaw clenches, but I say nothing. Even if I could recognize the symbol, it's so swollen and inflamed that you can barely make out the shape of it.

"Let's take a shower first," I say and lead her into the billowing steam. I take my time, cleaning her limb by limb, the suds washing off the dirt and grime from her skin. I avoid her hip, careful not to let the soap sting her fresh wound. I then pour a small dollop of shampoo into my palm, rubbing my hands together before reaching over to her head. She watches me and I can tell she's fighting off a wave of emotion.

"He shaved it off in front of everyone," she croaks, her eyes shining with unshed tears. "It was my first punishment."

I struggle to find the right words and instead let my tender touches speak for me.

I could say I miss the feel of her long hair in my hands. But why would I? When I'm faced with the most beautiful person I've ever seen. Her shaved head only accentuates her fierceness. No longer hidden, it now sits unabashedly at the forefront of her.

When we finally step out of the shower, I wrap a large, fluffy towel around her body. She leans on the counter, keeping her hip uncovered while I reach for the first aid kit under the sink.

I pull out what I need to disinfect it, crouching down to have a better look. Lenix stands stoic the whole time while I take care of the wound. I whisper soft words of praise and for once she lets me. Her fingers find my hair, teasing the strands distractedly as if just needing something of me to hold.

When the clean bandage is finally hiding the horrors of her past, I lead her back into the room and give her a large t-shirt of mine to wear. It's barely evening but it doesn't matter, I'm desperate to have her close and in my arms.

I pull on a fresh pair of boxers, climb into bed, and reach out for her, dragging her into my chest. Her body melts against me, one long leg over mine, her head tucked over my heart. Her hand finds my neck and face, the other finding my own and squeezing it three times. Her eyes close almost immediately. I watch her sleep for what feels like hours, lost in my own haunting thoughts, wondering how I'll ever be worthy of her love.

She is Lilith personified.

And I am the devil at her feet.

## 47

It's early morning as I stand in front of the guest room. I must have slept for over fifteen hours. I woke up disoriented, fear piercing my heart as my foggy brain took in the room I was in. Then I felt Connor beside me in bed and the relief was indescribable. I doubt we'll see news coverage of the fire. It's not over entirely, but hopefully having cut off the head of the snake will be enough to deter the others from ever retaliating. Most of the people in Sacro Nuntio are innocent… like my mother. No matter how much she hates me now. She's a victim like us all.

I knock on the door. A few seconds later it creaks open and Lucy appears in the small opening. Her face brightens when she sees me and I feel like sobbing. Opening the door wider, she falls into my arms and I hug her like I'm about to lose her all over again.

"Penelope," she whispers into my neck, squeezing me tightly. I have a small reflex to tell her, now that we're out, to call me Lenix but decide against it. She's been through enough change, she can call me whatever she wants if it means having her in my life.

"Can I come in?"

She pulls away and smiles. "Of course."

I notice she's wearing some of my clothes, a loose long-sleeve shirt and—

"You're wearing jeans," I say in disbelief as I walk into the room.

Women were never allowed to wear pants in Sacro Nuntio.

She giggles softly. "Yes. Yes, I am."

I'm suddenly so proud of her. To leave, knowing your whole life is about to be turned upside down, and I savor this small defiance she's allowed herself by choosing pants instead of a dress. This is only the beginning, she has a long road of discovery in front of her. While I was forced to do it on my own, I'm so relieved I can be here for her as she explores the outside world.

We sit on the bed, our knees touching each other, hands intertwined. I study her face for a few seconds, allowing myself to take her in as slowly and as long as I want to. Feeling like this is the first time I'm truly seeing her, without the weight of the commune hindering us.

Her curls are similar to how mine were, but looser, light brown instead of my black. Her skin tone is the same as mine, except hers looks like she's never really basked in the sun like I have. She has a splatter of freckles across her cheeks and has some of the most striking eyes I've ever seen. Dark green, with flecks of gold, seeming to change hues depending on the light.

I'm suddenly hit with such melancholy realizing how much I've missed, her most formative years now behind us. I need to close my eyes to stomach the wave crashing over me. When I finally catch my breath, I turn my gaze back to hers and squeeze her hands.

"I'm so sorry, Lucy…" I rasp.

"Don't," she says quietly, her eyes shining with tears. "Don't take the blame for the actions of others."

"I could have tried harder. I could have tried to get you out," I say in a choked whisper.

I chastise myself for just thinking about me and the fear that kept me gone and hiding.

She smiles softly. "Maybe I wasn't ready to leave until now. Would you really have been able to raise a child on your own?" she says with a shrug and then looks at me with a serious, almost knowing expression. "This was the path God chose for me."

I scoff, slightly angered. "How can you still believe in God, Lucy? After all of *this*?" I say waving my hand around the room to better drive in my point.

She watches me, her expression never wavering and gives me another small smile. "God did not do this to me. Fredrick did."

"God never protected us," I snip. The same fury I felt before killing our brother crawls back up my throat.

"But God brought us back together," she replies reverently.

My mouth opens but then closes, swallowing back my retort. Who am I to deny her some sense of peace, even if I personally disagree wholeheartedly. I can't be just one more person who tells her how to think or what to do when that's all she's known her entire life.

Instead, I smile back, my eyes softening, and pull her into my arms. "You're right," I say, her hair tickling my nose. "We're together now. That's all that matters."

When we pull away, I notice the sun shining brightly through the window. An idea pops into my head. I give Lucy an amused look. "Have you ever seen the ocean?"

Her eyebrows rise up her forehead, eyes shining. And suddenly, I'm washed over with the peace of knowing that no matter what, we'll be okay, she'll be okay.

No matter what, from this point forward, we have each other.

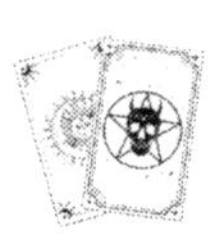

ALTHOUGH CONNOR PREFERS HIS POOL, the back of the house also faces the ocean. I considered bringing Lucy to the public beach since for some weird reason I enjoy it best. Most likely because of all the memories I have with Sunny there, or just the fun of people watching. But I decided against it, thinking she might need to ease into crowds and the shock of people wearing bathing suits showing a lot more skin than she's used to.

So I lead her down to the small patch of private beach connected to the property. She refused to wear any of my bathing suits so we settled on gym shorts that go down to her knees and a black t-shirt twice her size.

The awe in her eyes when she looks back at me as we both face the sprawling ocean makes my heart melt, like a small child discovering that the world doesn't end in their backyard. I swallow back the urge to cry, my emotions heightened with having her here next to me.

"Want to go in?" I ask, the soft ocean breeze caressing my cheek.

She looks back to the water, and then down to her toes digging into the sand.

"I'm scared," she says so quietly, I almost miss it.

She glances up at me, a sad smile on her lips, a few tears tracking down her cheeks and I can't help but to let my own tears show. It feels like those two words encompassed everything left unsaid—of the daunting mountain she still has to climb and everything she still doesn't even know exists in the outside world. I could say I can't imagine what she's feeling right now, but I do know.

I once *was* her.

I hold out my hand for her to take.

"I'm right here," I say.

Her smile widens and she takes a hold of my hand, walking tentatively towards the waves, letting her control the pace. A giggle rolls out of her when the water finally licks her toes and we slowly walk into the surf. She keeps us close to shore, the water never reaching higher than our thighs. It's our own private baptism into this new life. A rebirth worthy of this quiet moment of awe and gratitude, with the sun shining against the ripples of the waves.

We stay like this for a while, the water gently lapping around our legs.

If I could collect perfect moments, I would preserve this

one forever. Keep it safe in a locket to wear around my neck, close to my heart.

"This is what freedom feels like, isn't it?" Lucy says after a while.

I take a long and deep breath, my eyes focused on the horizon.

"I think so."

# 48

## Connor

I've kept myself busy in the study most of the day. I wanted to give Lenix and her sister some space. I'm catching up on everything that fell to the wayside while Lenix was kidnapped. I take a long drag of the joint, nearly burning my fingers and stub it in the crystal ashtray that used to belong to my father, and lean back into the leather chair.

I chose to wear a suit this morning, even if I have no

plans of leaving the house today. I needed to feel like myself, or maybe I needed the armor the suit provides. I needed to slip into the role of Connor Maxwell, leader of the Sin Eaters and not whoever I am lately when I'm around her.

The vulnerability feels itchy, but then I look at her and crack open nonetheless.

I'd rather not think about it, not when the guilt still weighs heavy on my chest, making it hard to breathe.

A knock on the door snaps me out of my spiraling thoughts.

"Yeah?"

Lenix's head pokes through, and she gives what almost looks like a shy grin.

"You busy?"

There's an awkwardness in her tone that unsteadies me but I hide behind my preferred mask and flash her a grin.

"Never for you, my darling," I respond, uncrossing my legs and straightening my posture, feeling somewhat uneasy.

She seems pleased by my answer and walks in, wearing a black hoodie that swallows her whole, falling mid-thigh, legs and bare feet on display. I fight not to stare too long.

She approaches me and I scoot back, giving her space to lean on the desk directly in front of me. Something about this moment feels off. But still, my hands can't help but find her thighs, caressing her warm skin while I look up at her.

The smile she offers is genuine, but there's worry in her eyes, leaving a bitter taste on my tongue.

"How are you doing?" she says.

"I should be asking you that," I volley back, my hand hovering over her hip. "How's your—"

"It's fine, I'm fine," she says too quickly, taking my hand and placing it back on her thigh.

"If you aren't, you know you can tell me." I continue to study her, and whisper, "Talk to me, Len." I almost cringe at the emotion in my voice but I steel my expression.

"I know," she says, looking away, biting her lips anxiously. She keeps her gaze averted. "Connor… I—" She takes a breath, seeming to fight for her words to come out. "I'm going back to my condo," she finally says.

A surge of possessiveness barrels through me and my fingers squeeze her thighs in response.

"Funny," I choke out on a huff. Because like *fuck* she is.

When her eyes finally land back on my face, there's sadness etched in the small wrinkle between her furrowed brows.

"My sister needs me."

*I need you.*

"And before you say, she can stay in the guest room. No, she can't. She needs a place to call her own. She needs a safe space."

"Staying *here* is safer," I growl.

"You know what I mean, Connor. Just for a few days. And besides…"

Before she says what I *think* she's about to say, I pull her into my lap and thankfully, she doesn't resist.

I take her face into my hand, my thumb stroking her bottom lip.

"Lenix, you're my wife—*mine*. You belong here with me. Nowhere else," I say vehemently.

That same lip quivers, and I'm being torn open all over again.

"Wasn't this all pretend?" she whispers. She seems so

small at that moment, shrinking to fit the feelings she's trying to hide from me.

My other hand wraps around her waist pulling her even closer to my chest.

"Does this feel pretend to you?" I take her hand in mine, holding it to my beating heart.

Pulling her bottom lip into her mouth, she rakes her teeth over it and slowly shakes her head.

She leans over and kisses me. Suddenly, I can't breathe.

The tenderness of her soft mouth on mine is nearly overwhelming, choking me into feeling… just *feeling*.

My thumb smooths over her knuckles and I'm struck with the absence of what should be there. I pull away and look down at her hand. "Where's your ring?"

She releases a small pained breath. "They took it," she says meekly.

I grind my teeth and breathe through my nostrils trying to rid myself of the anger roiling inside me.

"I'll get you a new one," I say, kissing her again but this time with a little more fervor, the heat of her tongue breathing life back into my veins. Pulling away, I study her face—serious but also worried. "I'm not letting you go unprotected, Lenix. I just got you back," I say, swiping my thumb over her hand, pausing for a long beat. "I'll go crazy."

The smile she gives me still holds the same sadness from before.

"I have to go. You know I have to."

I swallow hard, keeping my gaze steadily on hers. "Fine," I finally say. "But you're moving in, pack up your shit while you're there, I don't give a fuck. But this is your home now, Lenix. You sleep in *our* bed now. Got it?" My words might pack a little too much force but I've lost the will to care, not when the thought of being away from her for even a few days is making me sick. It makes me want to hit something just to feel my knuckles crack, and focus on physical pain instead of these flaring emotions ripping me apart.

"I need you, my darling," I rasp.

She stays silent for far too long, watching me, her eyes swirling with so many emotions that I can't even pinpoint one.

Finally, she smiles, kissing me softly on the forehead while my hand lays flat and wide on her back and I fight back the urge to close my eyes at the feeling.

"Okay," she says.

She tries to stand up, but my arm is an iron bar around her middle.

Looking at me with an indignant expression, as if I'm being ridiculous, I grin at her.

"Where do you think you're going?" I say, my voice low, fingers trailing up her thigh and sliding under her hoodie.

"What do you think *you're* doing?" she says slightly appalled but doesn't move or bat me away. "Sunny and Lucy are downstairs…"

"And?" I give her my best smirk.

Her legs part slightly and I finally discover that all she's wearing underneath are bikini bottoms. My thumb finds her heat, sliding up and down over the fabric.

"And… and." Trailing off, her breath hitching. The color of her cheeks deepens as her hips push forward. "That would be *weird*."

I can tell that it's a flimsy excuse but placate it anyway.

"Weirder than you sitting on my dick in the middle of a meeting?"

The guilty laugh that dances out of her makes me smirk even wider. Then her palm lands on my cock, and I groan.

She leans closer, sucking my earlobe into her hot wet mouth and I lose my ability to think.

Taking this small advantage, she wiggles out of my arms and jumps to her feet. "Patience is a virtue, Connie baby," she whispers tauntingly.

She turns to leave but before she walks away, I snatch her wrist. "Wait. Let me at least drive you there when you're ready," I say hurriedly.

Her expression is warm, her eyes soft when she nods, miles from how she was acting when she came in and I can at least find some comfort in that.

I let go of her wrist, even if all I want is her body next to mine, and watch her walk out of the study. I spend the next few minutes staring blankly at the spot where she disappeared wondering how I got here. And how I plan to stay here with her for as long as I'm alive and breathing—maybe even longer than that.

# 49

## Lenix

I wake up with a start, my shirt soaked through and sticking to my chest. My bedroom is pitch black and for a few harrowing seconds, I think I'm back in *that* fucking room. I place a shaky hand over my beating heart trying to calm down and look over to find Lucy still sleeping soundly beside me, Ewan dozing at my feet.

We've been staying at my condo for the past three days. The nightmares are getting worse, and I've hardly been able to get a full night's sleep since I've gotten back from the commune.

That's not true.

There was one night when I did sleep through the night. Connor's arms were wrapped protectively around my shoulders.

I miss him.

As much as I love my sister, I would rather be sleeping in Connor's arms than in my own bed without him. But I've already been robbed of the opportunity of being a big sister once. There was no way I was going to let Lucy travel this life-changing bridge alone. I need her to be okay. I need for her to find some small comfort in the outside world, not just another thing to fear.

I sigh and crawl out of bed as quietly as possible. Changing into a fresh shirt, I grab my phone and then pad into the living room. I rummage through my things for the half a joint I'm sure I've left somewhere. I'm trying to ease Lucy into my vices, not that I really consider weed a vice, but I need to be mindful of how sheltered she's been. One day at a time, I keep reminding myself.

Finally, I find what I'm looking for and slide the balcony door open, the crisp night air feeling luxurious on my still overheated skin. I sit down, pulling my knees up on the chair, wincing slightly when the movement pulls at the fresh scab on my hip.

I hadn't recognized the symbol at first, so my sister had to break it to me. The brand was made out of Fredricks's initials. The letter F and L turned into a sigil on my skin. Cold dread trickled down my spine when she told me. I considered taking a scalpel to it immediately, disgusted to have anything of him on my body, especially something so possessive as his initials. I try not to think about it, the sick feeling in my stomach almost doubling me over anytime it *does* cross my mind.

Sunny has stopped by daily since I've been back. I'm not sure why I always feared her reaction when she loves me so unconditionally. She's vaguely hinted at me making an appointment with her therapist, and I know she's right. Maybe I don't need it in the way she needed it, but it's trauma nonetheless. No matter how I try to tell myself that I'll be fine, the nightmares themselves are enough to make me feel on edge.

I mull this all over while I spark the joint, my thoughts quieting into a small background hum when the smoke finally hits my lungs. I look down at the cityscape as I smoke. My balcony is high up but I can still make out most of what's happening below, the street lights the only glow reflected against the parked car windows.

One of the cars snags my attention. I peer slightly closer as if me leaning over in my seat would really make a difference, but it's enough for me to make out an arm hanging out of the driver's window.

I laugh softly out loud and pick up my phone.

Connor picks up on the first ring.

"My darling," he simply says, his voice low and scratchy as if he hasn't used it in a while.

"I thought stalking was Byzantine's thing?" I say jokingly, keeping my voice quiet.

He chuckles, and I can picture the smirk on his face, my body lighting up at the sound. "Runs in the family."

I don't bother reminding him they're not related. I know what he means—just how Sunny is my family. From my seat, I watch him climb out of his SUV, closing the door behind him and leaning against the hood. I can almost make out his perfect face from here.

"Please don't tell me you've been staking out my apartment building for the past three days," I add teasingly.

"And if I have been?" he says in all seriousness.

I pause, finding comfort in that thought while I stare down at him from all the way up here.

"I'd say you were obsessed with me, Mr. Maxwell."

There's barely a beat before he answers, "I've always been obsessed with you, Mrs. Maxwell," he drawls.

My heart pitches out of my chest and plummets over the balcony, landing at his feet.

It scares me how good that sounds coming from his lips.

I clear my throat, stubbing my joint in the ashtray next to me, and swipe my hand over my shaved head, a nervous habit I'm starting to pick up.

"I miss you." I find myself saying.

There's silence on the other end of the phone and then. "Come home, Lenix."

"Soon," I manage to say through all the unshed tears, fears and doubts.

"In the meantime, get some sleep, my darling."

I nod as if he could see me. "Goodnight."

"'Night," he says before hanging up.

I watch him get back into his car before dragging myself back to bed, the weed helping to keep the night terrors at bay. Instead, I dream of Connor and of the words he softly spoke into the dark night.

IT TAKES me two more days to find the courage to start packing. I keep glancing over at Lucy guiltily as if she secretly hates me for leaving her all alone here.

"Stop looking at me like that," she says with a huff.

*Oops.*

"Like what?" I ask innocently.

Pausing what she's doing, she gives me an annoyed look. At that moment, the familiarities between us are glaring, even being apart for thirteen years can't deny that.

I laugh to ease the tension.

"I can't help it."

"I will be fine," she says, placing some more of my clothes into a cardboard box. "It is not as if you are leaving the city. You will still be close."

"I know…I just—I want you to be more than just *fine*," I say.

"I could say the same for you," she quips with a knowing smile.

And shit, I guess she's right.

"I think we both need therapy," I joke.

"Therapy?"

My smile drops and I groan, my hand swiping over my face in disbelief.

"You have so much to learn, Lucy," I mutter as I continue to pack up more of my things. "Please use the phone I got you okay?"

"I will try."

"Maybe I should stay."

"No," she says sternly, crossing her arms. "I can do this."

My gaze lingers on her while I stay silent for a beat. "You can do this," I say softly.

We spend the rest of the morning packing. It doesn't take long, I'm only bringing my personal belongings, leaving the rest to Lucy. I'm sad to see my pink couch stay behind, but it's for the best.

It's hard not to see the symbolism behind me packing up like this. I know I'm still Lenix. Even if most of my life was spent hiding the truth, she was still the most genuine part of my deceit. Even my shaved head feels strangely purposeful as if even my hair held too much of my past. Now I can start fresh, and become the fullest, freest version of myself.

Surprisingly, my relationship with Connor has become the pillar of this new chapter. The thing that feels the most legitimate. A beacon born from the ashes of my past.

I can't help but hold on to hope, while still feeling absolutely terrified.

Maybe I do believe in fate after all—when all this feels much bigger than just one choice after the next leading me here—leading me to him.

*Bound together.*

# 50

## Connor

My lungs burn but I stay underwater. I push off the pool wall with the full force of my legs while I swim lap after lap trying to keep my mind as distracted as possible.

Lenix is moving in today. Movers are taking care of her boxes and as much as I wanted to drive her here myself, she insisted she could do it herself after her day at the office. I had to bite my tongue not to bark orders at her like I do to everyone else in my life and reluctantly conceded.

I told Bastian he had to stop coming over unannounced now that Lenix would be living here. He gave me one of his looks like I was the stupidest person alive. I think that meant he agreed, I never fucking know with that one.

Now, I'm counting down the hours till she gets here like a prepubescent teenager having his first co-ed sleepover. I have to stop myself from pulling out the polaroid picture every other minute. I have no shame in saying that I've fucked my fist more than once in the past few days, my eyes glued to the damn thing.

*Fuck.* I've got it bad.

It somehow feels like karma for all the times I made fun of Byzantine and how whipped he became after meeting Sunny.

I get it now, as infuriating as it is.

I would set the entire world on fire just to keep her safe. Nothing really makes sense anymore without her here.

My head finally breaches the water and I suck the air back where it belongs in large lungfuls. I whip my hair out of my eyes and almost let out a startled shout when I notice a figure dressed in all black sitting in one of the deck chairs.

"Jesus fucking Christ, what are you doing here?" I hiss at Byzantine.

*I need to change the locks.*

I press my palms into the hot cement and push myself out of the pool from the side, water sluicing down my arms and body as I do so.

"You can't do that anymore."

"Do what?" he asks unbothered.

I grit my teeth. "Show up unannounced."

"I called you," he says with a shrug. "You didn't pick up."

I snatch the towel off the chair beside him and dry myself off, all the while giving him a hard glare from the corner of my eye.

"That's hardly the same thing, you idiot." I plop down beside him, stretching my legs out in front of me, grabbing my shades and propping them on my nose. When he doesn't say anything, I add, "Was there a purpose to this house visit?"

His hand strokes the scar on his neck absentmindedly. "Yeah," he says while his eyes stare off into the distance, then focus back on me. "Were you still planning on having that party for your birthday? The one you hired Sunny and Lenix for?"

*Christ, that feels like a lifetime ago.*

"Yeah, I guess. Why?"

"Sunny wanted to know, but I also think it's a good idea to keep up appearances. The mayor has been sniffing around ever since his uncle was found dead." He quirks a smile like the whole thing is amusing to him. "We should operate normally. Laying low makes us look suspicious, we don't want to give him a reason to suspect your involvement. The cult threat might be handled, but our intentions haven't changed. There's always going to be one more crooked politician to bribe in our favor."

I palm my face, rubbing my eyes in irritation. Fuck, I'm losing focus.

"You're right," I groan. "So that's in what?" I look over towards him. "Three weeks?"

He nods.

"Why didn't Sunny just ask me herself?"

He shrugs. "I think she didn't want to bother you. After everything."

"What does that have to do with anything?"

His face is blank while he stares at me. But I know him too well to believe he isn't currently chewing on his words.

"What?" I snap.

"I think we're all just a little confused as to what the fuck is going on with you two."

"We? Who the fuck is we?" I say, a hot flash of anger burning through my chest. "Why the sudden interest in my love life?" I grunt through clenched teeth.

"Is that what it is?"

My head swivels over to him as if he just confessed that he collects miniature ponies. This conversation needs to be over.

"She's my *wife*. That's all anyone needs to know."

He puts his hands up in a surrendering gesture, the placating move just angering me even more. "Sensitive subject got it," he rumbles.

We fall silent and I try to breathe through my nose, knowing there's no reason for me to be so aggressive towards Byzantine. But there's too much left unsaid between her and I to start answering his probing questions. *Fuck*, this day couldn't go any slower. I feel like a feral animal circling the same walls—waiting, prowling. She was only back for one fucking night until she was gone again. It's making me feel strange. I can't relax knowing she's not here, somewhere in this house where I can watch her—even if it's from the cameras around the house.

"Did you ever go back to see that psychic?"

I swallow back the venom that makes me want to snap and snarl and answer his question after a long sigh, which I hope conveys how little patience I have for all his questions.

"Yeah, I did." I can't help but rub my chest as I respond.

"And?"

I roll my eyes behind my shades, feeling fucking ridiculous. "She says birthmarks are…" I trail off, not sure how to explain myself. "Like an imprint left from how you died in another life."

His eyebrows rise in slight surprise. "Huh," is all he says, but then after a beat, he adds, "What's that got to do with Lenix?"

"That's what I said," I scoff, wiping sweat from my chest, the afternoon sun getting almost too hot. "She told me to ask Lenix herself."

"Have you?"

Ire licks up my spine but I suppress it, giving Byzantine a look from over my shades instead. "We've both been a little busy."

He lets out a small chuckle, cutting the rising tension building inside of me, then stands up.

"Well, this has been a pleasure, brother," he says sarcastically. "I'll see you Wednesday at the port, the new shipment from Russia is coming in."

"Yeah," I say distractedly as he disappears into the house. After everything that happened between Lenix and me, my talk with the psychic slipped my mind. I stare into the pool, now wondering if I should even mention it to her.

But there's a small curious voice in my head that wonders what it all means. If somehow it explains why our paths have crossed before, or the uncontrollable pull I have towards her.

I doubt she'll have the answer.

Deep down, I don't *need* to know. Not when our future together is now etched into my fucking DNA. If I had to be certain about one thing in my life, it'd be this: Lenix by my side.

Until death do us part.

# 51

I hug Lucy one last time. I'm acting like I'm leaving forever and not just moving to a house a short car ride away. I've stopped apologizing for it, it's only normal to worry about her. She might be twenty-four but in the real world, she's a newborn. Learning to crawl when everyone else has been running for years now. I don't tell her that though, it's better to keep my worries to myself.

"I miss you already," I mumble into her curly hair, and she laughs.

"You are being dramatic."

I huff, pulling out of her embrace and wiping away an errant tear. "That's who I am, I can't help it."

I look around the condo. It still looks like mine. I hope she'll make it into her own soon enough. I gave her access to my bank accounts and credit card. I don't care how much she spends, as long as she's comfortable. The moving company came earlier while I was at work, all I need to do now is to drive to Connor's.

I'm stalling.

I know I am. Hell, I think Lucy even knows.

The little gentle coaxing out of the door might be a clue that she's on to me.

"Now go," she says with a laugh. "Your husband is waiting."

A chuckle rolls out of me. "That sounds weird," I say with a smile from the outside hallway, my feet still dragging behind me.

"Well, isn't he?" she asks in all seriousness.

I drop my smile. "I mean… yeah… it's just… uh…" I don't even know what to say or why the word still feels weird to me, so I laugh it off, giving a small hand motion that's meant to say *nevermind*. "I'll call you tonight okay?"

"I think I can manage one night."

"For me?"

She pauses, my feet slowly inching towards the elevator doors.

"Alright, for you," she finally answers with a soft smile.

"Love you," I say, blowing her a quick kiss.

"I love you too, Lenix."

My chest squeezes tightly hearing her call me by that name and I fight back the tears, giving her one last wave before finally turning my back to her. My heart feels like it's bursting, hoping this is the beginning of my favorite chapter yet.

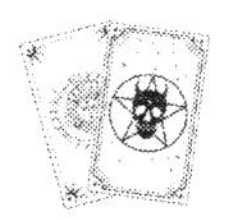

THERE'S ALMOST no traffic on my way to Connor's—or rather our—home. As if the universe gave me all the green lights and quiet streets to say *no more avoiding this missy.*

I know in my gut that this is the right decision. Doesn't lessen how scared I am of change. So much of what happened between us was under the guise of pretending, it's hard to decipher now what's real and what's not. All of my feelings toward Connor are complicated. I can't tell if deep down I always knew we'd end up together, or if the thought is so outlandish that my brain can hardly compute. I want to run and hide, but also be found. He's the most infuriating person I've ever met yet he also matches my energy like no one else ever has.

There's so much for us to discuss, so many things left unsaid. Our preferred mode of communication is to argue—or fuck… or fuck while arguing.

My heart begins to slam in my chest as I pull up to the gates, they open as soon as I turn into the driveway, and I can't help but smile despite the anxiety knowing he was probably watching the cameras.

I park, take a long inhale, then breathe out slowly. I can't even explain why I'm so anxious other than this is crazy. This *is* crazy right? My time back in Sacro Nuntio and everything that ensued, definitely solidified a lot between us. But it still feels unsteady, like I've lost all of my senses while trying to navigate this new terrain.

Feeling that Connor is somehow watching me from

inside I don't linger too long and push the car door open. I tried to dress casually cool but probably overdid it, wearing a black maxi bodycon dress—no bra—that hugs my curves and some pink wedge sandals for a pop of color. I hide behind my oversized sunglasses until I get to the door, but it opens before I can even reach for the doorknob.

Connor appears and for a split second I'm taken aback by his raw beauty, darkness personified with the smile of an angel. He looks utterly dashing in his navy bespoke suit and I find myself gawking while I remove my sunglasses to get a better look.

"Finally," he grunts, grabbing my wrist and pulling me inside. I stumble slightly into his embrace, his strong arms pulling me close while also pushing us against the wall. He presses into me and buries his nose into my neck, breathing in deeply. "*Fuck*," he mutters, his voice muffled by his mouth currently trailing up my neck.

I let out a small moan and tilt my head so he can get even better access. "If that's how you're going to greet me every time I come home, I'm okay with that," I say with a quiet laugh.

His head pops up, while his hands blaze a path up my waist. They curl around and over my breasts, then collar my throat in a loose grip. His eyes are hooded, the deepest black as he peers into my own, his throat bobbing up and down.

"Say that again," he growls.

My eyes flit left to right, while I try to recall what I just said, what he wants me to repeat. But then I stumble over the word in my mind as if it was waiting for me to pick it back up.

A slow, sultry grin pulls my lips up. "Home."

He stays silent for a long, slow second, our heated

breath intermingling until his lips slam into mine and I lose all sense of direction. Nothing else matters if only he continues kissing me like this. As if the entire world begins and ends with us—with me.

He palms my breasts with both hands and groans, "God your tits look fucking perfect in this dress."

Leaning over, he wraps his warm mouth over the fabric covering my peaked nipple, and I whimper, my head falling back onto the wall.

"Connor... *fuck*."

I slide my hands under his suit jacket wanting to remove it, trying to remove *any* piece of clothing keeping his skin from mine, but as fast as he was on me, he's now pulling away. He straightens his jacket, swiping over his mustache, while I look at him wide-eyed and breathless. Still glued to the wall.

"Excuse me?" I say incredulously.

His smirk is so cocky, I'd be giving him a hard shove in the chest if I could remember how to move.

"Patience is a virtue, my darling," he drawls with a wink and waves his hand around like an arrogant king. "I swear I heard that somewhere."

Finally recovering from the whiplash that is *Connor fucking Maxwell,* I push myself off the wall and fix my dress. "Yeah, well. You'll be waiting a long time if you ever pull something like that again," I mutter.

He chuckles affectionately and smiles, warm and open, but then he looks around.

"Where's Ewan?"

"In the car."

"Oh."

Then he's out the door, heading for my car. Moments later, he's back with the crate, settling it down on the marble floor. Opening it, he scratches Ewan's neck as my cat curls around his legs, meowing softly. When Connor straightens back up, he finds me gaping at the scene.

"What?" he says.

"Umm… I think I just hallucinated. What the hell was *that*? I thought you hated Ewan?"

He slides his hands into his pockets. "People change."

I blink in disbelief, not knowing what to say to that.

Smirking, he winks, holding out his hand. "Come, I've made us dinner."

I place my palm in his, and I swear I feel a small twinge of electricity zipping up my arm from where our hands are touching. I think Connor notices it too, his eyes snapping down and then up as if nothing happened, so I say the first thing that comes to mind.

"Did you just say that you've *cooked* for us?"

While he leads us into the kitchen, he glances over as his other hand pushes his hair back and out of his face. He almost looks… shy.

"Why so surprised?" he jokes. Maybe it's because of how much I'm starting to learn the intricacies of his personality, but his tone hints at some kind of vulnerability he's trying to hide behind humor.

"You never cook, remember?" I say as he ushers us into the kitchen, making me sit at the dinner table I've never seen him use.

"I guess I've never had a reason before," he says with a casual shrug.

I settle into my chair and watch Connor putter around the kitchen island. He opens the fridge and pulls out a bottle of rosé, pouring a glass and walking it over to me.

"That's nice of you," I say, now suddenly feeling a little shy myself. "Smells good, is that—"

"Lasagna," he interrupts.

I hum into my wine glass as I take a sip. "That's my favorite."

"I know." He takes off his suit jacket and rolls up the sleeves.

I smile but say nothing, knowing that he would have had to ask Sunny in order to know that, and just that little detail makes me feel all warm inside. I'm having a slightly hard time merging this domestic side of Connor with the ruthless gang leader he typically portrays.

I don't hate it. Not at all.

Then it hits me again.

That same all-encompassing feeling that overwrote my entire body when we stood side by side watching the chapel burn.

"I love you," I blurt out.

He stills, holding the lasagna atop large red oven mitts and *fuck* could he be more adorable?

"What?" he says, looking slightly stunned.

For a second I consider coughing and waving it off as if I didn't say anything of importance. But by the look on his face, I know he's heard me and that his question is rhetorical. The emotion in my chest, stomach, limbs, heart is too big, too expansive. So I settle into a safer version of myself and roll my eyes as if he's annoying me by making me repeat myself.

"I *said*," my voice dies down a little at the end, "I love you." I swallow hard, staring at him with slight suspicion, challenging him to say something stupid.

Instead, there's a sudden flash of relief and then he gives me the largest, toothiest smile I've ever seen on him, still wearing those silly red oven mitts paired with his thousand dollar suit.

I melt.

When the lasagna is safely placed on the kitchen island, he pulls off the mitts and stalks toward me. Placing his palm on the table in front of me, he leans over while I'm holding onto my wine glass like a life raft.

His kiss is tender, and somehow those kisses unsettle me more than anything.

When he pulls away, he smirks and says in a low and gravelly voice, "Wait here."

He turns on his heel and he's out of the kitchen before I can even blink.

I break into a cold sweat, trying not to obsess over the thought that he didn't say it back.

I stew in silence, listening to his steps echo in the foyer until he reappears, his cheeks slightly flushed. He rounds the table and sits in the chair beside me, pulling it even closer until our knees touch. His hands engulf mine, pulling them up to his mouth, his lip grazing my knuckles.

My gaze flickers to his and I feel even more frazzled.

But then my awareness zeroes onto something foreign in the palm of my hand, and I look down and slowly unfurl my fingers, my heart skipping a beat.

What I find is the most beautiful vintage ruby ring I've ever seen, the band intricately woven and encrusted with small diamonds around the oval setting. I look up at him in shock, tears suddenly blurring my vision.

"It's breathtaking," I say softly.

His expression falls suddenly serious, searing and unrelenting.

"Listen carefully to what I'm about to say."

I simply nod, eyes wide.

Taking the ring still sitting heavily in my palm, he slips it onto my ring finger—the perfect fit. "*This*," he says, while pointing to me and then him, "*is real*, Lenix. And it's for life. I adore you. I love you so damn much that it feels like I've always loved you, but I've just been too much of an idiot to realize it until now. It doesn't matter how it started, the only thing that matters is that there's no end between us."

My lip quivers and I pull him in for a kiss, his tongue swiping against the seam and I let him in, eager to taste him, to swallow him whole.

I love him, fuck do I love him.

He pulls away, breathless, forehead touching, giving me a quick kiss on the tip of my nose before his palms wrap around my face holding me there.

"Now, with that ring back on your finger, everyone will know you're Connor Maxwell's wife and will be treated as such."

"And how's that," I say trying to tease, but my voice cracks with emotions.

He smiles, his lips curling devilishly. "Like a living goddess." His expression softens, my face still cradled in his strong capable hands. "This is forever, my darling."

Then he's on his feet, wrapping an arm under my knees, lifting me into his chest, striding out of the kitchen and up the stairs.

"What about the lasagna?" I say with a giggle.

"Who gives a fuck about food when my wife is on the menu?" he says with a growl, kicking our bedroom door open with his foot.

# 52

## Connor

The weight of having Lenix in my arms connects me to a longing that feels like it's been there for fucking lifetimes—or even eternity. Who am I to say? All I know is that whatever happens to me after I die, I don't care, because I've already experienced bliss and it's her.

I near the bed, letting her knees drop and set her on her feet. Although, I would almost prefer to keep her like this—in my arms, leaning into my chest, her soft breaths fanning over my neck. I take a small step back, taking her in with a slow sweep from head to toe and back up again. As I do so, she steps out of her shoes and drops a few inches, her eyes rising slowly as she keeps her gaze locked on mine.

I reach out and trail my fingers down her arm, taking pleasure in the goosebumps I awaken and swallow hard. My nerves are crackling deep in my stomach, I'm thinking Lenix has similar ones from the shallow breaths she's taking.

Sex has always been easy between us.

But tonight feels different.

Like something monumental has shifted between us and now we're facing the vast expanse of the unknown—everything suddenly feels like the first time. Like learning a new language and slowly becoming familiar with the foreign words on my tongue, only to realize it's the most beautiful thing I've ever heard.

Her dress is as sinful as the person wearing it. It ravaged my thoughts when I first saw her, I could barely tear myself away from her.

My hands caress back up her arms and I hook my thumbs under the thin straps, eager to have her wearing nothing but my ring on her finger.

But then her hands reach over and pull my dress shirt out of my slacks in quick, impatient movements as if she's suddenly grown tired of waiting for me to take the lead. Her fingers fumble over my belt and a surge of heady anticipation shoots up my spine and obliterates my rational mind.

I grab her neck and jerk her towards me, her lips searing into mine and nothing has ever felt more right. She gasps, her mouth open and needy, her hands still pulling at my waist until I hear the zipper being pulled down. It rings loudly in my ears and my heart beats even faster at the sound.

"Connor, God, I've missed you so much," she confesses and *fuck* I could come with only those words resting softly on her hot wet tongue. But then her hand finds my aching cock underneath my boxers and my vision blackens with the simple pleasure of her touching me.

"Take that damn dress off before I rip it off," I say in haste. I'm so frantic that my thoughts barely make any sense—only one—and that's the feel of Lenix's skin against mine.

Instead of following my order, she pushes my pants down, my boxers following along with them while I wrench my shirt off my body. I do the same with the top of her dress, yanking it down forcefully and unveiling her perfect tits. I groan loudly and only have time to swipe my thumb eagerly over her hard peaked nipple before she's falling to her knees in front of me.

Her dress is still pooled around her waist and my pants still around my ankles but it doesn't matter. Not when the world around us dims when I see her hand wrap around my cock, the ruby of her wedding ring glinting like a supernova. I've never seen something so hypnotizing in my goddamn life.

I watch her fingers work my shaft up and down, her grip harder with every tug and I can't move, I can't look away. My eyes are glued on her ring and when her full lips join her hand, her tongue swiping down the length of me, I think my soul actually leaves my body.

"*Fuck*," I grunt, balls tightening, abs constricting. Reaching up, I fist my hair while my body shivers with the pleasure of my wife's mouth on my dick. She moans around my shaft and I have to pull away before I come down her tight little throat. When I do pull away, I ache from even this small distance, as if we've been stitched together, thread by thread and I'm trying to tear the stitches out from our skins.

"On the bed. Dress off," I command while toeing the rest of my clothes off.

She doesn't move.

At first, I think she's just being Lenix and balking at any type of command but then I notice her avoidant gaze and my gut wrenches. I immediately kneel in front of her, my fingers curling around her chin trying to get her to look at me but she resists.

"Lenix… what just happened? Where did you just go?" My tone is laced with worry.

Silence stretches between us, and I feel powerless. But finally, her gaze slowly shifts, her eyes finding mine. They shine as if holding on to too much emotion, and it's threatening to spill over.

"I hate having that…that *thing* on me, especially now, like this."

When the realization washes over that she's referring to her brand, I can barely control the rage still red-hot inside me. It's quickly replaced by sudden and near-suffocating guilt.

I failed her. I couldn't protect her.

It's my fault she has that fucking thing on her body for life now.

My jaw ticks. I need to breathe deeply through my nose before I can find the proper words she needs right now. Instead of the ones burning on my tongue that could ease my own shame from having done nothing but push her into harm's way.

"Between you and I, this means nothing. It's simply a mark that now exists," I say with determination.

"Tell me then, what else could you possibly see when I'm naked now?" Her voice is small and I would rather die a thousand deaths than to hear her like this.

I stare at her intensely, lacking the words to explain to her what I *do* see when I look at her. Her statement is so outrageously off base that I swallow everything I'm trying to say back down and instead, I pull her up on her feet.

"Take that dress off and I'll show you—but I need to see all of you."

She stays frozen for a few seconds, looking like she's trying to make up her mind and then she sighs softly, her shoulders dropping the tension she was holding. Standing up, her fingers finally slip under her dress near her hips and nudge it down over her ass, letting it drop to the floor. She holds her head high, eyes fixed on mine while she steps out of it, her fists tight on either side of her as if she's fighting against the impulse to cover herself.

I step into her space and hold her face in my hands. Smiling down, I softly kiss her parted lips, hoping it will convey how proud I am of her. How much she means to me, and the lengths I would go to see her smile back.

"I love you," I tell her in a hush. Watching her eyes close at the sound of my voice is reward enough. I pull away and tilt my chin forward. "On the bed."

Her lips form into a small pout and she gives me the smallest of eye rolls before heeding to my order, I can't help but chuckle at her small defiance even now.

Sliding herself up the mattress, she rests back on her arms that are stretched out behind her. She keeps her legs closed, one ankle over the other while looking up at me expectantly. I notice that the angle makes her right hip tilt away from me.

She's still trying to hide it from me.

I can't blame her. I'll never blame her.

But she's wrong to think I would ever think of her differently because of it.

I prop a knee on the bed and lean over, grabbing her feet. She's more pliable than I originally expected which makes the base part of me snarl in approval. She lets me push her legs wide apart, her cunt spreading open for me in all its holy fucking glory.

My eyes linger on her open thighs, hypnotized by Lilith herself reclining in front of me and I can't believe how lucky I am. And how fucking stupid I've been not to make her mine the second I saw her from across the bar at Sammies.

The same pang of guilt I've been harboring since she was ripped away from me crawls up my throat, but I quickly shake it off before Lenix can notice anything.

I trail a burning path up her body with my eyes, hovering on her rising chest for a few seconds and finally land on her own smoldering gaze. I keep still, a slow curl of my lips displaying the starving hunger I always have for her.

"I like it when you look at me like that," she says, her tone matching my own hunger.

"Like what?" I say slowly.

"Like you're obsessed with me."

My chest squeezes, and a low growl rumbles up my throat. My hand slips up her leg to her thigh, squeezing it, while I fully climb atop the bed, hovering over her. I cup her pussy in my right hand with casual proprietorship and wink with all the arrogance I know she hates to love.

"You're my wife, darling," I drawl. Keeping my palm

splayed wide against her warm cunt, I slowly push my middle finger into her and watch in absolute adoration as her pupils dilate from my ministrations. "*Obsessed* doesn't even begin to describe what I feel for you."

I feel her get even wetter around my finger and I move it in a slow winding circle before dragging it back out, using her own arousal to stroke her clit. Leaning over, I catch one of her nipples between my teeth, tugging it softly before letting my tongue lave over it and then sucking it back into my mouth. Her breathy moans are the strongest aphrodisiac, my erection straining against her soft stomach. I'm suddenly fighting against my restraints, needing to sink inside her with such force my vision blackens.

Her hands find my hair, her nails raking against my scalp, and I pepper heated kisses down to her navel, somehow finding the strength to hold myself back. I need her to feel unrestricted by the wound on her skin before going any further.

I move towards it and as expected she tenses.

I hold back my frustration. Not of her but of the situation we find ourselves in, wishing she could focus on how I'm making her feel instead. The thought gives me an idea, and I pull away, jumping off the bed.

"What are you doing?" Her voice sounds slightly impatient, but I don't look up, too busy rummaging in the pile of discarded clothes at the foot of the bed instead. My hand finally wraps around my tie and as fast as I was off of it, I'm back on the bed making my way up to Lenix's head.

"What are you doing?" she repeats slowly, now with a lot more suspicion.

"Don't you trust me?" I tsk.

Her eyes narrow, but still she lets out a quiet laugh and grin.

"I want you to focus on what you're feeling and not on," I let out a breath, "Everything else."

Not saying the word *brand* might be giving it too much power, but that's not what matters right now.

I wait, holding the tie taut in both hands until I watch her give me a slight nod. I don't waste my time tying it around her head, covering her eyes. Resting her back onto the pillows, I find her lips with mine, giving into another time-bending kiss. Her warm wet tongue seeks out mine and the sensation has a direct line to my cock. I let out a low groan, sucking her bottom lip into my mouth and releasing it with a pop before finding my way back to her hips.

I hear her breath hitch, a mixture of nerves and arousal and I swear to fucking God by the time I'm done with her, her chest will only be rising with pleasure.

I turn my focus on the brand. By the look of it, it's healing well but it's still scabbed over and looks sore. My fingers ghost over her hip, she flinches and I know it's not from the pain. I hold in a long exhale, deciding to leave it alone for now and shift my gaze to her open legs.

I kneel in between her thighs and push her even wider open, bending her at the knees with my hands. Leaning down, I drag my tongue from her entrance to her clit and my body hums like I've taken a hit of the purest drug. She moans my name in the softest of tones and I know, without a shadow of a doubt, I'll never hear anything sweeter.

Her clit is swollen, begging to be sucked, and I do just that, while I push two fingers into her pussy. She bucks against my mouth, and I thrust my fingers even deeper. Slowly, I slide them out, then back all the way in while my tongue strokes her clit in a sequence of tight circles and long broad licks.

I pull away but keep my fingers pumping rhythmically, my thumb replacing my mouth. I take a moment to watch her, blindfolded and all fucking mine. Leaning over, I kiss her softly along her clavicle and then up her throat, nipping her earlobe with my teeth.

"You asked me what I see when I look at you like this?" I say, my voice at least an octave lower than usual and I watch as she licks her parted lips, and whimpers out a small yes while she clenches around my fingers. "I see *you*, Lenix." I graze her lips with mine, kissing her nose, both her cheeks and then between her breasts. "Your body is a marvel, and I have the honor to be the only one who gets to look and enjoy it like this—when it's warm and flushed and just begging to be fucked." I add a third finger into her cunt. She gasps, rocking against the heel of my hand like she's trying to fuck herself on it.

"Don't stop," she says breathlessly and I can't tell if she's asking me not to stop what I'm saying or what I'm doing so I continue both, whispering every possible thing I love about her while my palm grinds her clit, my fingers dripping from her wet desire.

Her hand finds my shoulder, nails biting into my skin, her mouth open and moaning and so *fucking* irresistible.

"I'm going… I'm…" she trails off, her nails digging even deeper into my bicep.

When she comes, I'm winded by the sight of her. A stunning picture of sensuality that will stay burned in my mind forever.

The hunger to see all of her becomes unbearable, so I rip the tie off her face. She blinks in rapid succession, acclimatizing to the light while she's still coming down from her orgasm. Finally, her eyes snap to me and again, I'm split in half by the expression I find staring back at me.

"I love you so fucking much," she utters almost in shock, swallowing hard.

The need to be inside of her is almost painful, and if I wait any longer I'll lose my mind.

"Come here," I growl, dragging her to the edge of the bed. "Stand up for me."

She does what I say on shaky legs, and I press my lips to her stomach before slowly making her turn away from me. Her brand is almost at eye level like this and while she turns, I kiss the tender red skin surrounding it. I feel her jump slightly but she doesn't pull away. When her back is finally facing me, I see her notice the full-length mirror in front of us.

I find her eyes in the reflection and I pull her closer, my left hand moving wide up over her thigh and then up her stomach. "Look at you… so beautiful, and so fucking *mine*," I say with reverence while I stroke my cock with the other, my eyes never leaving hers.

"Keep your eyes on the mirror, my darling," I tell her while I tug her backwards. Keeping my legs close together, I make her widen hers while her sweet little pussy hovers close to my cock, keeping her weight up by her palms on my thighs. I fist my dick and drag the broad head over her wet clit, groaning at the sensation. "Watch as your husband fills you up, and tell me how good I feel when I'm so deep inside of you, the only thing you'll be able to pronounce is my name on those perfect lips."

I wrap my arm around her waist and pull her down. She lets out a broken moan and the heat of her around my cock is nearly too much. Suddenly I'm struck with the all-consuming need for us to feel even closer, the desire for our souls to merge together so I don't have to stand one more second being apart.

My gaze jerks to our reflection, and I'm fucking gone.

Her legs hang over my thighs, her pussy spread wide, my cock filling her up so completely that I'm nearly struck dumb by the image of us.

"*Fuck, Lenix*," I swear into her neck while I palm her tits in my hands. I tug at her nipples, making her gasp, and then my hands fall to her waist. I push her up and then back down. My hips hitch upwards with the movement, slamming myself into her while I watch her expression turn into a blissful heat and nothing has ever felt this fucking good.

My fingers trail up her spine and her whole body shivers, her pussy clenching around me and I go blind with lust. Picking her up, I stand and flip us over, dropping Lenix on her back on the bed while I bracket her with my body.

Her hands fall over her head, breasts bouncing with the motion, eyes glinting with the same desire I know darken mine. I sink back into her, thrusting harder and deeper now with a better angle. I catch a glimpse of her ring again, and I grow even harder—if that's at all possible. I grab her hand and thread our fingers together, feeling the ring dig into my skin and my mind is nothing but her and the way she's making me feel.

"You should see how pretty my perfect little wife looks when she's being fucked," I groan through clenched teeth, my hips slamming over and over into her. The sounds falling out of her lips are so erotic, I can barely utter another word, needing to hear every small whimper escaping her kiss-swollen lips.

"Connor," she moans loudly, her hands scratching into my shoulders, her legs locking around my waist as I continue to piston into her.

"That's it, darling. Come all over your husband's cock. Let me show you the fucking universe."

One small gasp, and then her back arches, her mouth widening into a silent scream. Her cunt pulsates around my shaft and I thrust deeper and deeper, needing to feel every single aftershock of her orgasm.

I follow quickly after. Grabbing her face, I kiss her harshly while I feel myself disintegrate into nothing. I spill into her, my cock throbbing and twitching with the sudden force of it, and then finally, it's over.

I'm left breathless. Mindless. Nameless.

While I try to piece my identity back together, I slump over Lenix, our skin sticking together as both our chests heave with the exertion.

After a minute—or maybe hours—I don't fucking know, I try to pull out but she stops me.

"I want to feel you like this for just a little longer," she whispers. I look at her and smile. She seems so sated and pleased, eyes clear and wide, that I'm suddenly stabbed by the guilt I've been trying to suppress.

"I'm so fucking sorry, Lenix," I manage to choke out, my eyes still locked onto hers.

Her face softens.

"For what?" she says while she pushes a few strands of hair off my forehead.

"For everything—for not protecting you. For failing you when you needed me most. For letting all this shit happen…"

I trail off when I see her smile, imbued with so much affection I can barely continue to look at her.

"Just shut up already," she says, her smile widening. "I can't give you my forgiveness when there's nothing to forgive." She then kisses me and the taste is tender—not resentful. "Let it go, Connor. For me? I need you. There's no space for this guilt between us."

I study her expression for a little while longer, swallowing hard and then finally nod.

"Thank you," she says.

When she finally lets me pull out, I fall onto my back, dragging her into my chest.

"Then I promise you this, Lenix. You'll never be safer than right here in my arms. I'll turn the Sin Eaters into a fucking world empire just to keep you safe. No one will ever dare touch you now."

She stays silent for a beat, seemingly lost in thought, her fingers tracing idle lines across the tattoos on my chest.

"What if I want to run this empire with you instead of just being protected?" she finally says while looking at me with a mischievous smile.

I run my fingers down her back and then up her arm, before saying, "Then it's all yours, Mrs. Maxwell."

# 53

Waking up from this particular dream feels like my body fell from a mile-high drop and then tried to brace for impact. My hand is pressed against my beating heart and it takes me a few seconds to find my bearings, especially when I notice the bed empty beside me.

It wasn't any of my usual nightmares either. But it held the same odd sensation of knowing what was about to happen or even recognizing the setting while still feeling foreign. Trying to remember now feels like sifting through fine sand, anytime I try to grasp at an image it slips through my fingers.

I scan the bedroom trying to center myself back to the here and now. It's still early morning, the shy yawning sun is barely peeking through the curtains, casting the room in shadows. I'm awake, but something still feels off. Like my consciousness is still wandering somewhere without me, like I have my foot in an invisible world I can't describe.

It's unnerving. Something I have no real control over.

My attention snaps to the ensuite and the sound of a running faucet, then a few seconds later Connor pads out holding a glass of water. Somehow, seeing him like this, his face darkened by the somber light of the room, rattles one of the images of my dream into flashing in my mind's eye. Of a hand—is it mine?—around a knife, sinking it into someone's chest.

My stomach drops.

"Oh my God…" I mutter, my hand flying over my mouth, my eyes still fixed on Connor walking back to bed. With the expression of vague horror, I'm probably sporting, his eyebrows dip in worry, quickly placing the glass on the bedside table and slipping close to me in bed.

"What's wrong?" he says while his hands smooth over my face, shoulders, arms, seemingly thinking I must be hurt, but finding nothing other than my rattled frame in an oversized t-shirt.

*What's wrong?*

Is anything wrong? I stay silent while I clamber through my anxious thoughts one by one trying to make sense of it all. Am I still struggling with killing my father that they're manifesting in bizarre visions and dreams? No, because this predates even the death of my father.

It doesn't make sense. Nothing about this is making sense.

My eyes drop to Connor's bare chest. I still haven't spoken. My hand raises up to skim the tattooed skin over his heart, and he jerks under my touch ever so slightly, as if trying to pull away but deciding against it. The ridge between his brows grows deeper.

"I think I might be going crazy..." I whisper, not knowing what else to say.

"Why would you say that?" he says, wrapping my shaky fingers into his hand, keeping them pressed against his chest.

I meet his gaze and sigh deeply. "I don't even know... I just keep having these thoughts... or visions? Dreams? I don't know..." I trail off.

"About?" he gently coaxes.

"Bloody knives," I say with a dry laugh, trying to take my hand away but he grips it even harder.

"What do you mean?" His voice now sounding a bit harder.

"I don't know, that's what I'm trying to tell you. I can't explain it."

"So explain what you can."

"You'll think I've lost it," I say, slightly annoyed that he's pushing this already odd conversation along.

He quirks a brow and gives me a look that seems to say *humor me, darling*.

"Okay fine," I huff, rolling my eyes just to annoy him back. "I've been having these *urges*—wait, no... not urges... more like sudden fears. Like one day I won't be able to control my actions." I peek a look at him, suddenly feeling so ridiculous but his eyes are boring into mine and I force myself to continue. "They used to come as daydreams when I was younger, then they eventually faded. Until they started back up again when I moved in here…" I close my eyes, taking a deep breath before continuing. "Like I'm going to stab you in the heart if I'm not careful…"

*Oh my god, I'm insane. I'm literally unwell.*

I open my eyes even if I'm not quite ready to face Connor's reaction. He stays silent for far too long, looking like he's mulling everything over and the more I wait for him to speak, the more I merge with the pillows and mattress beneath me.

"I never told you I went back to the palm reader," he finally says.

My eyebrows shoot up. "Really? When?"

"A day or two before you were taken," he says, averting his gaze, his free hand reaching for his nape in a self-soothing manner.

As much as I'm surprised that he would *ever* entertain anything that woman has to say, I'm not sure I'm following. "What does that have to do with what I just said?"

"Well…" he mutters, his gaze lifting to the ceiling as if trying to recall something. "She said that my birthmark was linked to how I died in a past life. And that—well, that you were somehow connected and I should ask you and not her what that connection was."

Suddenly, it clicks. "Wait… you don't think that we… that I… that you?" I close my eyes and take a deep breath attempting to make sense of what I'm trying to say. My gaze finds his again and I blurt it out, "*That I killed you in another life?*" The words come out as a nervous hiss, my rational mind doing backflips trying to get my attention but I ignore it.

Connor shrugs like none of this is a big deal.

"Don't you find all of this, *oh I don't know*, fucked up?" I say, rattled.

"What's fucked about it?" he asks in all seriousness.

"What do you mean 'what's fucked up about it?'" I repeat, blinking in slight shock before answering. "Let's say all of this is true and not a complete construct of our imagination, 'cause honestly who knows at this point." He lets me take my hand back and I wave both of them around to further my point. "You're telling me you have no reservations about us ending up together when I have visions about killing you in a past life?" I squeak out.

He gives me one of his cocky curls of his lips and flashes me a smile. "I probably deserved it."

"Connor," I roll my eyes again, but I can't ignore the sudden flash of relief his words have on me like I've been waiting lifetimes for him to say just that. "Be serious for a second."

He drops his smile and settles even closer to me. "I am being serious," he says, his tone and eyes darkening. "Do you really believe I was a saint in a past life, Lenix? Me? I have no doubt my soul has been damned from the very beginning. Even *if* you did kill me once, I probably had it coming."

I laugh incredulously. "God, this is so weird," I say, my gaze down as I play with the sheets laying over my thighs. When Connor doesn't say anything, I look back up and realize he's deep in thought.

"Maybe the only good I'm destined for in this life is you, Lenix," he finally says.

My heart squeezes so tight, it takes a second for me to find my breath.

"What do you mean?" I ask softly.

He blinks, seeming to snap himself out of the daydream he was lost in and looks at me with such adoration that I forget all major motor functions. He leans in and kisses me softly before settling back, his face falling serious again.

"I was the one who gave Martha the money that night."

For a split second, I don't know what he's talking about until the memories begin to piece together and I'm left completely astounded.

"Wait, you're saying that you were the reason I had a place to stay when I first ran away?"

Martha never told me where that money came from, and now looking back I can't believe I trusted a stranger so wholeheartedly but it was that or the streets and I was desperate. "You—you basically paid for my new life?" I say in shock.

When I look over to Connor, he seems slightly uncomfortable. "I wasn't going to tell you at first, I didn't want you to think you owed me anything."

"But why *did* you help me?"

"I don't know actually, I never really thought about it until now. It was just something I felt compelled to do."

"I can't believe it..." I utter in disbelief. "All this time... and I didn't know that you were such a pivotal part of me becoming... Lenix."

Suddenly, he's beaming. An expression I don't think I've ever truly seen on him, it's pure and honest and so unlike the Connor I know that I can't stop staring in awe.

"Why are you smiling like that," I say with a laugh.

He looks at me with the same adoration as before and I don't know if I can survive it.

"The same Lenix who's now my lawfully wedded wife. What a pretty little thought," he says with a smirk that could leave me in cinders. Then he pulls me into a heated kiss and I melt into him, forgetting about the what if's, the maybes and the speculations because there's only one thing I know to be real.

And it's *us*.

# EPILOGUE

**Three weeks later**

Leaning over the bathroom counter, I peer into the mirror while I apply one last coat of red lipstick and smack my lips together.

The positive side of having shorn hair is that there's no such thing as too many accessories. My earrings are big, bold and totally me, and the matching gold bracelet and necklace aren't subtle either. My black floor-length dress ties everything together perfectly.

From the mirror, I watch Connor strut into the ensuite, dressed in a tuxedo and my heart skips a beat. Damn, he looks good. Almost passing for a gentleman.

Though, not when he's staring at me like that he doesn't.

It's Connor's birthday, he turns thirty-five today, and also the night of the event.

The memory of him walking into Sunny and I's office looking to hire us feels like lifetimes ago, especially when his hands slide over my ass, then wrap around to my waist.

"You look dazzling, my darling," he says before kissing my naked shoulder.

I smile and wink at him, making a final inspection in the mirror before turning around and wrapping my arms around his neck.

"Thank you, Mr. Maxwell."

He groans in approval before pressing his hips into mine and peppering kisses across my neck. His mustache tickles the skin near my ear and I giggle, pushing him lightly on the chest.

"We should go. We can't be late," I say.

"Says who," he mumbles into my skin, his hands igniting a heat I know I'll have a hard time putting out anytime soon.

"Says your wife," I answer with a slightly scolding tone.

His head pops up, his hands still gripping my hips. "If you don't want me to bend you over this counter and fuck you 'til you can't speak, you'll avoid saying that word in that tone," he says with all the arrogance and raw power Connor Maxwell possesses.

And it works.

I swallow hard, refusing to admit how hot the image he just painted made me, and give him a sultry—veering on blasé—look from my own personal arsenal.

"I'll keep that in mind, husband," I say with a wink and saunter out of the room.

If only we had a bit more time, I'd take him up on it.

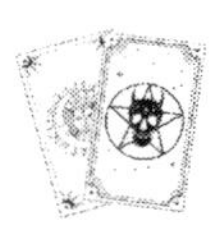

Connor opens my car door, his arm resting on the top of the roof, leaning into the passenger seat, holding out his hand for me to take. For a second, his engulfing presence and his perfect smile are the only thing I see, everything else fading away.

"Ready, my darling?"

I smile and nod, placing my hand in his, then stepping out of the car. There's a nervous tickle in my throat as we walk up the stairs into the Noxport Yacht Club as if this is the first time I'm being introduced as the dutiful wife to this powerful man. But it's not. People already know us as husband and wife. To the outside, nothing has changed.

What they don't know is—

This time it's real.

This time I can savor the words like a delicacy and enjoy the warmth it creates low in my stomach. I never knew I'd be so horny for monogamy—especially marriage. But even now, I know it's not really the title that lights me on fire, it's the man behind the words.

It's the way he looks at me when he says it.

The way I've never felt more wanted and cared for.

It's the way he sees *me*, and not the projection I've tried my best to hide behind.

From his lips, the word wife doesn't sound subservient. It sounds powerful, equal, and intoxicating.

I could get used to this feeling.

Once inside, Connor drapes my arm over his and leads me into the ballroom. The faces are familiar and it doesn't take long for him to begin charming the key players he invited. I notice Mayor Hawkins looking our way and my stomach dips, my muscles tightening with the effort of keeping my face pleasantly engaged.

"Don't worry," Connor whispers in my ear, kissing me softly on the shoulder. "Nothing connects us to Morrissey's murder. He can't touch us."

I release the breath I'm holding and peer back at him, smiling over my champagne glass.

"You seem so confident," I say.

"It's because I am." He grins and continues to study me. "Tell me a secret," he says out of the blue.

My eyebrows rise in surprise, and I look around as if to say *now?*

I almost dismiss him—his demand feels too random until it dawns on me.

"Are you trying to distract me?"

"Indulge me," he answers, shrugging and taking a sip of his drink, the very picture of an indulgent aristocrat.

At first, I don't know what to say, until the perfect secret slides into my mind and I smile mischievously while staring back at Connor. He notices my expression and he raises an eyebrow, clearly curious.

I lean into his ear, and he wraps his arm around my waist, pulling me closer into him.

"Do you remember the night you caught me watching porn near the pool?" I whisper.

His fingers fist around my dress as he lets out a low chuckle. "How could I forget?"

"Well," I say while I slide a hand over his arm, my fingers curling around his neck. "I wasn't watching porn, I was watching the video of us we took in Vegas."

His body stills under my touch, the fist holding my dress growing tighter, pressing me even harder into his firm body. I feel his head tilt towards me, hot breath fanning across my neck, his lips grazing my earlobe making me shiver in delight. "You kept it?" he growls so low, I can barely hear him.

I lean back ever so slightly so I can gaze into his eyes, and as expected they're hooded and so dark I can barely keep my cool, but nonetheless, I nod.

"And you've been watching it ever since?" he adds.

I nod again.

"*Fuck Lenix*," he groans, his eyes falling closed as if trying to collect himself. "And you're telling me this now? *Here?*"

I put on an innocent face. "You're the one who asked for a secret, Connie baby" I purr with a mock pout.

He stares at me for a long stretch of time, seemingly dumbfounded but then he finally blinks and swipes a hand over his face, a wide grin appearing.

"I don't think I'll ever love you more than I do right now," he says before tugging me into his arms fully and kissing me like we're not in a sea of the stuffiest people in Noxport.

I laugh into his mouth, pulling away to catch my breath. "You're so easy."

"Are you kidding? That's the hottest thing I've ever heard." His gaze turns searing, his voice now even lower than before. "Just you wait 'till I get you alone, my darling."

His hand slides over my ass, squeezing it hard before he releases me. He reverts back to his usual charismatic self, easing back into whatever conversation we were just ignoring like I didn't just tell him I used to fuck myself to a video of him for the past two years.

Now, looking at him. I can't believe how wrong I was about it all.

I must have been blind not to understand that what we had wasn't just simple attraction. The feelings were always there, I just pretended not to see.

From the very beginning—it's always been real.

*I've* always been real.

## *More from Naomi Loud*

Dive into Sunny and Byzantine's story in *Was I Ever Here*, the first book in the "Was I Ever" series.

## COMING SOON

Lucy and Bastian's story is next!

If you don't want to miss out on any announcements make sure to follow me on Instagram, TikTok & Facebook.

And if you loved Was I Ever Real, I'd be forever grateful if you could leave a positive review on Amazon. Your support is why indie authors can continue doing what we love. Thank you!

You can also join my newsletter to receive updates, teasers, giveaways and special deals.

www.naomiloud.com

# ACKNOWLEDGMENTS

First, I would like to thank Meghan and Summer. You two have been my pillars of support during the creation of this book and Connor and Lenix wouldn't be nearly as hot a couple without your constant help and suggestions. You have no idea how much I appreciate our friendship and how grateful I am to have met such amazing people through this little community we've built for ourselves. Love you both so much. You're stuck with me now, I don't make the rules.

Thank you to my readers, the positive reception I got for Was I Ever Here was more than I could have asked for and I am so grateful to everyone who gave my debut novel a chance. I hope you all love Was I Ever Real just as much!

Thank you to my husband Aldo, my forever person who is always so proud of me and supports me no matter what. Here's to the best year yet! We definitely deserve it.

Thank you to my alpha readers, Summer, Meghan, Alexandra, Kristie, Tasha, Bella, and Autumn as well as my betas readers, Janine, Dani, Erica, and Laura. The more I write, the more I realize how creating a book is a team effort. Was I Ever Real wouldn't have become what it is today without all of your help.

Thank you to my proofreaders Salma, and Christana. My sensitivity reader Lo as well as who Lenix was based on, my sister Joelle. And most importantly, thank you to my editor Louise who I always feel goes above and beyond. I feel like you just get me. Always so grateful for all your help and insights.

Lastly, thank you to my graphic designer Mallory. You always seem to understand exactly the vision I have for the book, and then come back with a finished product that exceeds my expectations. Thank you!!

# ABOUT THE AUTHOR

Naomi Loud is an author of angsty dark romance. While her first love are words; spirituality and magic are the lenses through which she experiences the world and this heavily influences her writing. She lives in Montreal, Canada with her husband and three cats but secretly wishes she could live underwater.